The Windlands Tales

John Ernest Briggs

The Adventures of Window Breesian

Part One:
The Path To The Northlands

Part Two:
The Search For The Northlands Treasure

Part Three:
The Search For The Angels Of The Very East

Some of these adventures may not have been true at the time they happened, but most of them are true by now.

Book Two of the Windlands Tales

THE ADVENTURES OF WINDOW BREESIAN
Part Two:

The Search For The Northlands Treasure

By

John Ernest Briggs

Illustrations by the author

Including a Reference Appendix

Willowix Publishing

The Adventures Of Window Breesian
Part Two:
The Search For The Northlands Treasure

Willowix Publishing
WillowixPublishing@gmail.com

ISBN: 987-1-7325181-2-4

Library of Congress Control Number: 2019905948

Printed in Century Schoolbook font

To Kristin Reynolds [Feather Blonde]
and
Crystal Reynolds [April Moon] –

Whose observations, suggestions,
and inspiration made this book much better
than it would have been without them

THE ADVENTURES OF WINDOW BREESIAN
Part Two: The Search For The Northlands Treasure

+++++++++

+++++++++

INTRODUCTION TO PART TWO

Window Breesian, the young adventure-seeking man from the Windlands, has found his way up the secret path through the Deep Woods to the Northlands. After his adventures in the dangerous city of Calisay, and the attack at the Deep Woods clearing, he and his fellow travelers have now decided to travel next to the ocean on the western coast.

Circles, the silky-furred Woot, wants to search for the King's lost treasure. Panni, the beautiful runaway Traepelle Castle dancer, wants to be free for the first time in her life. Rings, the huge bear-like creature, is going along because he enjoys a challenge and the friendship he never knew before. Raine, the man stranded from his home in the stars, has just joined the others on their adventure.

Together they travel across the Northlands, meeting new friends and enemies, visiting new and wondrous places, and sharing new adventures as they continue their search for treasure, friendship, and discovery.

Some of these adventures may not have been true at the time they happened, but most of them are true by now.

John Ernest Briggs

PROLOGUE

+++++++++

[ON THE ROAD TO THE TREASURE]

Somewhere across the lands from the Windcoast, to the Northlands, and far to the Very East, the moon was shining, as it often did, into the bedroom window of Tresette and Vermillion. It was a tall, wide window with a rounded top, and was framed by soft curtains quietly moving in the warm summer breeze.

The breeze came in through the window and gently caressed the faces and ruffled the blonde-brown hair of the twin girls as they lay on their bed, in their sleeping-shirts, waiting for their mother to read them some more of their favorite story.

"Isn't it funny, Mama?" Veri spoke up. "I can see Window and his friends better with my eyes closed than with them open."

"So can I, Mama. Why is that?" Tressi wondered.

"That is because there is a special place behind your eyes where pictures live," their mother explained.

"I have lots of pictures in my special place, Mama," Veri shared. "I can see some of them right now when I close my eyes."

"How do the pictures get there, Mama?" Tressi wanted to know.

"When you listen to me reading to you, your ears put them there."

"Oh, Mama, that sounds like something Window's Uncle Breeze would say," Tressi doubtingly replied.

"Well, then it must be true," Mama smiled at the girls.

"Yes, then it must be true!" the girls happily agreed together, with a giggle.

"Will you help our ears draw some more pictures for us, Mama?" Veri asked. "And read us some more of the story?"

"Certainly, Veri. Settle down, now, and get ready for the next part. Do you remember where the travelers are going on the Northway?"

Together, the girls answered with excitement, "To Meriselle, to look for the King's Treasure!"

"But, do you think that Window and his friends will find the Treasure?" Veri questioned her mother.

"You know very well what happens, Veri," Tressi reminded her sister.

"Well, maybe... but I want to be surprised."

"Quiet now, Darlings. You can't look for a treasure with a lot of talking going on."

"Well, I think that this <u>story</u> is a treasure. I never want it to end," Veri replied.

"Well, it won't end for quite a while yet, Darling Daughters. There is a lot more to go. Now, close your eyes and let's go searching with Window."

"I guess that you can even find a treasure with your eyes closed," Veri realized.

"You can if your mama reads it to you," Tressi explained.

"Thank you, Mama," Veri followed her sister's thought.

"Yes, thank you, Mama," Tressi politely agreed.

"Alright, Darlings, quiet now."

The girls' mother sighed gently to herself and picked up the book from the clothes-stand. The bright light of the table lamp reflected from the jeweled pin in her hair and flashed on the ceiling like stars in the warm night sky.

She opened to the next chapter and, once again, continued on that adventure she knew so well.

"Chapter Eleven, On to Meriselle."

Their mama's voice was soft and soothing, and, as she read, on their pillows, Tressette and Vermillion came along with her, painting pictures of wonder and adventure as they went.

"The five travelers' first night together was a joyous one..."

+++++++++

MERISENNE PROVINCE
ATLANDIC OCEAN
MERISELLE
THE NORTHWAY

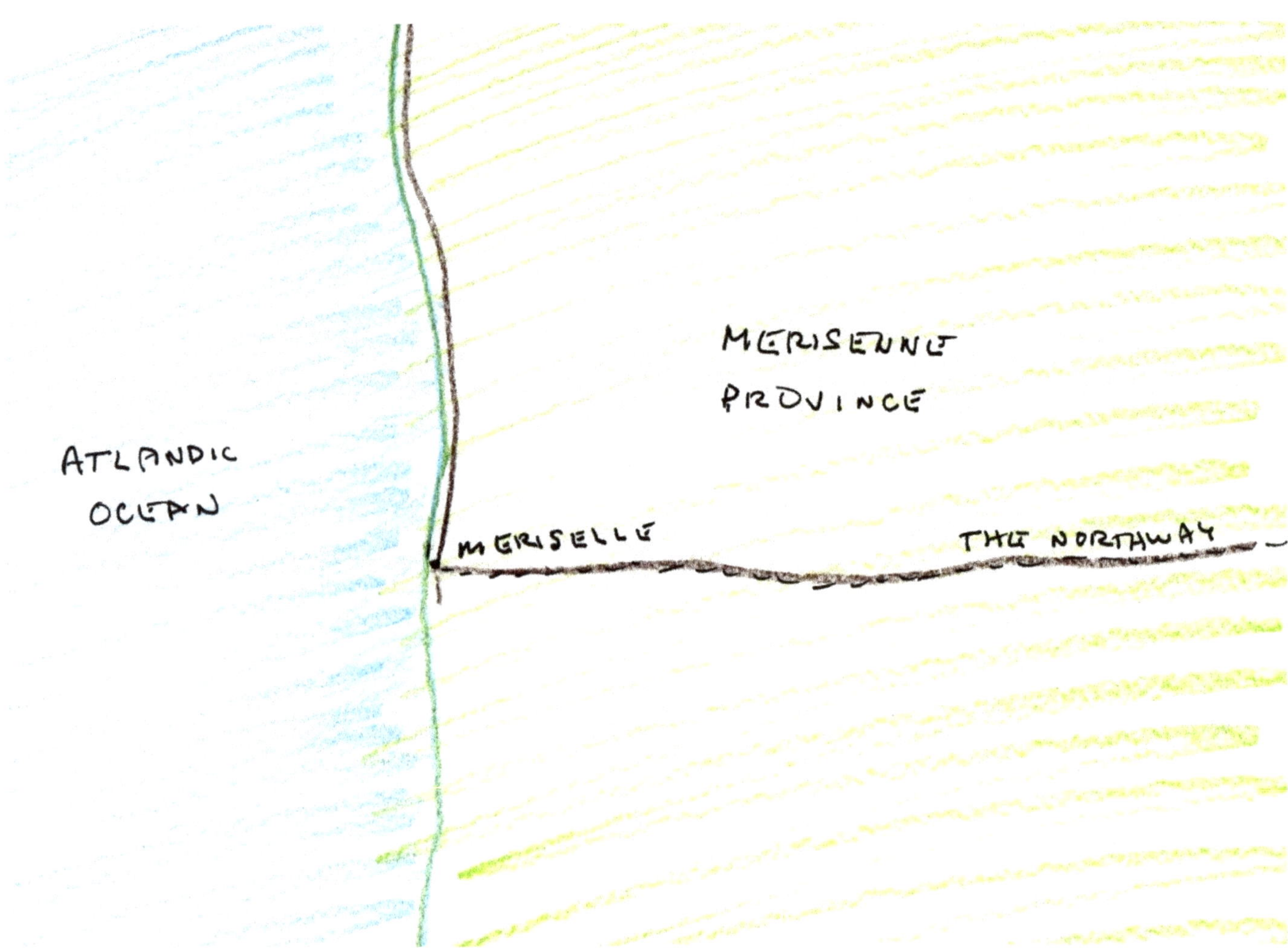

4

CHAPTER ELEVEN

ON TO MERISELLE

The five travelers' first night together was a joyous one. Much of the pain had gone from Window's remaining cuts, and they were already starting to heal. He felt much better. Rings dragged all the wood he could find to the campsite and helped Panni build a huge fire, "To celebrate," as Circles put it.

Panni served some of Sara's sugar cookies to everyone. Even Rings enjoyed one – well, he enjoyed three.

The travelers talked far into the night, until finally Panni fell asleep while leaning against her pack. The others soon lay down and joined her. Raine sat up against a tree. He refused the offer of a blanket, saying that the glowing light around him would keep him warm and comfortable.

When he awoke in the morning, Window's injuries were very much improved. All pain was gone. Only a slight redness remained, and Window no longer had a fever. It seemed like magic, but Raine assured him that it was not.

At breakfast, Raine told the travelers more about his life as a star-messenger. His ship was a small vessel, best suited for carrying light cargo at high speeds over long distances. Its sun-sails were larger than even those of a heavy cargo vessel, giving the ship extremely high speeds when piloted by an expert sailor.

Raine had been traveling, alone and secretly, within a system of seven stars called Fantessian Resenne. He had just delivered a secret message from the government of a world named Linnaia to the Prince of their enemies, the Lettes, who lived on an outlying world. As he left the Fantessian system, a ferocious storm overtook his ship and carried it for weeks across unknown distances. His ship was severely damaged and could not be repaired.

Raine used his ship's final power to come to the ground without injury, but the ship was still up in the sky, far above the clouds, adrift without a pilot. Raine's location was unknown to his commanders and could not be revealed. His only hope of discovery is by chance. It could take a very long time to find him. It could be that he will never be found.

As a messenger, Raine knew thousands of languages, and was trained to understand and speak any language at all, even if he had never heard it before. He could immediately converse in Atlandan or Freelandan or any other language.

His finger-rings held power that he could direct by manipulating them in different ways. It was not magic, but science, he assured the other travelers.

Circles didn't really understand much of what Raine had told the group, but he liked the man from the sky. He thought that Raine's light blue skin was fascinating and he especially liked Raine's finger-rings.

Raine wore the rings near the ends of his fingers and thumbs on both hands. The rings were each a slightly different color of gold on his left-hand fingers, and of silver on his right. Those on his thumbs were of a shiny, but rather dark metal Window didn't recognize. The rings were plain bands of metal, but each held a tiny gemstone on the part of the ring that faced inward, towards the palm of Raine's hand. The stones were each a different color, and although very small, they made it look as if Raine's fingertips were sparkling with colored light.

Circles asked Raine if he could use his science-rings to help them find King Alezan's Treasure. The starman said that he could help them with his rings, but he would not. "As a messenger, there are only certain things that I am allowed to do for those I meet on other worlds. Finding treasure is not one of those things. Besides, Circles, if I find the treasure for you, then it will not be your adventure and your treasure. So, I will just come along and keep you company, and watch as you find the treasure."

Circles wasn't sure that he liked that answer, but said that he guessed that he understood.

"There is one thing that I will do for you, though, and I will do it soon," Raine told them.

"What is it?" Circles immediately wanted to know.

"It is a secret for now," was his answer. "Tonight, when we camp, you will all learn what it is."

Of course, as the happy travelers returned to their trek west through Ryeland, most of their morning and afternoon was spent wondering what Raine's gift, as they called it, would be. Circles thought that it would be finger-rings that would start a fire, even in the rain. Then he changed his mind, and hoped it would be a special metal horn, that when blown, would bring the Silkie to them.

Window hoped that it would be a detailed map of where they were going. He was very concerned that they really knew almost nothing about the lands that lie ahead of them. Rings thought that it might be a device to warn them of any dangers nearby. Panni walked quietly, not having much to say about it. She was keeping her wishes to herself.

Raine was a fine addition to the traveling group of treasure hunters. He walked along with the others, mostly just listening and enjoying their company. He was friendly to them all, and did tell a great story about a time he was almost captured on a world of reptile-men. As they walked, Window noticed that the heel of Raine's boot made an interesting triangle-shaped print in the dust.

Circles asked Raine if he had a weapon to protect himself, and was told that his finger-rings would keep him safe from most

dangers. Window hoped Raine would never find a need to use his
rings in that way.

The road through Ryeland, although long, was an easy one.
The only difficulty came when the travelers reached another river.
This time there was no bridge, only ancient broken support beams
half buried in the mud at the river's edge. The travelers' main
concern was to keep the clothes and supplies dry as they crossed
the river.
"Can you swim?" Window asked Rings.
"A little bit." was his response. "If you help."
So, as they crossed the river, everyone swam alongside Rings
and helped keep him afloat, and the packs of supplies, that they
had stacked on Rings' back, from getting wet. They were pretty
successful. But just as they made it to the other side of the river,
Rings' giant nose got splashed with water, and as he plodded up
the far riverbank, he started sneezing. His whole body shook with
every sneeze, and the packs and bags on his back went flying. The
water on his fur flew out, as if he were a giant dog trying to dry
himself. It was really funny.
Everybody started laughing and couldn't stop. Each time that
they almost recovered, Rings would snort and sneeze some more,
and everyone would laugh again. Fortunately, none of the food or
equipment was damaged.

At dusk, the travelers again camped along the side of the road.
They were filled with anticipation and excitement as they finished
their meal of dried fruit and pin-nuts.
Raine stood up and asked Panni to join him. Earlier in the
afternoon, as Raine and Panni had walked together, he had
spoken with her privately. He told her of his idea, and she was
thrilled. He asked her to think about it for a while, and if she was
sure, he would present his gift that night.
Raine again asked Panni if she was certain that she wanted
her life to change in this way, and she agreed. She was overjoyed,
and could think of no better gift he could give to her. And, she
hoped that the others would like it too.

Raine stood before the group and spoke to them. "Often it is not, but sometimes change is a choice we get to make. Panni has chosen a change, a gift from me, a gift to her, and to all of you as partners in your travels and adventures." Window and the others were almost shaking with anticipation.

Raine and Panni walked a bit away from the fire and stood beneath a large tree where everyone could still see them. The blue glow surrounding Raine, which was not visible in the daylight, lit up Panni's face. Circles thought that he may not be an Angel, but he certainly looked like one.

Panni stood in front of Raine, facing him. Raine touched his palms and fingers together and slowly moved them apart. As his hands separated, shining between them, from the sparkling stones of one set of finger-rings to the other, was a bright rainbow of colors. The colors moved and shimmered and glittered as if they were alive.

Raine held his hands out in front of him, the palms facing inward towards each other. The rainbow of light seemed to jump between his hands, as if he were holding its ends.

Panni closed her eyes and stepped forward. Raine raised his hands and Panni's head passed right into the flowing rainbow. She stood for a minute or so without moving. Raine quietly asked her a question and she nodded yes. He removed his hands from around her and slowly put them together until they touched. When he took his hands apart the rainbow was no longer there.

The travelers were enthralled. Panni seemed to be all right, but Window was a bit worried. His worry was soon replaced with joy.

Panni stepped back to the fire, and smiling as big as she ever had, announced to her friends, "Raine has taught me to understand and speak Atlandan! And, not just a little, but completely! It is as though I have spoken it my entire life."

Everyone was thrilled and applauded wildly. Her friends took turns saying things to Panni in Atlandan to see what her response would be. They laughed and smiled as they did, and were soon convinced that she really could speak the language completely.

They asked her questions, and told her jokes, and did anything they could think of to enjoy her new skill. It was fantastic. Panni had gained still another freedom.

That night, around the fire, Panni was the guest of honor. She told stories and rhymes, and everyone shared in her joy. It really was amazing. Panni had trouble falling asleep that night, but she didn't mind. She lay awake, reveling in her joy of Raine's gift.

The next day, as they walked on towards Meriselle, the other travelers took turns walking with Panni. Of course, Circles and Rings had been able to talk to her before, in Freelandan. Only Window had never been able to speak with her in any detail.

It was a bit odd for Window, after the weeks of trying to communicate with Panni, and having difficulty. Raine had taught her so well, that she now knew the language even better than Window did. At first, he was almost reluctant to talk to her, but then, he quickly forgot his hesitation, and fell into a joyous conversation as they walked together.

Window remembered the question, about watching birds, that he didn't ask Panni before. He asked it now. It was only a simple thing, but a wonderful thing. She and he talked about birds, and then about nothing in particular for a long time. It was so nice to be able to really talk to her.

The others thought that Raine's gift was wonderful as well. Now their group could all talk and all understand each other at the same time. Circles would no longer have to interpret to Panni. Panni would no longer have to miss any of the stories or conversations in Atlandan. It was the perfect gift for her – and one from so very far away.

As Window walked along and spoke with Panni, he felt that she had more to say to him, but privately.

That night, Window would find out that he was right. After their evening meal, the travelers spent their usual time of sitting by the fire and talking or singing. But, tonight, Panni and Window stayed up after the others had gone to sleep.

Window had looked forward to being able to speak to Panni ever since they had first met. Now, he wasn't sure he wanted to.

Panni sat next to Window in the firelight. Her face was as smooth and beautiful as ever – her eyes shining with hope and promise. Window's dark eyes, reflecting the dancing flames before them, were alive with the movement of the fire.

Panni's voice was soft and clear as always, but now she was able to say all that she wanted so say. No longer would she have to search for words and stop because she didn't know how to express something. No longer would she be afraid that she was using the wrong words, or be uncertain of what Window was saying to her. At last, she was able to speak all that she had been thinking for so long.

She spoke to him as in a letter.

"My Dearest Window, I am Pantine Tresette. I was a dancer – now, I am a traveler, too. I met you several weeks ago when I was desperate and alone. You gave me my life. You have shown me caring and love. You have given me hope and joy and freedom."

"I have been waiting to talk to you, Window. It has been very difficult for me. My mind and my heart have run ahead of yours, I am sure. My thoughts have been trapped and unable to get out, just as I was in the Traepelle Castle. I had been captured and lonely so long I could hardly breathe. But, you freed me and gave me life. And, now I can tell you my thoughts."

"I have been planning what to say to you. It is long, but not complicated. I am sure you won't mind. Since you have freed me, I have learned a lot about love and hope and treasures and many other things. Now I know that love and treasure are sometimes the same."

"In my many hours of loneliness in Traepelle, before I ran away from my captivity, I wrote a poem of who I am, or dream to be. I want to tell it to you. I want you to know who I am. It is called *The Dancer*."

Window kept his eyes joined with Panni's. She spoke as though her voice came directly from her heart.

"She is magic she is love
She is silk and rings and things
She is hunger she is fire
She can cry and she can sing
Spinning twirling like a storm
In a looking glass of light
Follows stars across the sky
She dances in the night

Lace and legs and eyes that shine
Silken hair and diamonds bright
Gowns of crystal-spun delight
Keeps her heart locked safe inside
She is magic she is love
She is silk and rings and things
She can cry and she can sing
She dances in the night"

"I am that dancer, Window. That dancer is me. I was captured within myself, but now my heart has been opened."

"When you were attacked in the Woods, I was frantic I would lose you. As you have been ill, I have been desperate. My connection to you is consuming and unending."

"I know who you are, Window. You are love and you are hope. And, you have become my love and my hope."

"You are steady and assured. You have a spark that I hold dear, Window – a spark that I crave and that pulls me close, and will not let go. I will never be free of you, Window, I will never be free of you."

"I know that you love me, Window. I know that you do."

Then she asked the question that she already knew the answer too.

"Could you love me more, Window? Is it possible that you could? I would like that."

Tears ran from Panni's eyes as she asked. Window's tears matched hers. He answered her softly, in both voice and in affection. "My love for you is forever, Panni. But, I can only love you just this much. I dare not love you more. But, my love for you is complete." I would give my life to you if I could."

Panni's body shook as she tried to calm herself, to comfort herself. She had known what his answer would be.

She had only one more thing to tell him. Panni held Window's face in her hands, joined with his eyes, and looked deep inside him. Her heart almost died as she spoke. "Some at the castle say that we are all dancers in circles. We dance with someone for a while and then release. I am dancing with you now, Window." She took her hands from his face and pulled his hands into hers. "I hope that it is a very long dance."

Panni leaned to Window and kissed his lips. He closed his eyes and shared the joy of their connection. They floated together for a long moment.

Panni stood up and walked to her blanket. She threw off her skirt and wrapped the blanket around her. She lay down, and without looking back at him, Pantine Tresette closed her eyes.

Window sat up all night, gazing into the fire, and watching the flames dance before him.

+++++++++

It would take several more weeks for the travelers to reach Meriselle. They walked on happily, Circles often riding on Rings' back, the others pressing steadily on, hour after hour, sometimes talking or singing, sometimes keeping their thoughts to themselves. Window's injuries, and those of the others, were completely healed. The horror of the forest attack was fading from their minds and their attention turned ahead to their adventure at the ocean.

As the miles continued to pass beneath them, the trees, bushes, and grass were starting to get a bit thicker and healthier looking. Window was sure that they would soon be leaving Ryeland and entering the Merisenne Province, which was the area that continued on to Meriselle and the ocean. Window's thoughts jumped back to when he was in school, and he learned that Calisay and Meriselle were named for the Freeland king's daughters.

As Circles perched on Rings' back, he started taking the far-scope Rings had given him and searching up the road ahead of them. He was looking for the ocean, although Window had assured him that they were nowhere near the ocean yet. After a day on so, Circles gave up looking for the ocean, and started searching for Silkie, off in the distance to the side of the road. He was very disappointed that they had not found the Silkie.

Circles also tried flying his kite while he rode on Rings' back, but that didn't work out so well. While Circles was trying to get it into the air, the kite spun down and whacked Rings on the nose, and that was the end of the kite flying.

The countryside continued to grow greener and more fertile. Small herds of wild cattle and sheep appeared in the grassy fields along the road. Colorful birds flew overhead and the whole world seemed to be coming to life.

Finally, late one morning, they came upon a stone marker by the side of the road. It was plain, with four flat sides, and about as tall as Window's chest. On the marker was engraved the Freelandan letter M.

"We are here," Window announced to the others. "We have arrived at the edge of the Merisenne Province."

Window thought that it should take about nine more days to reach the ocean, if he was correct — one day's travel, and one marker, for each letter in the Freelandan spelling of Merisenne. He expected to pass eight more markers on their way to the sea.

As the travelers proceeded into Merisenne, off to their right they saw the remains of what must have been a province watchtower before the wars. A mile farther up the road, they passed the overgrown ruins of a small village, its remaining building now almost buried beneath the wild field grass and sten-bushes.

The Northway continued through the Merisenne Province as Window had expected, each day's journey marked with a new letter and each marker guarded by a destroyed watchtower.

As they went on their way, the travelers encountered more animals – cattle, sheep, wild pigs, and other once-domesticated animals that had apparently been existing in the wild, for all of the years since the Northern Wars ended.

One afternoon, the travelers stopped to rest next to a small lake. As they sat in some shade by the water, many of the big, white ducks that were swimming in the lake came over and quacked for food. Circles tossed them some bread strips and the ducks went wild, honking and quacking and chasing after him as he hurriedly tried to climb into a small tree to get away from them.

The hungry ducks stretched their necks up to try to reach Circles, but he was just high enough to be safe. Eventually the ducks left him and went back to the water. Circle's friends just sat and watched the episode with gentle smiles on their faces.

As the travelers left the lake and continued on their way, Circles looked back. One of the ducks had left the others and was following them. Three times Circles ran back to the duck to chase him away, but every time the travelers started walking again, the duck would follow.

The next time Circles went to chase the duck away, Raine went with him. The starman squatted down next to the duck and spoke to him in odd tones and pitches of his voice. With a final loud quack, the duck turned around and waddled back towards the lake, no longer interested in following them.

"I wish that I could talk to birds," Circles lamented.

"Maybe I can teach you someday, Circles," Raine told him. "Maybe I will be able to do that."

"I would like that, Raine," Circles replied. And then he asked, "Do you think that you will be able to talk to the Silkie?"

"I can talk to almost anything," was Raine's response. "Except maybe a rock," he joked to the little Woot.

"I'll bet that your finger-rings could even talk to a rock," the admiring Circles suggested.

"Well, not a rock, Circles, not a rock. There are many things that my rings cannot do."

"I wish that I had finger-rings so I could do magic things. You are very lucky to have them."

"My rings can do many things – but they cannot get me home. Besides, it is I who envies you, Circles, because you do not know what you already possess. Someday you will understand how special you are."

"Yeah, well, maybe," Circles countered, not knowing what Raine was talking about. "But I still wish that I could talk to the birds."

Panni hadn't had much to say to Window for a few days, but as the travelers passed by the fourth road marker on the way to the ocean, she came up next to him.

"Look at that field-jay over there, Window. Doesn't it look pretty, with those white wings and blue wing-bars? I love the way it sings, too. When I was a girl at home, I used to try to whistle, just like the birds in our yard. I used to say that when I grew up, I was going to feed all of the birds so they would come stay in my yard and sing to me. Once I had a dream that I could fly, and I flew away with them."

"It is a beautiful bird, Panni. Thank you for pointing it out. And thank you for joining me. I have been a bit lonely walking the last couple of days."

"I know what you mean, Window. I have felt the same way."

"Maybe we could walk together for a while. I would like that."

"So would I, Window. So would I."

Panni reached over and squeezed his hand. They walked on together, speaking of birds and treasure and nothing in particular. It was a happy afternoon of reconnection for both of them.

As they drew closer and closer to the ocean, the travelers' excitement grew. None of them had ever seen an ocean, except Raine, of course, and they were all really looking forward to it.

Circles wanted to go swimming. Rings wanted to jump into the water, from someplace high up, and make the "biggest splash in history."

Panni wanted to sit in the sun and feel the sea breeze on her legs. Window wanted to gaze out to sea, and imagine where his father was at that very moment. They all wanted to sit and rest for a long, long time.

As the travelers came around a slight curve in the road, they were met with a very unexpected sight. Off to their left, were rows and rows of simple, white, upright gravestones, off to their right, rows and rows of low, grey, gravestones.

Window had forgotten. This was the location of the first great Northlands battle of the Continent Wars. The Atland army had come up to the Northway from the southwest, bypassing the city of Meriselle, and engaged the Northlands soldiers here. The Northlands forces were defeated, but both sides took tremendous losses.

The travelers all just stopped and stood without saying anything, looking at the stones. Everyone seemed reluctant to go near them, even Raine. Apparently, he also had some experience with death, up close.

As they stood and watched, five big ocean gulls appeared from the western horizon and flew into view.

"Hey, look," Circles called out. "Birds from the ocean. We must be pretty close."

Everyone kept their eyes on the beautiful birds as they circled overhead and then flew down and landed in the cemetery on their right, alighting on the top of some of the gravestones.

"Let's go see if we can catch one," Circles suggested. Everyone thought that this was a silly idea, but no one had anything better to say.

They walked ahead and into the rows of wide, low stones to their right. Rings was too big to fit between the rows, so he stayed on the road. The others gently sat on the grave markers, and watched as Circles chased a few of the birds around for a while.

Circles soon tired of that, so he had another suggestion. "Let's eat," he called back to his friends. Panni agreed, and soon they were having a quick lunch and quietly planning their final few miles to the city.

The travelers' meal was restful. They relaxed and watched the sea birds hop from marker to marker, looking for something to eat. Circles tried to lure one of them with a piece of bread, but the bird just grabbed it and flew away
By the time they had finished eating, each of the travelers had become comfortable among the markers. It was another beautiful late-spring day. They were almost to Meriselle.

As the travelers continued towards the ocean, the sea-birds became a common sight. Circles thought about trying to hit one with an arrow, but changed his mind.
At last, they reached the final road marker. They could easily smell the salt of the sea as it came inland on the ocean breeze.
Window assured the group, "Tomorrow we will reach the city, and the ocean."

+++++++++

The last day of their journey to Meriselle started with great anticipation. After several hours of travel, Circles stood up on Rings' back and looked ahead with his far-scope.
"I see it! I see it!" he happily cried out. "I see the ocean! It is big and blue. It is really big, and really blue!"
They hurried ahead, and reaching the top of a rise in the road, saw the city and the sea both laid out below them. The travelers stood in awe and looked to the west at a panorama of green grass, broken, white stones of the city, and the bright blue of the water.
Panni took Window's hand. "It is beautiful, Window. Thank you for bringing me here. I will never forget this day." Window gave her a delighted hug.
Circles jumped down from Rings' back and ran on ahead. Raine didn't say anything, but just watched, sharing in their excitement.

"Keep an eye out for treasure, everybody. We wouldn't want to miss anything," Window said jokingly.

Circles took him seriously, and called back, "Oh, I will, Window, I will."

Spread out far before them were the broken ruins of the once-grand city of Meriselle. No building remained standing. They were all destroyed by the Atland army long ago. The wooden framed buildings were completely collapsed, and those structures that had been made from the slabs of bright, white stone from the ocean's edge, had been knocked down. There were a few trees among the ruins, but most of the former city was covered with bright green grass.

Beyond the ruins, from their far left to their far right, was a horizon of bright, blue, ocean. The midday sun shone down, and reflected from the water and the white stones of the ruins.

The travelers decided not to wait, but continue ahead to the ocean immediately. They hurried down the long hillside in front of them, Circles running ahead of the others again. More sea birds called overhead, as the treasure hunters reached almost to the edge of the city.

About half-way down the long slope to Meriselle, the ground flattened out briefly. On this flattened section of ground, the road passed through a grove of large, ancient-looking trees. As the road went under the shade of the trees, it temporarily widened. In the middle of the widened space was another stone marker.

Well, it seemed to be a marker, but when Window got close to it, he excitedly cried out, "This is it! Circles, Panni, this is it! The sundial! The sundial! The last picture from my grandma's springcookies that I couldn't think of in Calisay. This is it. It had the same angled design for the three and the six, and the same sun design at the top. I am sure it is the same sundial!"

Panni and Circles knew all about the cookies. They rushed up to see just what Window was talking about.

At first, Circles was excited about the discovery of the sundial that appeared on the cookies, too. Then something else jumped into his mind.

"Hey, Window. What is a sundial doing in a grove of trees where the sun can't shine on it?" Circles wanted to know. "And it didn't happen by accident. These trees have been here a long time."

Window was surprised by the question. "I don't know, Circles. Maybe whoever put it here didn't really care what time it was."

"It's a good thing that they didn't care what time it was, because, look," Circles continued. "It's not pointing in the right direction."

Circles was right. Window checked the position of the sun behind and above them. His years of hiking and camping had taught him well. The shadow blade, and top of the sundial, which should have pointed directly to the north, did not. It was turned somewhat to the northwest.

Circles wondered aloud, "Why would anybody put a sundial pointing in the wrong direction?"

"Maybe a tree blew down and knocked it to the side," Panni suggested.

Rings had an idea, "Maybe a big animal like me walked through here once, and accidentally bumped into it."

Raine once again stood silently, and didn't join in the speculation.

Then Circles answered his own question. "Maybe it's in the wrong direction for the sun, but the right direction for something else."

"What do you mean," Window reacted, "Like what else?"

"Oh, I don't know," Circles thought for a moment. "Like a treasure, perhaps." He smiled broadly at everyone.

Window looked at the sundial again. The mark at the top of its circle of hours was definitely pointing to the west of where it should be.

Circles went on, "I wonder what is off in the direction that the sundial is pointing." He pulled his far-scope from his pack, and looked out, between the trunks of the trees. "It looks like nothing but open ground, except for over near the ocean, where there are trees and maybe more ruins."

Window answered, "I don't know what is over there, but when we travel to the ice lands in the far north we may see. We will be traveling up the coast right over in that direction. Look, you can see the road from here."

Through the trees, off in the distance to their right, they could see the road that followed the coast. If the sundial was pointing to anything, they would pass by it as they went north from the city.

"What time is it anyway," Circles wanted to know.

"Time to go to the ocean," Window replied. Everyone agreed.

As they left the grove, Window turned to Circles. "I guess that we shall see where the sundial is pointing, Circles, we shall see."

Circles thought for a moment, and then asked, "Hey Window, how come that sundial was carved into your grandma's cookie board – and the Calisay bridge and tower, too?"

Window just looked at Circles, gave him a puzzled grin, and shrugged.

The happy travelers followed the road and passed into the ruined city. The road itself was undamaged, but as they continued to the ocean shore, they passed among hundreds and hundreds of destroyed buildings, all overgrown with sea-ivy and ocean grass.

The road led them to the highest point of ground at the shore. It must have been the location of the Meriselle lighthouse, used to guide the Freeland ships that sailed to and from the harbor. Off to their right, they could see where the harbor had been cut into the rock.

As the travelers reached the high ground above the shore, they stopped at the ruins of the ancient lighthouse. The lighthouse had been built of massive slabs of bright stone taken from the quarries to the south, and at one time, must have been a beautiful creation. Now, the large, flat stones of its base and walls were lying on the ground, at various angles, and were partially covered with ivy.

Right at the highest point of ground overlooking the water, there were several huge slabs of the soft white stone that lay flat on the ground. Window unhooked Rings' harness and it slipped from his back. The treasure hunters sat down on the stones and gazed out across the beautiful ocean before them.

With the sun still high in the sky above, the bright, green grass at their feet fluttered gently, and the caws of the sea birds joined with the relaxing sound of the waves breaking on the sand below. The sweet sea breeze blew over them, washing away their physical pain and their emotional pain. It was a scene of wonderful calm and comfort.

After a few minutes of sitting and watching, Panni took off her shoes and slid down the slope to the beach below. She kicked sand before her as she ran, twirling, up the shoreline, running in and out of the water.

Circles followed Panni down to the sand, riding on Rings' back. Rings waded into the water and sat down. The waves lapped up against him.

Circles swam around Rings and splashed him a few times. Rings lifted a giant paw and slammed it down into the water. The resulting waves flipped Circles over in the water and some went up his nose. After that, Circles just floated quietly on his back and Rings was left alone to enjoy the cool of the sea.

Raine and Window remained high above the water, on their benches of stone. Raine seemed lost in his own thoughts. Window's memory flew back to the time of his first summer with Mary. They had raced to the top of Kite Hill in Windtown and sat laughing as it started to rain on them. Window wished that Mary could be with him now.

Rings and Circles left the water and sat on the sand together and talked. Panni returned up the slope and lay down on one of the sun-warmed stone slabs near Window. She closed her eyes, the sun bathing over her face and arms and legs. The beauty of the sea washed over them all.

Later, when Circles and Rings returned to the lighthouse stones where Window had waited, Circles had a question. "Where will we find a treasure buried around here, Window? Where could it be?"

"I don't know, Circles. Too bad that we don't have a map."

"Too bad that your grandma's springcookie board didn't have a cookie showing where the treasure is buried."

"Yeah, Circles, too bad." Window closed his eyes.

That night, the travelers used only enough wood to build a small fire, but no one minded. They prepared their camp among the soft, flat, lighthouse stones. The setting sun shot flames of fire into the darkening sky as it fell below the distant sea to the west. The moon had not yet risen, and soon the nighttime sky was ablaze with stars.

The sea breeze remained warm as the night surrounded them. The travelers sat in the starlight and thought and talked and thought some more as they completely enjoyed their first night at the ocean.

Panni loved the stars. At the Traepelle Castle, she and her dancer friends used to spend every warm night out on the evening room balcony. They would slip from their overclothes and enjoy the breeze on their bare skin as they looked to the sky. The Calisay dancers didn't have a star book to tell them the names of the star pictures, so Panni made up her own.

She would lie back on one of the smooth balcony lounge settees and imagine the stars above her as pictures of animals and things. She would see a bird, or a running deer, or a dancer in the starlit sky, and give it a name. Watching the stars comforted Panni, and gave her a sense of freedom, which she did not have.

Now, here at the ocean, Panni reveled in the beauty of the stars on this moonless night. As she had so many times before, she lay back and gazed into the sparkling night sky. The breeze caressed her face and fluttered her hair, as she once again let her imagination fly to the stars.

After a while, Panni noticed Raine, off by himself. As he dangled his feet over the edge of his flat stone bench, the soft blue glow of his skin stood out against the dark horizon. He, too, was looking up at the stars, and seemed to be studying their positions. Panni went over and sat down by him.

"What do you see when you look at the stars, Raine?"

"I see the beauty of the world, Panni, and the loneliness of the world, too."

Then he added, "And sometimes, when I look at the stars, I count those that I have visited. But, tonight, I cannot see any I have ever been to. I am far away from my own world. I am lost from my home."

Panni waited a moment and then gently asked, "What is the best world you have ever visited, Raine? "

He considered her question carefully. "Each world has its own delights, and its own terrors. It all depends which you choose to see. But, my favorite would be my own world. I miss it dearly. I hope that I can see it again soon."

Raine continued, "Your world is beautiful, Panni. Some places I have been are not so inviting. "

"And your world, Raine, what is it like?"

"It is a lot like this one, Panni. That is why I am fortunate to have found it. Thank you again for letting me come with you. I would be very lonely without you and your friends."

He looked up at the stars again, and then continued, "Back on my world, starpilots have a rhyme that they sometimes recite. It tells a bit about me."

Quietly, Raine shared it with her.

> "I do wander wonder far
> Past the silent break of dawn
> Travel far and sail on farther
> To the stars and yet go on
>
> I have seen the highest mountain
> Higher than a bird can fly
> I have crossed the widest ocean

To the edge beyond the sky

I have braved the coldest winter
Only to be colder still
I have watched the sunset signal
Seven moons above the hill.”

  Raine’s voice faltered, but he went on, a silver tear running down over the blue of his face.

“Stargates beckon lonely traveler
Back from where the Starpaths roam
Waiting fires warm the doorstep
Waiting voices welcome home”

  “It is cold and lonely sailing the stars, Panni. I am fortunate to have met such caring friends.”
  Panni glanced up at the sparkling night sky above them, and searched for a moment. “I see the star you pointed out to us, Raine, the one on the path to your home. I hope that you can return there soon.”
  “So do I, Panni, so do I.”

  Just then, Circles came over and joined them.
  “Raine, you have been to many worlds, and I’ve been wondering, do you know who made them, or how our world came to be as it is?”
  The starman marveled at the thoughtfulness of the little Woot, and answered as best he could. “I do not know that, Circles. Your world was here before I arrived.” And then, he added. “I guess that you will have to discover that for yourself.”
  Circles looked a little disappointed.
  “Why don’t you sit here with me for a while, Circles, and I will tell you some stories about places I have been.”
  Circles smiled, sat down next to Raine, and scooted up close to him.

Panni left the two friends, and walked back towards their fire. Rings was asleep against a big stone. Panni found Window, sitting alone. He seemed to be waiting for her.

"Hello, Window. Isn't this a beautiful place? May I sit with you for a while?"

Window and Panni stayed up late that night, naming star pictures, and feeling the warm sea breeze on their faces.

+++++++++

[AT RIVERHOLD]

Far across the Merisenne Province, the Deep Woods, and the Windlands, beyond the Outlands and the mountains, Wendy Kesselle was dreaming. Wendy loved Angels, and tonight, that's what she was dreaming about.

Her grandmother sometimes told her stories about Angels, and Wendy always hoped that they were true. It seemed like such a nice idea to have something magical to watch over you.

One of Wendy's favorite stories of her grandmother's was about Angels who rode on the Silkie in the moonlight. Silkie, her grandmother had told her, were giant beasts that roamed the far Northern Plains. Wendy didn't know where the far Northern Plains were, but, well, she figured that they were in the far north, and since it was just a story, it didn't really matter.

Anyway, tonight Wendy was dreaming...

Caroline and Valentine were the youngest of the Angels. They had yet to be assigned to a part of the world. They sat in the sun, on the stone bench at the bottom of the long staircase from the palace, and wondered when they would be sent out. The others

+++++++++

Window opened his eyes from his sleep, and sat up. There was
a thin slice of the moon glowing near the horizon. The stars were
still bright across the entire sky, like a glistening ceiling in a great
hall. The fire had gone out, but the air was warm. The breeze
from the sea ran through his hair.

Window looked out towards the ocean. There was someone there, beneath the canopy of stars. It was Panni.

Panni was there, on one of the large, flat, soft white stones from the lighthouse. She spun, she twirled, she turned. She moved as if she were floating on the breeze.
Panni's almost-silver hair trailed out behind her, flying as a silken bird in the wind. Her soft skirt followed her graceful legs, her arms carried her as though she was weightless. Her skin shone moon-white in the dark. She closed her eyes and turned again. Panni was dancing!

POLARTICA
THE
ICELANDS
ATLANDIC
OCEAN
MERISENNE
PROVINCE
MERISELLE

CHAPTER TWELVE

UP THE WESTERN COAST

"Come on!" Panni yelled back at them. She was almost to the water, running as fast as she could. She had left her thin half-blouse and skirt on the blanket and tied her drying towel around her waist. She threw the towel to the hot sand just before her feet splashed into the sun-warmed ocean. Window and Circles ran after her and, one after another, they all flopped into the oncoming waves. They were bounced and tossed and splashed in the bright morning sunshine.

Panni squealed with delight. Circles showed off his floating skills, and soon Panni and Window were picking him up and trying to toss him back and forth. His wet fur was too slippery to hold on to very well, and so Circles would continually be dropped, and splash down into the water, but then, immediately rise to the surface again. He got a lot of water up his nose, but didn't seem to mind too much.

From his seat on a lighthouse stone, high above the swimmers, Raine watched his friends enjoying themselves. He and Rings were having another restful morning, as the other three travelers played in the water. Rings opened his eyes just long enough to notice that the world was still there, and then he closed them again. The travelers had discovered that sleeping was one of Rings' best skills.

The happy travelers remained at the Meriselle lighthouse ruins for three days. In the mornings, they would relax in the sun and breeze, or go swimming. In the afternoons, they would go exploring. Well, Window, Panni, and Circles would go exploring. Rings and Raine preferred to stay at the camp, Rings sleeping, or gazing out to sea, and Raine, apparently, just thinking.

The three explorers searched all around the destroyed city, but found little of interest. Most of what was left of the buildings was so overgrown with sea-ivy that it was nearly impossible to uncover them. They did find what they were sure had once been the Province castle, but it, too, was completely in rubble. Circles wanted to bring Rings back with them so he could move some of the toppled castle stones, to look for the King's Treasure, but then, even he realized that the search was impossible.

On the remains of one stone wall, Panni found a large carving of the symbol of King Alezan – crossed swords and the sun between the blades of the swords. The treasure-hunters were excited for a moment, but soon again, realized that no one would mark the location of a hidden treasure with a large royal seal.
After two days of searching through the city, the explorers spent the next afternoon looking up and down the ocean beach to the south and then to the north. They weren't expecting to find any treasures, but enjoyed the sun on their faces and the sand beneath their feet.

At suppertime, on the third night, Window and Panni laid out all of the remaining food they had in their supply packs – and it wasn't much. They had originally planned to be back to Oldsmith's by now and, even though Raine didn't eat much, they would soon be out of food.
There were still lots of crackers, and a few of Sara's baked sugar-sticks from her shop in Calisay, but the fresh fruit and the dried fruit, the cheese and dried meat had all been finished days before.

"Can you use your finger-rings to make food, Raine?" Circles wanted to know.

"Well, I could help us get food, but I would rather not, unless it was an emergency. I want to preserve the power of my rings as long as I can."

"You mean that they could lose their power?"

"Yes. They will last a long time, but eventually all of their strength will be used up.

After hearing that, Circles knew then that the power in Raine's finger-rings must be from science, as he had said, and not from magic, as Circles was hoping.

On the fourth day, the travelers left the city. As Window finished securing Rings' harness, Panni and Circles stood on the lighthouse stones and looked out to sea from them for the last time. Their stay in Meriselle had been a very good one, but now, once again, their thoughts had turned to treasure and adventure.

Their plan was to travel north of Meriselle, along the road that went up the coast. They would go to the lands in the very far north where Brarries, like Rings, had lived before coming to the Deep Woods. Rings wasn't sure, but he thought that maybe some of his relatives could still be living up there somewhere.

The lands of the far north were called Polartica. At the southern edge of Polartica was the area known as the Ice Lands. Rings told his friends that much of his family had moved from there to the south, because of massive glaciers there that were advancing from the top of the world. The glaciers were bringing the snow and ice closer and closer to the south. There were only some low mountains between the advancing ice and the plains of Merisenne and Ryeland.

The others weren't immediately sure that a trip to a place of ice and snow was a good idea, but everybody agreed that they wanted Rings to have his wish of going there come true. They hadn't thought about it before, but then realized that Rings' fur made him naturally suited for cold weather.

Also, Circles always enjoyed winter in the Deep Woods, so he, too, was ready to go north. Woots are naturally slippery, and so, young Woots would spend much of the winter months playing in the snow, sliding down hillsides and along frozen creek beds. Circles was really looking forward to the trip.

"How far is the far north? Window asked Rings as they made their plans.

"I'm not sure, Window. But I think that a week or two will bring us there. We just need to reach the mountains and then go to the other side."

"How will we climb over the mountains?" Circles wanted to know.

"We won't have to, Circles. There are gaps between the peaks that we can pass through. Besides, they are not large mountains, only small ones."

The group started out on the coast road leading to the north. After traveling just a short distance from the city, they came to the destroyed harbor of Meriselle, which had been the only port in all of the Northlands. The docks and moorings were all collapsed and fallen into the water. The skeleton of one sailing ship still could be seen sticking up from its grave below the surface, its lonely remaining mastpole reaching out to the sky as though the ship were making a last grasp at life.

On the top of the mast was perched a beautiful golden sea-tern. It fluttered its wings and reminded Window of what it must have looked like, so long ago, when a flag flew at the top of that mast. It was sad to think of a beautiful sailing ship being sunk.

Window had never seen his father's ship, the "Kathryn B." but knew that its mast flag was light green, his mother's favorite color. He thought of his parents for a while as the travelers proceeded up the coast.

The road north from the harbor wound along the edge of the sea, sometimes passing through small groves of trees but mostly the lands were somewhat barren. As they walked along, the bright blue of the ocean kept them company on their left. To their right, the land was mostly open space, sprinkled with an occasional patch of underbrush.

Circles had taken the arrows out of his quiver and replaced them with his far-scope, so he could easily carry it with him. He would march along, spot something in the distance, and then take out his scope to get a better look at whatever he had spied.

In the middle of the afternoon, he saw something especially interesting. After looking through his scope, Circles took off running up the road ahead of his friends. He returned in a few minutes, carrying, high above his head, a stick he had pulled from a bush. Its slender twigs were all bent, and hanging down towards the ground. It was loaded with scores of large, bright, juicy-looking, red berries.

"The sea-berries are out!" he happily announced. "Our food problems are over!"

"Are those berries good to eat, Circles? How do you know?" responded Window.

"Everybody knows about sea-berries. They are the best. We learned back home that sea-berries are the most delicious berries in the world. You will see. You will see."

Circles had discovered a large patch of the berries, and they really were delicious. It seems that back in the Deep Woods, mama Woots would put their babies to sleep, telling them stories of the berries from by the sea. Woot children grew up, hoping to be good enough to be rewarded someday with sea-berries for lunch.

"I thought that they were just made up stories for the children," Circles went on. "But here there are. Mama was right!"

Soon the travelers came upon other delights. There were groves of ocean-fruit trees, and patches of sweet ground-berries. Everybody helped pick the ripest looking fruit and juiciest looking berries, and soon the food tins and bags were full. Raine seemed to especially enjoy the chore. He told the others that, every summer, when he was a boy on Moonfarm, he always helped pick the fresh sky-berries. He hadn't done that in a long, long time. Today, he felt connected to his faraway world, as he carefully collected the dark purple berries from the scatter-patches on the ground.

"Has anyone seen any bread-trees?" joked Window. "We could use some of that, too. Oh, well, maybe we will find one later."

Lunch was very enjoyable that afternoon. Most of the conversation was taken up by Circles reminding the others to keep an eye out for treasure. He figured that they were passing along the part of the coast that the sundial was pointing toward, and he felt that King Alezan's treasure could be hidden around here somewhere, except that there didn't seem to be any place to hide a treasure, just a lot of open land. As they continued on their way, Circles stowed his far-scope, and as he walked, he looked down at the ground a lot. He didn't want to miss any clues.

The trip up the coast went smoothly. By the middle of the next morning, they came upon the ruins of a small village. Just beyond the village, a small, low, grass-covered promontory jutted out into the ocean. It had probably been used as a lookout to warn Meriselle of enemy ships that were approaching the city along the coast from the north.

The small lookout watchtower at the neck of the promontory was completely collapsed. Out on the headland, surrounded by grass and pointing out to sea, were four dark-metal cannon, mounted on stone bases. They stood in a row, about ten feet apart. The cannon were undamaged, and gave the impression that they had been standing there, dutifully guarding the shoreline for a thousand years.

The stone bases of the cannon were triangular in shape, with the cannonpieces mounted at the upper tips of the triangles. The four guns looked lonely, silently pointing out to sea, alone and unchanging.

Window couldn't believe it. He was so amazed that he didn't shout or speak excitedly. He just calmly told the others, "Those are the cannon. Those are the cannon – the ones on the springcookies!" He just looked at the others and quietly repeated, "Those are the same four cannon."

Circles didn't seem surprised at all. "And I'll bet that there is
some treasure around here someplace, too," he asserted. This
time the others couldn't be sure that he was just imagining things.

The treasure hunters searched through the ruins of the nearby
village, and the watchtower rubble, and of course, the cannon.
They thought about any possible connection between the cannon
and the sundial and what it might mean. The only conclusion
upon which they agreed, was that, somehow, Window's
grandmother's cookieboard had come from the Northlands.

"Remember, Window," Circles unnecessarily reminded him,
"Oldsmith said there were three Treasures of King Alezan – his
gold and silver coins, his statues and other large ornaments, and
his crown and jewels. One part was hidden in Calisay, one part
was hidden in the eastern mountains, and one part was taken to
Meriselle.

Panni suggested, "Let's think about, if we were the King's sons,
which part of the treasure we would take to each place, and how
we would hide it."

"It seems to me," offered Window, "that it would be very
difficult to transport a bunch of statues and other large things
across the Northlands by wagon. It would take many wagons, and
be impossible to keep from being noticed. So, I think that part of
the treasure was hidden in Calisay. The coins and jewels would
not take nearly as many wagons to carry them."

"That means, of course," Panni continued, "that either the coins
or the jewels came to Meriselle."

The others agreed, except for Raine. He just listened as the
others went on. Window wondered if the starman knew anything
that could help them in their search.

Rings hadn't had much at all to say about the treasures, but
now he spoke up. "If I were bringing a treasure to the ocean, I
wouldn't have taken it to Meriselle. The King's son should have
realized that the Atland Army would capture or destroy Meriselle
before it left the North. And, even if the treasure hidden in the
city was not found by the Army, it would still be lost to the Royal

Family. I would have hidden the treasure somewhere else, where I could retrieve it later, or maybe even tried to take it out of the Northlands. I am sure that the son didn't want to just bury the treasure and leave it."

"So," Panni asked, "where could the King's son have gotten on to a ship, except at the harbor at Meriselle? There everybody would have known it was him, and would have seen his wagons of treasure being loaded on board."

At the same time, everybody looked out to the promontory and the cannon.

"Maybe down there, at those mooring posts," Circles answered.

Circles was right. Several hundred feet beyond the cannon, sticking out from the sand, were the remains of a walkway, and a dock, and several large mooring posts. It was clear that large sailing ships could have tied up there years ago.

"Or maybe the King's son was unable to get the treasure on board a ship, and it is still hidden around here somewhere, waiting for us to find it," Circles offered hopefully.

No one said anything. Then Circles burst out, "Let's go check the cannon again. Maybe we missed a clue."

The treasure hunters hurried to the headland and carefully examined the cannon one more time – and this time they found something! The last cannon in the row, the cannon nearest the mooring posts, had a small insignia scratched into the back of its base, hidden by the grass near the ground. It was the crossed swords and shining sun of King Alezan.

"Why would just this base have the insignia on it?" Window wondered out loud.

"Maybe the treasure is buried right here, or maybe it is back in that direction somewhere," Circles spoke next.

Rings didn't wait to find out. He extended the thick, long claws on his right paw and scooped them across the ground, just behind the cannon's base. It only took two or three scoops for him to dig down two or three feet into the ground.

And there it was! Still half-buried in the dirt behind the cannon, something bright sparkled back at the treasure hunters in the noonday sun – it was a gold coin!

Panni's heart was beating so fast she could hardly breathe. They all just stood for a moment and stared at the coin.

"Circles, I think that you should have the honor," announced Window. "Why don't you jump down there and pick out that coin from the dirt. It looks like you have found the King's Treasure!"

Circles was thrilled as he hopped down into the low little treasure hole. He proudly held up a large gold coin. It must have been part of King Alezan's hidden treasure. Everyone cheered and applauded. It was a wonderful moment they shared.

Unfortunately, their excitement was short lived. Although Rings dug a lot deeper behind the cannon base, nothing else was found. The King's Treasure was only a single coin.

Everyone was immensely disheartened. They had thought for sure that they had found the treasure. They had not.

And not only that, but upon examining the coin, Window realized that it could not have been even a part of the King's Treasure. It was not a Freeland coin – it was an Amerand coin. Window's grandmother had once showed him a similar coin. On its face was a likeness of an Amerand nobleman that Window didn't recognize. On its reverse, was the likeness of a large Amerand sailing-ship.

Panni was the first to make the connection. "Gentlemen," she addressed her friends. (She loved using that word, since she had learned to speak Atlandan.) "It looks as though we were right. I'll bet the treasure that was to be hidden in Meriselle was King Alezan's gold and silver coins. And, instead of going to Meriselle, the treasure was taken here. But the treasure is no longer here."

Panni continued, "And I think that the coin and the cannon are pointing the way it has gone. I think that the King's Treasure was taken out to sea on an Amerand ship."

So that was it. The travelers had found part of the King's Treasure. Well, not really. Rings dug in front of the cannon, and in several more places, but nothing else was discovered. They all agreed that Panni was right. The treasure of gold and silver coins had been taken from the Northlands by an Amerand ship. Why that ship had been there, or to where it sailed, they could not know.

The unhappy treasure hunters sat on the grass against the cannon and had lunch. They were pretty quiet and just thinking until Circles spoke up. "Window, let's see if we can figure out the connections between your grandma's cookieboard and places in the Northlands. The board must have been carved in the North, with all those things we have seen."

Window agreed, and reminded everyone of the twelve pictures on his grandmother's cookieboard – a kite, the Calisay bridge, the Calisay tower, the Silkie, a sword and shield, an Angel, a flag, a windmill, some flowers, a ship, the Meriselle sundial, and the cannon.

"Let's group the pictures by where they are located in the Northlands," Window suggested. "The sundial and the cannon are over here by the ocean."

"And the ship, too," Panni threw in.

"The bridge and tower are located in Calisay, and the kite could belong there, too," Circles continued. "How about the shield, Window? Did it have an insignia on it?"

"Yes, but I can't be sure what is was. It could be King Alezan's crest. I know that it had crossed swords, or maybe lances on it, but I don't remember any sun between the blades. Anyway, I suppose that the shield could be put in the Calisay group."

"Maybe the Silkie could be grouped with the ocean pictures," Panni thought out loud. The Silkie are supposed to be in this part of the Northlands somewhere.

"I was just thinking," Circles put in. "I'll bet that these cannon are still used by the Angels to tie their Silkie's reins to, so the Silkie don't run away when the Angels are resting."

That comment gave everyone a good laugh, and they all relaxed a bit. Then, one by one, as the conversation continued, they realized that, although they didn't find the treasure, they still had their friends, and their travels to the far north to look forward to. Their spirits lifted as they regained their joy of adventure.

"Hey Rings, are there any missing treasures in the Ice Lands?" Circles wanted to know.

"It is so cold there that there are not many flowers, so I guess you could say that a flower would be a treasure there."

Rings went on, "What about the flowers on the cookie, Window? What kind were they?"

"They each had four or five long, pointed petals that stood straight up into the air, and long, pointed leaves that did the same. I have never seen anything like them, at home, or here in the Northlands."

Panni summarized their thoughts so far, "If we group the Silkie with the ocean group and the shield with the Calisay group, that leaves the flag, and flowers, and windmill, and Angel in a group. Where have there ever been windmills in the Northlands? Does anybody know? I didn't see any as we searched along the shore in Meriselle."

"And how about Angels?" Circles added.

Rings joined in again, "Window, what was on the flag in the picture?"

"The flag held two identical designs, side by side. Each design was formed of a horizontal line crossing a vertical line. And, at the intersection of those two lines, two shorter lines crossed diagonally. It gave the suggestion of two bright stars twinkling. Does anybody know what flag that might be?"

No one did.

Rings spoke again. He was enjoying the challenge of trying to figure out where a treasure might be. "Well, everyone keep on the lookout for that flag design, those pointy flowers, a windmill..."

"And an Angel," Circles threw in. Then he went on, "I'll bet that those things are all somewhere in the east by the mountains, where the third treasure was hidden. I think that the cookieboard is a map to the King's Treasures."

"I just don't see how my grandma's cookieboard could be connected to any treasure," Window reacted.

"I don't see how it couldn't be," Circles concluded.

+++++++++

As the travelers loaded up their supplies to continue to the north, they noticed dark clouds off to the far west over the ocean. The clouds swirled and grew, and blew towards them. By the time they had walked just a mile or so up the coast road, a storm was upon them.

It was an uncomfortable wet walk for the rest of the day. There simply was no place to take shelter, no hillside or big trees that would have helped keep them dry, so they just walked on in the rain.

After a while, Window looked at the others. Circles was on Rings' back, hanging on to his harness, and trying to not get blown away. Everyone was so wet, and looked so sad and miserable, that it almost brought a smile to Window's face.

Then Panni glanced over at Window, and soon those two were laughing with every squish of their shoes. Then Window noticed that Raine seemed to be a lot drier than the others. Apparently, whatever caused the blue glow around him, kept some of the raindrops from landing on him, too.

The air turned cooler and the travelers struggled to keep going. Panni wished that she was back at the Meriselle lighthouse, in the sun.

The rain continued for a few more hours, and then the storm passed. The travelers decided to camp early for the night, and to try to dry out. Fortunately, as they continued following the road next to the coast, they came upon a small forest just off to their right. Here they could find wood for a fire.

They stopped and unpacked a few of their things. As Window was checking to see that his notebook had stayed dry, he noticed the date on his calendar

"Hey, everybody," Window called out. "It's the first day of summer. Happy Summer's Day, everyone!"

"Let's celebrate with a big bonfire!" Circles suggested.

"Yes, let's do, Window," Panni requested. "Back at the castle, we dancers always had summer ribbon parties on the lawn. It was a time of fun for us."

Rings and Raine went into the trees and pulled piece after piece of wood to their camp, which was on some high ground right next to the water.

Although the wood was wet, with a little help from Raine's finger-rings, the fire was soon blazing into the sky. It seemed that the smoke billowed almost up to the clouds.

Window untied the spear from Rings' harness and stuck it into the ground. Raine took some of their rope and stretched it between the spear and a small tree nearby. Soon all of their wet clothes were hanging over the rope and drying by the roaring fire. Their world was getting comfortable again.

As the others sat and enjoyed the bright heat of the fire, Panni brought out the last of Sara's sugar-sticks. They all clicked them together in honor of Sara and Oldsmith, before sticking the crumbling, sweet pastry into their mouths.

Circles started singing and soon the whole group was welcoming in the summer months with good cheer. Window was reminded of the songs and stories at the forest clearing. It already seemed like that was a long time ago.

As the fire crackled loudly, and the smoke from the wet wood continued to rise into the night sky, Window noticed that they were about to have a visitor. From the direction of the trees across the road, a large grey snake was slithering towards their camp.

Window motioned to the others and they all just watched as the shiny creature crawled across the grass, around the fire in front of them, and right up to the ocean side of the blaze. The flames reflected from his scales, and made him look as though he was wearing sparkling armor.

The snake didn't seem to be paying them any attention. It just curled up by the fire with its head raised above its coils, and enjoyed the heat on its face. Circles started singing another song, and the snake bobbed its head in time with his singing.

"I guess he likes it," Circles happily spoke to the others. "Does anybody know any snake songs?" Not surprisingly, no one did, although Panni knew a song about a turtle.

Window had taken his medallion from his pocket, and sat, rubbing it, as he often did. He held the medallion up in the direction of the snake.

"Hey, Mister Snake," Window called to it. "Have you ever seen this before?" The snake turned in Window's direction and seemed to be looking at the medallion. Then it turned back towards the fire and lowered its head down onto his coils, and closed its eyes.

Circles spoke up, "Hey, Raine, can your finger-rings talk to snakes?"

"No, Circles, snakes are creatures that science cannot talk to. If you could talk to a snake, I guess that it really would be magic."

"What would a snake have to say anyway?" Circles asked no one in particular. There was no answer.

"I miss the Fire-claws." Circles added. "Now <u>there</u> are some animals that know how to enjoy a fire." Window smiled at him, knowingly.

Window opened his pack and got out his notebook. He checked it in the firelight. Fortunately, it wasn't wet from the rain. Window still had no idea where his medallion had come from. His grandfather's list of expedition members stared at him. Maybe Private Hollen's grandson was the mysterious traveler at the Summer Breeze. Maybe it was his medallion.

+++++++++

[IN THE SHADOWS OF BRISTON]

Three thousand miles to the southwest, Ajer Hollen stood in the shadows. It wasn't really necessary tonight, though. The fog from the Atlandic had come in a few hours before and the Port of Briston was buried in it. He could have stood right out by the streetlight and still no one could have seen him.

Of course, he couldn't see very well either, but he could listen. As soon as the door of the warehouse was slid open, he would know that Mr. Dollar was ready. Dollar and his partner, Mr. Drake, had been following the port thieves for three days. Tonight, would be their only chance to capture the robbers, and at the same time, recover the Calenne artwork.

It had been ten days since the port loading dock of the "Suzie Lacane" had been raided. Sometime after midnight, a band of dock pirates had somehow located the four large crates of newly commissioned land portraits meant for the Governor's Buildings in Calenne, and hauled them away. What they planned to do with them, Hollen didn't know and didn't care. He just had to get them back. His future at the Grand Port of Briston depended on it.

Dollar and Drake were known to many as the best detectives in all of Atland, maybe even in the whole of the Old Countries. They were the ones who solved the mystery of the murder of the wealthy shipping company owner in Triston last year, and they were the ones who recovered the kidnapped Hearten Duke, a few summers ago.

Now they needed just about two more minutes to force the Calenne thieves out into the open. Hollen was ready. All he had to do was to make sure that the main gate remained locked. He gripped the heavy iron bar he had brought to discourage anyone from approaching the gate. He heard Dollar slide open the big warehouse door. He could feel the blood pound through his chest and the sweat run down his arm.

Ajer Hollen was ready. He had better be. Here they come!

+++++++++

Thoroughly dried out, the treasure hunters headed north again in the morning. The road grew rocky, and although it was now summer, the air was getting cooler. Miles ahead of them, they could begin see low mountains in the distance.

The next day they stopped for lunch in front of a stark, high cliff along the water. As they ate their slices of ocean-fruit, two lone birds flew overhead. They were sleek, white, ice-birds from the snow lands to the north. They dove down close to the travelers, and circled above them. Panni tried to coax them to come take a piece of fruit from her hand, but they did not.

Then, as one of the birds dove close to her, she threw a piece of the fruit into the air. The bird caught the fruit in its mouth. That started a lot of fruit tossing by the travelers, which would have looked pretty funny to someone watching them, if there had been anyone watching them.

The next day as they continued up the western coast, the ground grew still more rocky and the road disappeared completely. The travelers went on, keeping their eyes on the ever-growing mountains ahead.

As they stopped for lunch again, they heard more birds cawing overhead – except the cries were not from birds this time. They came from the water. In the ocean, about a hundred feet from shore, were five or six, silver-grey Pinnipeds. They would stick their round heads above the surface, splash with their flippers, and squeal at the travelers. Then they would dive under the water, only to reappear again at a different spot.

"Look, Window, Pinnipeds!" Circles cried out. "I love Pinnipeds."

"What do you know about these sea creatures, Circles? Did your Mom tell you stories about them eating the sea-berries?"

"How did you know that, Window? That is exactly what happened. And everybody in the Deep Woods knows that if you want to have good luck, you should rub a Pinniped on the nose."

"I have never heard that," Rings offered to the conversation.

"I have been to a world where water creatures like these live in vast undersea cities," added Raine. "But those creatures weren't very lucky."

Circles started to climb down a ridge to the water. "Be care...," Panni started to call to him, but then marveled as Circles almost hopped down the rocky slope to the water.

"Raine, can you call them over to me?" Circles yelled back to him.

The starman made a series of loud *"Haah! Haah!"* sounds and a couple of *"Waay"* sounds. The friendly sea creatures swam over to the edge of the water near Circles. One of them stuck his face up towards Circles as the Woot leaned out over the water and stretched out his hand. With a great smile on his face, Circles soon turned back to the others and announced that he was going to have a very lucky day.

"Too bad there is no treasure around here to find, Circles. You would find it for sure, now," Window called to him.

"I am so lucky now, maybe I can find treasure that isn't even here," Circles responded.

So, as they continued on their way, Circles carefully searched the ground, looking for clues or treasures. As they walked on the rocks and barren dirt of the shore, off in the water, the Pinnipeds followed them up the coast for a while. Then the lucky sea creatures all squealed loudly at the same time. Circles waved to them, and they splashed the water one last time, and disappeared beneath it.

The march to the north went on. The air was getting cooler and cooler. Window put on his heavier overshirt and his jacket. Panni pulled on her longpants and wore her long-sleeved overshirt on top of her tunic. The others were still comfortable. Rings loved cold weather. He said he felt better with each passing mile.

By late the next morning, the five explorers had reached the base of the small Ice Lands mountains. They seemed to just rise out of the ground and slope up before the travelers. They were mountains of stone and hard clay. Nothing grew on them. They just slanted smoothly up into the air, reaching maybe only a thousand feet into the sky. They began near the ocean and stretched off to the east as far as Circles could see.

Rings thought that the mountains were like a huge barrier that separated the Ice Lands from the rest of the Northlands. The cold and snow of the approaching glaciers were trapped on the other side of them, unable, at least for the present, to affect the weather of the rest of the lands to their south very much.

At the very western end of the mountains, right along the shoreline, the ground remained relatively flat and easy to traverse. The travelers could feel the cold air leaking around the end of the mountain range as they started the final miles of their trip to the far north. They walked carefully as they made their way between the ocean on their left, and the towering rocks on their right.

In just a few hours, the travelers had passed by the mountains and had entered the icy snow-lands of the north. What they found surprised them. The air was cold, but unlike on the southern side of the mountains, here there was lots of greenery. Short trees, bushes, and grass grew plentifully between patches of ground snow. Small grey birds and sleek white birds flew everywhere. There were small streams of very cold, but flowing water.

The sun shone down on the snow world, and the travelers were really quite comfortable. Panni pointed out a large ground-rodent that was running behind a hedge of light-green leaves. There were even colorful morning ground-flowers poking out from patches of light snow at the base of some low hillsides.

It was a surprisingly beautiful world around them, but the fantastic sight was out before them, farther to the north. Stretched out along the northern horizon, from the far west to the far east, was a gigantic wall of ice.

THE ICELANDS

CHAPTER THIRTEEN

ACROSS THE ICE LANDS

Rings stood with the others and gazed out at the massive wall of ice before them. Panni hung on to one of his harness straps as she enjoyed the view.   The travelers were all silent for a minute as they each absorbed the expanse of the vista of ice to the north.

The advancing wall of ice was probably a mile or two from where they stood. It soared almost straight up from the ground, a ragged, frozen cliff, hundreds of feet high that disappeared off to their right.

Circles took out his far-scope and soon announced, "It just goes on and on and on."

What they saw was the head of the glaciers Rings had told them about. The glaciers came from mountains in the far north of Polartica, advancing a few hundred feet each year, slowly moving to the south, and swallowing everything in their path. The sometimes-mild temperatures of the southern Ice Lands had allowed the leading edge of the glaciers to occasionally melt enough so huge sections of them would crack and break off. The large chunks of ice would fall to the ground, leaving the leading glacier edge to be a tall, rough wall of ice.

The glacier wall went on for more than a hundred miles, and formed the northern boundary of the shrinking Ice Lands. The wall of mountains the travelers had just passed, formed the land's southern boundary. As the years passed, the glaciers had been

advancing closer and closer to the mountains, making the snow
world smaller and smaller as it was caught between them.

"What will happen when the ice reaches the mountains,
Window?" Circles wanted to know. "Will the ice stop, or will the
mountains be pushed down? And if the mountains are pushed
down, and the ice keeps advancing for a thousand years, will the
Northlands be destroyed – and The Deep Woods and the
Windlands, too?"

"I guess that could happen, Circles. Maybe there will be an age
of ice, and all the lands we know will be gone. Then, when the ice
melts someday, a brand new world will be here."

Although Panni was bothered by the idea of that distant
possibility, Circles spoke up as without a care, "Well, in the
meantime, there's going to be some mighty great sledding and
sliding going on around here!"

Panni smiled at her friend's positive attitude. "I think that this
is my lucky day, also, Circles." Panni responded, "Just to have you
with me."

"I like you, too, Panni," Circles answered her. "I like you, too."

Suddenly a white, ice-fox jumped out from behind a row of
bushes and ran off into the distance.

"Wow, this place is really something!" Circles called out to
everyone. "Let's go exploring. Ringer, where did your Brarrie
families used to live?"

"Far to the east of here, I think. Let's head off in that
direction, especially since there really isn't any other way to go."

So, they turned to the east and walked across the snowy
ground, with the wall of ice far to their left and a wall of stone on
their right.

The sun continued to warm their faces and bodies somewhat as
the travelers marched east across the Ice Lands. But by nightfall,
it had become much colder and so they decided that a fire to sleep
by would be a very good idea.

As the sun set behind them in the west, the lands became very
quiet. The birds left the sky, and the Ice Lands became a place
with very little sound.

They picked a camping spot at the edge of a small lake. The sky was clear and the moon shone above them. There was no wind and the water on the lake was very still. It made no sound as it gently lapped up on the shore near their fire.

As the travelers sat and warmed themselves by the flames, the world took on a magical quality. The quiet of the lake was comforting. The stillness of the air, and the beauty of the moon over the lake, calmed each of the travelers into a quiet reverie.

Raine stared out over the tranquil waters and was reminded of a faraway world he had once visited. Panni's thoughts turned to summer dances in the Traepelle garden. Window remembered a long-ago quiet walk in the snow with Mary. And, Circles imagined that he was snow-sliding down the steepest slope on the Ice Lands mountains. Rings took a final look out across the lake and closed his eyes to sleep.

They were all awakened from their quiet thoughts by the lonely, far-away call of a bird. It seemed to be coming from across the lake, and passing by them, traveling to the mountainside behind them and echoing back.

"Let's go find that bird," Circles suggested. "It sounds lonely. Maybe we could be friends."

He stood up, put his hands to his mouth, and called out across the lake, *"Cah-caw, Cah-caw."*

To everyone's surprise, about ten or twelve seconds later, Circles call came back to them. In the still night air, his voice had traveled all the way to the glacier wall and returned, perfectly echoed from the flat ice cliffs.

At first, Circles thought that the bird was answering him, and he called to it again. After another wait, those calls returned to them, also. But that was not all.

Circles peered out over the lake towards the direction of the returning calls. A pure white snowbird was silently gliding over the water towards them. Its moonshadow followed below it on the surface of the still lake. The beautiful bird landed on the ground near the fire and looked up at Circles.

"I did it! I did it!" Circles excitedly cried out. "I talked to a bird!"

Circles was excited beyond belief. He quickly pulled open a
berry tin and took out several juicy sea-berries. He held out his
hand and the snowbird hopped right up to him and, one by one,
took the berries from Circles' hand, and ate them.

Then the bird bobbed and hopped in a little dance. Circles
bobbed his head in answer to it. Finally, the dancing bird made a
couple of loud clicking sounds and took off. Everyone watched as
it glided back across the lake into the darkness. Circles spoke to
everyone, "See, this was my lucky day! I can thank that
Pinniped's nose. This was my lucky day!"

"Maybe I should have rubbed that Pinniped's nose, too,
Circles," Panni mentioned to him.

"You should have, Panni. You should have."

Circles spent the rest of the evening practicing birdcalls.

Their second day in the Ice Lands started out much colder than
their first. Panni wrapped herself in a blanket as they continued
their march. Window put on a second overshirt beneath his jacket.
Before long, he too, was wearing a blanket around his shoulders.

The sun was out in the morning, but by the middle of the day,
the sky was overcast and a light snow began to fall.

They came upon a trail in the snow that was smooth and led to
the east where they wanted to go. Apparently, some trail-using
creatures lived in the area, although they didn't see anything but
a few snow bunnies and a couple of big, ugly-looking burrow-rats.

As the snow continued to gently fall around them, Panni
noticed something up ahead – Snowrunners. They were little
deer-like creatures with tall, wildly curved antlers. Their feet
were wide, padded paws, perfect for traveling over snow and ice.
They were about as tall as Circles, and could run over the snow
without difficulty.

A group of seven Snowrunners was ahead, at the top of a low
hill, silently watching the travelers. As they neared the base of
the hill, the creatures turned and started off towards the
mountain rise to the south.

"How can we get them to run," Circles wanted to know.
"Snowrunners should be running, not walking."

"Why don't you chase them," Panni suggested, not thinking that Circles would take her seriously.

"Okay, I will," he responded, and took off after the slender little ice-deer.

Circles struggled up the hillside towards the creatures. He was trying to run, but his feet sank into the snow with each step and he was soon stuck, halfway up the rise.

"Maybe I should have rubbed that Pinniped's nose two or three times," he called back to the others, as he slowly pulled himself out of his predicament.

The Snowrunners disappeared towards the mountains and the travelers continued their trek to the east.

Camp that night was at the edge of a forest of green winter-trees. Raine enjoyed building their campfires, and so as he coaxed a spark from his finger-rings to grow into a crackling blaze, the others finished their usual chores.

Panni usually prepared the food, which she enjoyed. Window and Rings collected firewood, and Circles would tie up rope to hang towels and cooking utensils on, and generally arrange the camping area.

That night, around Raine's roaring fire, Circles had an idea.

"Let's make up a new rhyme, one about the Ice Lands. We may be the first to ever do that."

Everyone agreed to try it, although Rings wasn't very enthusiastic. As each of the campers suggested ideas, Window wrote them down in his notebook. Then they all took turns changing the ideas into rhymes. Circles wrote most of the first verse. Window and Raine wrote most of the second. Panni wrote the third verse by herself. Eventually, they decided on the final form of the poem.

When the rhyme was finished, Circles was given the honor of reciting it before the whole group, which he happily did. It was called "Before the Ice Age."

Circles stood before the fire and spoke from memory.

"Before the Ice Age we were here
Before all trees were gone
We sang and marched across the land
As snowbirds still flew on

Before the Ice Age, grass was green
And rivers flowing blue
We sang and laughed and wondered what
The Ice Lands ice would do

And when ten thousand years from now
The skies begin to warm
We hope to see you here again
And sing another song"

When he finished, everyone applauded, and Circles took a bow.

After that, things got quiet for a while. Then, as they sat by the fire, Panni noticed something.

"Hey, Rings, your legs are turning white! The brown color of your fur is fading, and your legs are turning white! It seems that the fading started at your rings of white fur around your ankles, spread to your feet, and now is moving all the way up your legs past your knees."

"I thought that it might happen to me, Panni. Although Brarries are all born with brown fur, in the Ice Lands, as they grow up, their fur changes to white. My mother told me that Brar-pups have dark fur so they can be seen in the snow by their parents. Those of us who were born in the Deep Woods just stay brown most of the time, but sometimes turn partially white when the snow comes."

"How come your fur doesn't turn green, like the grass and trees?" Circles wanted to know.

"Because there is a rule in the Deep Woods that only Woots are allowed to have green fur."

"What do you mean, a rule? Where did you hear that, Ringer?"

"I didn't hear it anywhere, Circles. I just made it up now."

Circles smiled at the joke and went over to Rings and started punching him on his leg as hard as he could. Of course, Rings

could hardly even feel the blows that Circles was delivering.
Rings pretended to be in great pain, and started howling. Circles
continued the attack, and everyone else started laughing.

Finally, Circles grew tired of punching Rings and plopped
down on the ground next to him. Rings reached out and pulled
Circles to him and gave him a hug. Circles could hardly breathe
and started coughing. Then, everyone started laughing again.

Window remembered that Circles' fur was supposed to turn
color someday, too.

"Hey, Circles. When will your fur get its new color?"

"I think I am old enough now, so it could happen at any time. I
hope it changes soon, so I will know what kind of Woot I am."

"We already know what kind of Woot you are," Window told
him, "and when your fur changes, make sure that the rest of you
doesn't change too much."

+++++++++

[BEYOND EASTPOINT]

*Far across the mountains and plains to the south, and the
Northlands Provinces to the east, Cadence and Arrow were
having a conversation.*

"How old are you, Arrow?" Cadence wanted to know.
*"About three hundred, I think," his friend quickly
answered. "I can still remember the first time I ever came
out this far beyond the Fence. It was a really sunny day,
and Ribbon had brought us all the way to the western end of
the High-way."*
"I wonder what ever happened to her."
"Lost, like all the rest, I suppose."
"Yeah, too bad. I liked her."

"Arrow, how long do you think it will take us to get back?"

"Well, we are almost to the Tower, then it will be another day to the Fence."

"Okay, and two more days after that, to reach the Ruins."

"What's the hurry, anyway, Cadence? There's nothing to do when we get there. We don't head north for another week."

"I hate going up there. What's on the other side of those clouds, anyway?"

"The really, really Ancient Lands, I guess."

"Yeah, I guess."

"Arrow, when we get there, I want to stop at the Bridge for a while."

"Okay, Cadence. Maybe you can carve something into a support beam somewhere."

"I need a new idea – something dramatic."

"When did you start doing all of those carvings?"

"Oh, about five years ago, or so. I figure I've done about a thousand of them by now."

"So, I guess when we are gone, your designs will live on."

"Yeah, I hope that somebody will see them someday."

"And then they will write songs and poems about the Ancient Lands carvings. Just think, Cadence, some kid back in the Newlands could someday be singing about your designs – or maybe some kid in the Very East."

"Oh, the Newland's songs are much better. Those kids in the east are too practical. They should learn to have more fun – and dream more, too.

"I had a dream last night, Arrow."

"What was it about?"

"I dreamt that I was flying over the mountains to the east, and I discovered an ocean."

"Cadence, we already know that there really is an ocean over there.

"Yeah, well, it was just a dream."

"Like that one you had about Underland?"

"Whatever happened to Moonbow?"

"Lost too, I guess."
"Too bad, I liked him."
"Me too."

"Ya know, Arrow, the world has really changed a lot since we have been here. Sometimes I like that, and sometimes I don't."
"Yeah, me too."
"I wouldn't like it if you got lost, Arrow"
"Oh, I won't get lost, Cadence, not from you."
"How can you be sure, Arrow?"
"Well, let me put it this way, if we do get lost, let's get lost together."
"Okay, Arrow, and I will bring the treats."
"An excellent idea, Cadence. That is an excellent idea. Hey, pass me one of those cookies, will you?"
"Do you want a plain one, Arrow, or one with a picture?"
"Better make it two cookies, one of each."

Far across the mountains and plains to the south, and the Northlands Provinces to the east, Cadence and Arrow were having a conversation.

+++++++++

Two more days of travel to the east, and Rings' fur had almost completely turned white. He looked like a massive snowball rolling across the snow and the green snow-grass.

Panni asked him, "Rings, why were there white fur rings around your ankles, when the rest of your fur was brown?"

"My mother used to tell me that it was so she could find me in the dark, but I think that it was there for no reason at all. I think that it is just one of those mysteries of life that no one can ever solve. Some of my cousins have white fur patches, too, like a white spot on their forehead, or a white stripe across their rumps."

Panni was impressed to hear her Deep Woods friend speak of the mysteries of life. She had struggled with her own life's mystery when she was at the Traepelle Castle. She couldn't understand why she was held captive, when she hadn't done anything to deserve it. Sometimes she wasn't able to stop thinking about it and it just filled her mind for weeks at a time. Only when she finally decided to do something about it did the thoughts start to leave her. She hadn't solved her mystery, but had grown beyond it. Now, although the direction of her life was still uncertain, she didn't worry about it. She felt free and excited by the possibilities.

On the fifth day across the Ice Lands, the travelers noticed that the air was becoming warmer again. There was very little snow on the ground, and they were passing more and more small forests where the trees grew taller than those they had seen before. Birds and small ground animals were everywhere, and it seemed that the world was somehow coming more to life.

They soon learned the reason for the change. Circles noticed something and mentioned it to Window. "I hear water splashing, Window. It is far away, but I can hear it."
"Does it sound like a waterfall, Circles, or rain, or what?"
Circles wasn't sure, but it wasn't long before they solved the mystery.
Soon, the five treasure hunters could all hear the sound of water rushing and splashing. As they came over a small hill, they discovered what was causing it.
Ahead of them was a field of hot water geysers, eight in all, Circles counted. They seemed to be taking turns, shooting steaming hot water high into the air. The water whooshed as it shot from the ground, and splashed as it fell back onto the rocky surface surrounding the geysers.
The air around the travelers was hot and moist. In this one spot, the Ice Lands' glaciers were pushed away by the heat from far below the ground. Surrounding the field of geysers, just out of the reach of the steaming water, in almost a circle around them, there was a garden of flowering plants and bushes. There were

bouquets of brilliant blues and fiery reds, gorgeous pinks and happy yellows, dramatic violets and greens.

There were flowers of all types, tall stems and short, large petals and small. Window didn't recognize any of the blooms as ones he had ever seen before. The travelers had seen flowers in the Ice Lands before, but nothing like this.

"Hey, everybody," Circles announced. Rings has found his treasure of flowers."

Rings smiled at his friend, "And I didn't even have to bother a Pinniped."

"I didn't bother that Pinniped, Ringer," Circles answered him. "But, you are bothering me right now." Then, to soften his comments, Circles ran over and picked a giant, light-violet blossom for his friend. He stuck it in Rings' harness, and patted him on the leg.

The treasure hunters found a dry hillside within view of the geysers to stop for a rest. Raine took a special interest in the flowers and examined several of the types up close.

As they ate, Panni told them how, for a time, when she was at the Traepelle Castle, she had the duty of cutting and arranging flowers for the nobles' dinner table. The castle gardener would save the best blooms for her, and her displays were always very pretty. Window thought about the fantastic Flower Day bouquet his mother could make with flowers such as these. She would certainly love to have a garden like this one.

Raine liked flowers, too. He explained that he had started collecting flowers from the worlds he visited, to brighten his ship a bit. Then, as he traveled between the stars, he had time to spend studying them. His plan was to use the flowers from different worlds to create beautiful new blooms. Now he wondered if he would ever have that chance.

The travelers decided to rest by the geysers for several hours. It was very pleasant for Panni and Window to remove their heavy clothing for a while, and just sit and enjoy the comfortable temperature, the beautiful flowers, and the whoosh of the water being thrown high before them.

When the breeze would change directions, the travelers would
sometimes be lightly sprayed with a hot mist. The moisture on
Panni's face made it glow with life.

Rings slept, and the others just relaxed. Then Circles decided
to "go swimming," as he called it. Before anyone could try to talk
him out of it, the Woot was running around and between the
geysers, trying to guess which one would erupt next.

Window warned him three times to stay away from the hot
spouts or he could be burned. Fortunately, when one of the
geysers would erupt, the water was shot straight up and very high
into the sky. So, wherever Circles was when it erupted, he had
time to run away from the spot where the water would come down.
He got a little wet, but, only once, was he really splashed by the
falling water. Circles said it wasn't that hot, and it didn't seem to
bother him.

On the southern side of the geyser field, the water from the
spouts collected in a stream that flowed off in that direction. As
they rested, the travelers were treated to a wide variety of
animals that came to the stream to drink. Circles counted two
different types of foxes and of badgers, three different types of
squirrels, and four different types of rabbits. Then he was
surprised by the visit of two Snowrunners.

The creatures' large, padded feet, made for traveling on snow,
spread out wide on the hard ground. They were beautiful
animals, as their legs and slender bodies moved gracefully below
their intricate antlers. The two Snowrunners drank from the
stream and then stood very still as they looked over towards the
travelers.

Circles walked over to Raine and asked him a question. Then
he started across the geyser field in the direction of the 'Runners,
as he called them.

As he neared the 'Runners, Circles spoke to them, using a
phrase of odd sounding words. Apparently, Raine had told him
what to say. The animals remained standing where they were.
Circles continued to speak as he walked right up to one of them
and reached out his hand. The Snowrunner lowered his head in a
sign of acknowledgement. Circles gently rubbed his hand down

the neck and back of the animal. The 'Runner quietly accepted the touch of the Woot. Just then, an ice-fox appeared across the geyser field and both Snowrunners darted away.

"How did you do that?" Window wanted to know when Circles had returned to the group. "How did you get that Snowrunner to let you touch him?"

"Oh, I asked Raine how to say something to him in its own language. I just told the Snowrunner that my name was Runner, too, just like his. He seemed to like that. Do you remember, Window, I told you when we met, that Runner was my real name?"

"I do remember that, Circles. I guess that you are Snow-Runner, now.

"Well, Snow-Walker, anyway," his friend responded.

Another couple of hours and the travelers were on their way again. As they left the field of geysers, the air became cool, and then after a few miles, cold, as it had been. Before they camped for the night, the snow of the Ice Lands had returned and they were, once again, surround by the wintery world of the far north.

The next day was overcast and very cold again. Rings told the group that he hoped that they would soon reach the area where his Brarrie family had come from. They walked along, trying to think of some different songs to sing, but it seemed that in the past many weeks they had sung every Deep Woods song anybody knew. Panni knew more songs from the Traepelle Castle, but didn't want to sing any of those.

Early in the afternoon, Circles asked Rings a question. "How will we know for sure, Ringer, when we are in the lands where your family came from?"

"There are two ways to tell, Circles. One is if we come upon a Brar-nest. They will be easy to see because they are so big. The other way to know we are in the lands of the Brars, is if we look up to the top of a big ridge of snow and we can see three big, white Brarries standing there, like those three over there on that hilltop."

Circles raised his eyes to the snow-covered ridge that Rings was motioning to. And there they were! Standing side by side and looking down on them, were three huge balls of snow – three Brarries!

"Hey, everybody," Circles called out. "Look up there! We have found them."

"Probably, they have found us," Rings responded excitedly. "But it doesn't matter. Let's go get acquainted."

Together the travelers hurried up the ridge towards the three huge creatures. They were each even bigger than Rings. Each one was totally covered in long white fur, with their black eyes and black noses sticking out from under it.

"And don't forget, they won't know any of your languages. I will have to speak to them in our Brar-tongue," Rings reminded his friends.

Then Rings remembered the messenger starman, "Oh, Yeah. Hey, Raine, do you think that you could talk to them? They would find that very surprising. They might even think that you were from some other, magical, far-away world, which I guess you are."

"I will greet them as best I can," Raine replied, and as he walked, held his right hand up to a spot near the outer corner of his eye. A slight flash of blue light jumped from one of his finger-ring jewels and sparkled against his skin.

As the travelers approached the creatures, the Brarries remained still. They seemed to be waiting politely at the crest of the hill.

Raine continued to walk closer to the Brarries, after the other four travelers had stopped. He bowed before them, and spoke in a language of rough sounding growls and huffs. When he had finished his greetings, each of the three Brarries put its right paw out in front of the other, and together, they bowed a return greeting to the starman.

Rings was pleased with Raine's greeting, but he couldn't wait any longer. He almost galloped the rest of the way up the hill to greet his "cousins," as he was soon calling them.

It was a happy reunion of sorts between Rings and the three Brarries, whose names were Dester, Lim, and Rinne. It had been about forty years since the families of the Deep Woods Brarries had left the Ice Lands. These three had heard stories of those that had left to live in the south, but were all too young to have known any of them.

The cousins were happy to have the visitors from the south. They accepted Rings and the others immediately, and invited them to come along to the snowraces.
"Oh, is it a special day of races for the Brarries?" Circles asked Rings.
"No, it is a regular day of races for the Brarries. Racing is what Brarries spend most of their time doing."
The travelers followed the cousins across a frozen stream, and to the other side of a snowy field. There they found something that Rings remembered his mother telling him about,
It was a series of long, low hills used by the Brarries as racing and sliding hills. Just like Rings, almost all Brarries were very competitive. Every afternoon, many of them would meet at the racing hills, and spend a happy few hours racing up one low, snow covered hill, sliding down the other side, and racing up another – on and on, across eight different hills and low valleys.
The cousins led the travelers to a high ridge off to the south of the racing hills, from where they could watch. Already there, and waiting for the racing to begin, were three Snowrunners, three big ice-hares and a couple of fluffy, grey tree-rakes. The travelers sat near them on a cleared off dry patch of dirt next to about a dozen tiny, reddish, ground-bears. Apparently, all of these Ice Lands neighbors of the Brarries liked to watch them race, too.
Before they sat down, Panni noticed Circles eyeing the ground-bears. So, she warned him, "Don't try to catch any of them."
"Oh, all right," he promised, but he still looked as though he would like to grab one. On another hill, on the north side of the racecourse, seven other Brarries watched as well.

At the west end of the racing hills, the Brarries were ready. Dester and three other cousins were about to start at the bottom of the first hill. Rings had been given the honor of starting the race. His job was to hide over the first hilltop, and when he poked his head up so the racers could see him, they would start their scramble up the first hill towards him. Of course, after poking his head up, Rings had to quickly get off of the hill before the four giant racers reached the top of the hill and ran into him.

The seven cousins, who were sitting on their haunches and watching, began slapping the bottoms of their front feet together. This made a deafening noise that cracked across the snow to the travelers. It was time for the race to begin.

Rings slowly climbed the back side of the first racing hill and, as his nose reached into view over the top, the four racers began their mad scramble up the front side. Rings slid back down his side of the hill and almost rolled out of the low valley between the first two hills, to get out of the racers' way.

Ice and snow flew everywhere as the cousins tried to run up one hillside and slide and run down the other side.

The watching Brarrie cousins stopped slapping and started huffing and hooting. It really was rather exciting. Circles was yelling for Dester to win. Window, Panni, and Raine just watched, very entertained by the whole thing.

The racers went up and down icy hillsides in a cloud of swirling snow. One racer, Linner, tripped at the top of the third hill and rolled down the other side, landing in a pile of white fur at the bottom. He tried to recover, but he was well behind the others, so he stopped at the top of the next hill and cheered on Dester.

As the racers reached the eighth hill, Dester was tied for the lead with a cousin named Ruely. And Dester might have won, but just as he started up that last hillside, the fourth cousin, Fanner, slid down behind him and landed on his back foot and leg. Dester got caught under Fanner, and Ruely scooted up the last slope ahead of them. As Ruely slid down the back of the hill to victory, the watching cousins started slapping again, along with their hooting and huffing.

That began three days of the travelers' stay with the Brarries. Dester took them with him back to the Brar-nests, and they met all of the other twenty-six cousins. There were more Brarries in the Ice Lands, who lived many miles to the east, but these Brarries didn't see those others very often.

Rings, and the rest of the travelers, were accepted readily by the Brarries. They especially enjoyed talking with Raine, who told them stories of some other very large animals he had met. He didn't mention that those animals were not on this world, but on worlds far out among the stars. He thought that might be a bit confusing to them. None of the cousins had ever even heard of a man who could speak their language, so that was surprising enough.

Every day, while staying with the Brarries, the travelers would play in the snow and ice. Circles even ran the entire racing hill course, although it took him about half an hour to make it over all eight hills. Of course, sliding down the back side of the hills was his favorite part.
Panni, Window, and Raine made some giant snowmen. Rings accidentally knocked one of them down, so the three builders accidentally pelted him with snowballs.

On the third day, Dester took them all for an afternoon sled ride around the area. Rings ran alongside, as Dester pulled the others in a big sled, woven from tree branches, up and down hills and over frozen streams and fields as fast as he could. It was a very exciting ride for them all. Even Raine said that he had never done anything like that before. Once, the sled started to slide to the side and almost turned over, but, other than that, it was a very smooth ride.
For a while, Circles tried to stand on the snow and hang on to the back of the sled as Dester pulled it, but he soon fell headfirst into a drift, and got snow up his nose.

The highlight of the day came as Dester pulled the sled near the mountains at the southern edge of the Ice Lands. When he stopped for a moment to rest, they noticed, off near the base of the mountains, three snowmen. These were not pretend-men made out of snow, but huge, white, furry, man-like creatures who lived in the Ice Lands near the mountains.

Dester explained to Raine that they were usually friendly but kept mostly to themselves. Of course, Circles wanted to go meet them, but Dester said that wasn't a good idea. So, Circles stood up in the sled and waved at them. To everyone's surprised, all three of the snowmen bowed in their direction, before turning and walking away.

So, after three enjoyable days with the Brarries, the travelers decided that it was time to go on. Rings had had his reconnection with his cousins, some of whom really were his cousins, and would be able to tell his family in the Deep Woods all about it.

Panni and Window were a bit tired of the cold, and felt that they were ready to head back to the Northern Plains. Circles didn't care, and Raine quietly and happily accepted whatever the others wanted to do.

As the travelers were leaving the Brar-village, all twenty-six cousins stood, in two long rows of thirteen on each side, forming a long passageway. The departing travelers walked between the Brarries and out into a snowy day. It was a very nice farewell by Rings' family of distant relatives.

Now that Rings had found his relatives, he was ready to return to the south, too. The cousins told him of the easiest way for them to travel between the mountains. They would go that way, but first, the travelers had one more adventure they wanted to share before they left the Ice Lands. They would climb on to the top of a glacier!

Dester had told them the best way to do that, too. They were to head to the northeast. In about two miles, they would reach the base of the glacier. At that spot, the head of the glacier was pushed against a very large hill, or small mountain, which was part of the beginnings of the mountains to the south. The travelers could walk up the ground from the south and step onto the glacier.

It was cold and snowing as the travelers found their way to the spot. The glacier wall towered high above them. It was hundreds of feet high, sticking almost straight up into the air. Standing in the way of part of the glacier was the massive mountain hill they were looking for. It rose into the sky even higher than the glacier.

The explorers carefully worked their way up the steep incline of the back of the hill towards the top of the wall of ice. It was a long, difficult climb. Rings went first, to flatten the snow. Panni stumbled. Circles slipped and fell. Window and Raine helped as best they could. The freezing winds grew in strength as the climbers reached higher and higher ground.

It was a long struggle to reach the height of the top of the glacier, but when they did, it was an easy walk onto the ice. One by one, they took the last step and soon were all on the glacier's back.

Under their feet, and out before them, was a glistening frozen ocean. They held hands as they looked out across the ice, sharing the moment. But, as exciting as it was to ride on a glacier, Circles had a still better idea. "Let's go all the way to the top of the hill, and look out over the ice from there." Even in their exhausted, near-frozen state, the travelers all agreed they would like to try Circles' idea. They would never have a chance like this again. They would climb even higher than the glacier.

The climbers returned from the ice flow to the mountain hill and continued to work their way higher. A hundred feet above them, through the swirling snow, they could make out a ridge at the very top of the mountain.

The buffeting winds burned Window's face as he pulled still another blanket out of a harness pack and threw it over Panni's shoulders. She pulled it against her body and face as they pushed on. Circles buried himself against Panni, and climbed on with his eyes closed. The others dug strength from deep within themselves, and went on and up, higher and higher, nearer and nearer the summit.

After twenty minutes of terrible cold, they reached the base of the final mountain ridge. They struggled up the ridge and stopped at the top. They had made it. They were at the top of the ice world.

Off to the left, the ground dropped away in a slow arc, and below them, they could see miles and miles to the north.

They were standing in snow a few inches deep. The freezing breeze swept across their faces from their right, and then turned down over the edge of the rounded cliff in front of them. To their left, a lone tree, bent and beaten, swept to one side by years of such a wind, shivered because so few of its needles were remaining.

Window stood and looked out across to the north. He gazed in wonder at the miles and miles of small ice-grey mountain peaks spread in a panorama before him, and across the entire horizon. The overcast sky of low, flat clouds seemed as a roof over their heads, and came down to meet the distant mountains, making it impossible to tell where the mountains stopped and the sky began.

Next to Window, on his left, Rings sat on his haunches in the snow and seemed to look as if he were watching for something – but the scene was unchanging. It had a mesmerizing effect on them both, a calming effect of never-ending beauty and majesty. Window wondered how such beauty could exist in a land of so little color.

For a long time they watched, then suddenly Window remembered the others. He turned and found them, standing together, a bit behind him, to his right. Raine, as usual, stood quietly, but Window sensed that he, too, felt the calm. Window wondered how many times before the starman had viewed such a sight of simple elegance on some world far away.

Panni was next to Raine, her hair blowing across her face as she shivered against the cold. Circles pushed against her side, causing her to instinctively pull him closer. It seemed to warm him a bit, so he buried himself still deeper under her arm. Window thought suddenly how very heroic they looked, their rough clothes and fur being blown about, as the cold wind brought out the strength in their faces.

For a long time they watched, each with his own thoughts, each carrying himself out across the miles and safely back again. Once, after a time, Window glanced back again to the others and caught Panni's eyes on him. She didn't turn her gaze, as he looked right at her. He felt her trust and faith in him, and realized, as never before, how grateful she was to him for being the one to open her eyes to so many things.

The awareness came to Window of the perfect connection he felt to those with him. He knew he could never feel any closer to them than he did at that moment. He reached out his left hand and grabbed on to one end of a pack strap hanging from Rings' back. The Brarrie purred and shifted his feet to move himself closer to his friend. Window looked out again at the sparkling vista before them, and sighed quietly to himself as he took a deep breath.

"I love this place," he said at last, mostly to himself. Rings purred softly in agreement.

"I'm cold," added Circles.

They turned from the ocean of ice before them, and worked their way back down the long, steep hillside. From there, they continued to the south, and headed towards a split in the rocks that would lead them through the mountains, and eventually back to the Northern Plains.

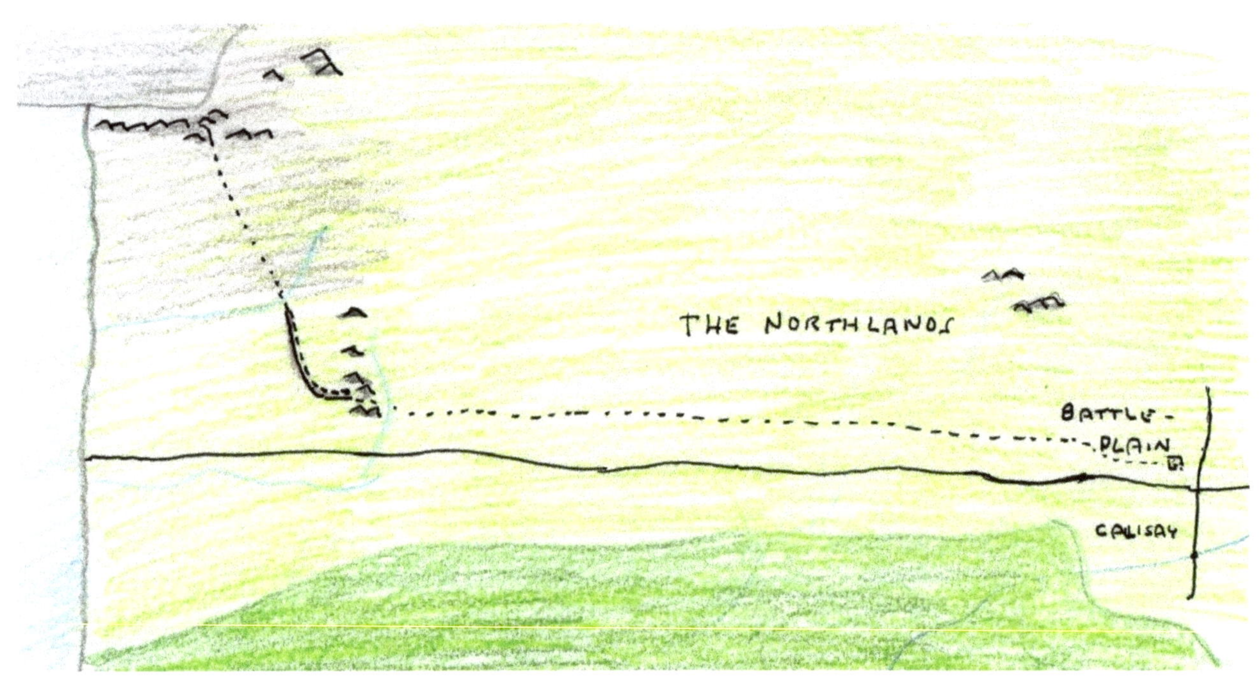

THE NORTHLANDS
BATTLE-
PLAIN
CALISAY

CHAPTER FOURTEEN

TO THE BATTLEPLAIN

"Oh, I am so happy to be warm again," Panni called out to her friends. She pulled off her overshirt and shoved it into her pack.

They had come through a narrow pass between the Ice Lands mountains, and in just a few hours, the change in the world was dramatic. The cold and snow of the glaciers was gone, trapped by the mountains behind them. The summer sun was high overhead, making the travelers comfortable in the very slightly cool breeze of the northern lands. Only Rings missed the cold. The others felt renewed for their long trek back towards the Battleplain Cemetery.

Their plan was simple. They would go to the southeast, across the rough lands north of Ryeland, and then turn east towards the middle plains of the Northlands.

They were unsure if any people or other creatures lived in the lands they would be crossing, but Window warned them all to be prepared should any trouble arise. The old rhymes told of creatures in the mountains they would pass, but no one could be sure if they would meet anyone, or anything.

The lands they entered were green and alive with wildlife. Badgers and foxes and deer were everywhere. Hawks and small eagles, that lived in the taller trees, were often flying overhead, joining the other birds that kept the travelers company as they continued on their way.

Of course, there were no roads to follow, so the travelers had to work their way across the wide grass fields and low hills between the forests to their right, and the spine-like row of low mountains that were far away to their left. It was a pleasant journey for everyone. They were in no hurry, and except for an occasional shower, the weather was beautiful.

Rings' white snow-fur was quickly regaining its color, and the group seemed to be back to normal. They continued to sing as they marched on, with the conversation again focusing on the Freeland coins that they hoped to find at the Battleplain Cemetery. After their search for the King's Treasure in Meriselle, a small box of coins didn't seem like much of a treasure, but still they wanted to find it.

Raine continued to say very little, and mostly kept the others quiet company. Window noticed sadness in his eyes, but Raine never spoke of it. Panni was enjoying her adventure immensely, with her painful days of servitude, seemingly, left far behind her. She had gained lots of self-confidence and her future now seemed completely open to her.

Window was feeling pretty good, also. His adventure to the wilds had taken him far beyond anyplace he had ever imagined. He missed home and family, and he missed Mary, but he loved his new friends and would be happy to go anywhere with them.

Circles, too, was refreshed and renewed. He practiced shooting his bow and arrows almost every day, and still explored the horizon with his far-scope. He often spoke of their trip to the ocean, reminding everyone how pleasant it was there. And since Rings was still happy to carry their supplies, including the fresh apple-like fruit they picked from some lonely orchard-trees, and wild potatoes Rings dug up for them, it was a satisfied group of treasure hunters that walked together.

On the seventh day after leaving the Ice Lands, the travelers saw a distant watchtower off towards the mountains to the east. Then, as the day passed, they came upon other signs of people living in the area. They saw two more towers, and, also in the distance, several small huts, with fences holding cattle. Rings thought that they probably belonged to Northlanders who were chased from their homes and farms during the war. They must have moved farther to the north, to avoid the Atland army, and remained there permanently.

The next afternoon they came upon a road, twisting through the greenlands to the south. They followed the road, leaving it temporarily as it passed through small villages. The travelers thought that it was best to just keep to themselves, and not initiate contact with anyone.

The road wound on towards the southeast, in just the direction they wanted to go. As the road continued, it grew closer and closer to the mountains. On their third day on the road, it turned sharply to the east, and headed directly towards a split between two rounded peaks.

Window's concern was that the mountains might be dangerous. The wild men that attacked his grandfather's expedition and those that attacked Oldsmith and Revell came from mountains much farther east, near the Battleplain, but these mountains could be dangerous as well. Also, besides song and stories of Silkie in this part of the Northlands, other stories, from before the Wars, told of vicious creatures that came down from the highlands and raided farms and villages.

Circles carried his bow and arrow quiver with him constantly. Window made sure that his sword was hanging from Rings' harness, where he could quickly reach it. Panni's dagger still pressed snuggly against her waist.

"I hope that we can get through the mountains in one day's travel," Window announced, as they rested for an hour by a slow-moving stream. "Let's try to get close to the mountains today, and start very early tomorrow morning, so we will have as much daylight as possible to travel through the pass in the rocks."

The travelers agreed. They pressed on until they reached the beginnings of the mountain pass where they stopped to camp for the night.

That evening, as they sat around their campfire, Circles was talking about the Silkie he still hoped to find. "Raine," he asked the starman, "Do you know where the Silkie are?"

"My finger-rings could probably find the Silkie, but they are not meant to do that."

"Why not, Raine?"

"Come sit by me, Circles, and I will tell you all about them."

The little Woot moved next to the starman. The flames from their campfire reflected from the soft blue of Raine's face, and the sharp white of his eyes, as he spoke to his friend.

"In my world, there are different kinds of jeweled science-rings. There are building-rings and growing-rings and battle-rings, and many others. Since I am a messenger, I have messenger-rings."

"What can messenger-rings do?" Circles wanted to know.

"My rings are specially made to help me talk with any person or any creature as I deliver my messages. With my rings, I can quickly learn myself, or teach others I speak with, any language at all. That is so our messages are clearly given and clearly understood. Clear messages have helped immensely in a great many difficult situations."

"What else, Raine?" What other things can they do?" Circles pressed on.

"I may use my rings to protect myself, and those I have messages for, but no one else. Since I was not assigned to deliver messages to anyone on your world, I decided that I would consider you and your friends as my assignment. Usually, my stay on a new world is very brief, but this time it is uncertain, so I am a little unsure how to handle it."

Raine continued, as Circles listened intently. "Since many of my messages are exchanged between warring peoples, I am also allowed to help those I am contacting, if they have been injured in battle. That is why I could help heal Window's cuts. I considered the attack of the creatures upon you in the Woods, as a battle with an enemy. And then, I can also do many little things with my rings, like starting fires and cooking food, if it is to help take care of myself."

"But what if I fall and break my leg or something?" Circles wondered?

"If one of you is hurt, but not by an enemy, I may not help you with my rings. I may only use them to help you with things that have to do with exchanging messages. That is why I may not help you search for treasure. Well, not with my finger-rings, anyway. If I don't use my rings, I can do whatever I want. But," Raine chuckled a bit, "I usually don't go out traveling and treasure hunting with those to whom I bring messages. This visit with you is very special, indeed."

"Can your science-rings do any magic, Raine – like turn you into a Pixie?"

"What my rings do only seems like magic, Circles. But it is not."

"What else, Raine? Can your rings do anything else?"

"Because I must deal with so many different people and creatures, in very difficult situations, possibly even in the middle of a battle, my rings can also help me tell me if a person is trustworthy. That is why I approached your group on the Northway. My science-rings assure me, Circles, that you and your friends are all very honorable. Both the science of my far-away world, and my own judgment, tell me that you and your companions are the best friends I could ever hope to find."

Circles face beamed with pride. He looked across the fire circle, to where Panni was watching him.

"One more thing about my finger-rings, Circles. Sometimes I can even tell some unknown things about those I meet."

"Oh, Raine, what about my future? Can you see my future?"

"I can't tell you everything I know, Circles, but I <u>can</u> tell you two things about yourself and your future. One is that you are a very special Woot. Some of what is special about you, you have already seen. You are an adventurer and a dreamer, and that is important in anyone's life. Other special things about you, Circles, you will have to wait and see."

Circles leaned closer to the starman, "What about my future?"

"In our lives, we have many choices, and in most things, your choices make your future. So far, you have made excellent choices, Circles, even though you have been unsure of just who you are. Your own choices have already taken you far, very far indeed. As you make more choices, always just trust yourself. Don't ever make choices that others pick for you."

"That sounds like good advice for anyone," offered Window, who had just come over and joined the conversation.

"Well, I guess that you are right, Window," Raine replied. "We should always trust ourselves when we choose."

Circles had heard enough about finger-rings for a while. "Right now, I choose some more of those mountain-berries we picked this morning," he decided. Then he called out to everyone, "Who else wants some?"

Every one of the travelers made their own choice regarding the berries, and they all chose to have some.

"I don't know about these berries affecting my future much," concluded Circles, as he finished his snack, "but they are affecting my present very nicely."

Raine gave him a very caring smile.

Well before the next morning sun was high enough to peek over the mountains, the travelers were already on their way. As they approached the entrance to the pass through the rocks, Window again warned everyone to stay alert, and to be ready should any dangers appear.

The road ahead looked smooth, but the farther it went, the higher the rock hills and cliffs on each side of it rose into the sky. Everyone kept their eyes on the heights above, hoping not to see any eyes looking back at them.

Rings walked ahead of the others, followed by Circles and Panni. Window and Raine came last, Window keeping his hand on the hilt of his sword, which he now wore on his belt.

An hour or so passed. There was no sign of trouble. The travelers' concerns lessened a bit and Circles started singing. It was a silly song about a cow and a chick that ran away from the farmer's barn. Soon everyone was smiling, and when Circles got to the part about the goose, Panni started humming along.

Lunchtime came and went, but the travelers pressed on. In the afternoon, clouds blew in over their heads and the day became rather dark. Sometimes their path between the cliffs and rocky slopes widened a bit, but mostly they felt somewhat trapped between the high mountain walls.

The travelers' concerns turned to fears as they came upon an area of the pass that was littered with bones. It appeared that an unusual number of animals had died right on the road or next to it. The travelers were slightly heartened because it seemed that all of the bones had been there for quite some time, so their owners had not recently died or been killed. Of course, even a bunch of old, weathered, bones had a sobering effect on the group of treasure hunters.

But finally, as the late afternoon sun dipped beneath the rocks behind them, they could at last see, ahead of them, the opening that led into the wide grasslands east of the mountains.

The happy travelers started the last several hundred feet or so towards the opening from the mountains, and then suddenly stopped. Up in the rocks on both sides of the trail, they saw eyes looking down at them. Hidden on the slopes and cliffs were twenty or thirty creatures that stuck only their rough, ugly faces out from behind the rocks and silently watched the travelers.

Window looked over at Raine. The starman's rings were sparkling at the ends of his fingers. Colored light was jumping out from several of the jewels as he prepared them for possible trouble. Window wondered what the science-rings were capable of. Panni pulled her dagger and held it tightly in her fist.

One of the animals stood up from his hiding place. It was a ragged, little, man-creature. The creature raised his arms over his head. He held a large rock in his hands, with six twisted fingers on each hand wrapped tightly around it. The other rock-men did the same. Twenty-five deadly stones were ready to rain down on them.

"Oh, Window, what should we do?" Panni asked first.

Before Window could answer, there was the sound of an arrow whizzing through the air. It was immediately followed by the whack of the arrow burying itself into the leg of a man-creature. Another arrow zipped up towards the threatening animals. It struck another of the men in the shoulder. The creature fell backwards.

Window spun around just in time to see Circles let his third arrow fly high up the rocky rise to their left. It was Circles! He was shooting the Marrent's arrows at their attackers.

The mountain creatures quickly turned and scurried off into the rocks. They didn't mind attacking a small group of outnumbered travelers, but they didn't have any interest in fighting against dangerous pointed sticks that flew through the air at them.

"Circles! Circles! You chased them away," Panni called to him. "Circles, you were fantastic!"

Everybody crowded around the little hero. "What made you do it, Circles? What made you shoot? Weren't you afraid?" Window asked excitedly.

Circles was breathing heavily. "Sure, I was afraid, but I liked Frazzle and Locker, and I didn't even know them. I couldn't bear to think of losing any of you. I just couldn't let it happen. I had to do something. I would do anything to keep you safe." Tears came to Circles eyes.

Panni pulled the little Woot close to her. "Oh, Circles, you are wonderful! You are wonderful!"

Circles held onto her arms tightly. It was a very long minute before he let go.

And, as their adventure continued, it was a very, very long time before the others got Circles' caring for them, or his bravery, out of their thoughts.

+++++++++

By sundown, the travelers had crossed through the mountain range, and followed the road out into the grasslands of northern

Selletenne Province. They were at the far western edge of the
vast Northlands grasslands that was known as the Battleplain, as
it approached still more low mountains on its far eastern border.

Their choices were to head south until they reached the
Northway road again, and then turn east, or to travel the much
shorter distance directly across the plains and through the light
forests that were sprinkled across the grasslands. It was decided
to travel across the open ground to the Battleplain. They would
start in the morning.

So, after their usual quick breakfast, the treasure hunters
trekked to the southeast across mostly open grasslands. Here the
grass was so tall that Circles rode on Rings' back most of the time.
Near sundown, they waded an upper branch of the same river
they had helped Rings swim across when they were on the
Northway, on their way to Meriselle.
Window liked traveling over the flat, open plain. He enjoyed
being able to see far to a distant horizon. The open space made
him feel free and unbounded.
As they walked through the tall grass, Window got out his
notebook to check on what his grandfather and Oldsmith had said
about finding the Battleplain. Again, he read down the list of his
grandfather's expedition members. And as before, he asked
himself the question he had been hoping to answer since leaving
the Windlands. "Was one of these men, the grandfather of the
traveler at the Summer Breeze? Could it be Private Cassidan?
Had Cassidan's grandson ever walked over this same plain,
looking for treasure in the North?"

+++++++++

[ON THE OPALINE TRAIL]

*There was dust everywhere. Russ Cassidan pulled his
neck scarf over his face, and lowered his hat and his head to*

the wind. Behind him, almost thirteen hundred longhorn steers were slowly moving across the last of the open plains before reaching Opaline, in the southern Windlands. The drive had started in Barrettown, about a month before, and he was happy that in a few more days, he would be taking a bath at the Double Days Hotel.

This was the third drive Cassidan had been on this year. The other two started farther south, in Kinsedo, but this one followed the Twin River Trail, which made it, by far, the toughest. There were two mountain passes west of Jayville to endure, and three rivers to cross, besides the Twin. They had lost at least twenty head at the Junction crossing alone.

The life of a cattle driver was a difficult one. Living on the open plains for months at a time, and riding from sunup to sunset, would be hard on any man. But doing that, while trying to keep more than a thousand hungry steers headed towards the cattle pens at Opaline was a real challenge. And, this was his third year of driving the steers. Cassidan spent his winters at Wiresand in the Uplands, but the warmer months meant the lonely life on the trail.

Tonight though, he and the other drivers would have a chance to relax a bit. About ten miles ahead, lay the town of Rusher. It was the last town they would reach before their final push to the north.

Cassidan looked back to the southwest. In the distance, he could see clouds heading their way, and certainly traveling fast enough to quickly overtake them. The sky ahead was clear and blue, but behind him, it was getting darker and darker. He knew that if a storm caught up with the herd, he was in for a very long night.

The drive master rode up from behind him and pulled alongside. "Straff says that we are in for a big one. Forget about Rusher tonight. We are going to have our hands full here."

So that was that. No home cooked meal, or cards and beer tonight. He scanned the land ahead. They needed protection for the herd – but where? As far as he could see, the ground was mostly flat and treeless – just a few gullies and sidehills. Looking back again, he could see the southwestern sky turning darker and darker. It was going to be a bad one. The rim of his black range hat covered most of his face, but his spurs would do him no good tonight.

The quickly approaching clouds looked like mountains of grey-black snow, piled higher and higher against the deep blue background. The dust whistled at his throat. The continual cries of the cattle kept him constant company.

Looking up again, he noticed that there were no birds to be seen anywhere – miles and miles of sky, but not a single bird. "They are all too smart to be caught out in the open in a storm," he explained to Holly, his horse of many years. She had been his companion on every one of his drives. "I'll bet they are all back in that big stand of trees by the Davison, sitting warm and dry in the underbrush by the river, quietly waiting for the sky to bury them in dust and rain."

Then, across the plain to the west, he could see it coming. The rain was hitting the ground, and kicking the dust ahead of it – like a stampede of cattle coming towards him. A cold blast of air hit him in the face. Beneath him, Holly stirred uneasily.

Suddenly, the darkening sky was filled with a crack of sparks, as a trail of fire joined the clouds to the ground. All at once it was upon them – rain that hit the ground so hard that it thundered beneath Holly's hooves. The wind whipped the rain across Cassidan's face, and through his jacket and shirt. Thunder almost knocked him from his horse.

Cassidan had worried that the herd might stampede, but that would not happen now. The steers were stopped dead – too confused by it all to even run wildly.

The wind pushed him. He tied his hat still more tightly under his chin, and hugged his saddle lines to keep from being tossed to the ground. Holly dropped her head and nervously tensed against the wind and rain.

The sound of the storm was deafening. He could hear nothing of the cattle, then looked up from under his hat, and could see nothing of them either. Beneath him, the dirt had instantly turned to mud, as spike after spike of lightning struck the ground nearby. His head ached each time a crash blasted his ears. Holly strained against her reins, and was breathing wildly.

Cassidan wondered about the others – especially Rogers and Harden. This was their first drive. Maybe it would be their last. They might be in need of help. They would have to help themselves.

The storm went on and on – louder – stronger. He was afraid to dismount. It was always dangerous to be on foot near the herd, and now anything could happen.

The wind tried to make up his mind for him – pushing and pressing him. Holly had turned away from the storm as best she could, but he still feared he would be blown off of her.

An hour passed. The sky turned to night without him being able to tell the difference. On and on the storm raged. There was nowhere to hide, no place to run.

Cassidan noticed that he was nearer the herd now. It had moved, or he had moved. It was impossible to tell which.

He held his arms as straight and tight as he could, to keep himself in his saddle. The storm would not give up. There was another tremendous blast of wind, and, beneath him, Holly slipped in the muddy ground. She was falling – he had to try to jump clear. "Hang on to the reins!" he yelled to himself, as nine hundred pounds of animal quickly dropped to one side. Cassidan tried to push away. If Holly fell on him, he would be badly hurt or killed.

His landing was soft. The ground was a slick soup of mud. Holly fell on her side and tried to get up, but there was no footing. She tried again and again, but could not. Then she just seemed to relax. Holly put her head down and Cassidan lay next to her, shielding her face with his body. He wrapped himself around her, and closed his eyes. It was just him and her – waiting.

With each crack of lighting, Holly's massive body would jump and then relax as he tried to soothe her. Her breathing slowed a bit – her muscles calming themselves as he spoke directly into her ear, "It's alright, Girl. We'll be alright."

With each lightning flash he could still see the cattle a few dozen feet away, huddled together against the storm. He wondered, "Would the herd still be there in the morning, or lost across twenty miles of impossible ground? Would a flash flood from some distant hills sweep the cattle all away, with him among them? Would he and the supply wagons be spread like plains dust, and buried forever beneath the summer prairie grass?"

Russ Cassidan curled tighter against Holly. Another crash of lightning split his ears. It was going to be the longest night of his life.

+++++++++

The travelers stopped for the night at the eastern edge of a small forest. Before going to sleep, they sat around their fire as they had done so many times before. This time, however, their evening turned out a little differently than usual.

Panni was teaching Raine a guessing game that she used to play with the dancers at the Traepelle Castle. He wasn't doing very well because he didn't know the names of many birds and animals from this world. Panni kept teasing him about his lack of knowledge and he pretended to be upset.

Overhead, a full moon shone down from the east. It was a quiet night on the Northern Plains.

In the middle of the quiet, Circles started to sing one of his pretty, Deep Woods songs. Panni and Raine stopped guessing and listened. Window leaned back against a tree next to Rings and closed his eyes. Circles' voice soared out from the camp and across the grasslands. It was a beautiful night and a beautiful song. When he was finished everyone just sat quietly for a minute.

Circles glanced back across the fire towards the others, and then he saw them, far out on the grassy flatland. He didn't have to imagine them anymore. His dream had come true. Out on the Northlands plains there were five gracefully tall Silkie standing in the moonlight.

Circles broke the quiet excitedly. "Look! Look! The Silkie! Out in the moonlight! The Silkie! There really are Silkie! And they are here! Just look! Just look!"

Everyone jumped up from their quiet rest and turned to see the enormously tall beasts. The Silkie were far away from the camp, but still easy to see. Their bodies looked a bit like very fluffy deer, with four fluffy legs and their backs almost as high as Window's shoulders. But, their most dramatic feature was their necks. Their tremendous necks alone were much taller than the rest of their bodies. Their necks stood tall and straight, high above their backs. As they walked, they moved with controlled elegance, those wonderful necks moving smoothly along with the rest of their bodies.

The Silkie's heads were also rather deer-like, although their faces were not as pointed. They had tall, pointy ears that stuck up even higher above their heads. Their legs and backs and necks were totally covered with fluffy, silky fur. The moonlight above them completed the alluring sight the travelers saw.

The others all expected Circles to jump up and down or otherwise continue to show his excitement, but to their surprise, he again became very quiet. His dream had come true. He was thrilled, but quietly so, and kept his quiet thoughts to himself. The others all felt the same wonder and magic of the great beasts and so the travelers all sat and kept their thoughts to themselves as they watched the mesmerizing sight before them.

"Wow," Circles at last spoke again, in rather unbelieving awe. "They are really something."

Window's eyes followed the creatures as they slowly moved across the horizon, "The stories were right. They are majestic and beautiful."

"I can see why the Angels would ride on them, Circles," Panni quietly added. "They are magical to look at."

Circles was thinking aloud. "I wonder if we can talk to them somehow? Or maybe we could ride on them."

Window smiled at his little friend. "You are a wonderful dreamer, Circles. I have learned a lot from you."

Out on the grasslands, the Silkie held their magnificent necks high, as they galloped off, beneath the moon, out of sight to the east.

Panni smiled at Circles. "It looks like we will all have something to dream about tonight, Circles. Maybe we will all have Silkie dreams tonight."

"I know that I will, Panni. I know that I will."

And he did. He slept as happily as he ever had.

The next morning found the travelers on their journey again, out into the grasslands in the direction the Silkie had gone the night before.

Circles could speak of nothing else but the Silkie. At breakfast, he told everyone that he liked them even better than he liked the ocean.

"And I like the ocean a lot," he reminded them.

"So do I," Panni threw in.

As the five travelers made their way out from the forest area into the flat plains to the east, the grass beneath their feet became shorter and less dense. Here, the lands were scattered with odd-looking plants and a few flowers. Circles found some very tasty roots to eat when he dug under a bush that looked like paw-branch. The sky was full of billowing white clouds, and the air was warm and clear.

They stopped for lunch under some trees just beyond a small stream that had crossed in front of them. As they were eating, Window noticed that Raine was holding his right hand up near his ear. "Circles," Raine spoke his name, but was really speaking to everyone, as he pointed out farther to the east. "They are coming. The Silkie are coming."

Everyone stood up and peered out into the grasslands. At the very edge of his vision, Circles could see them. Soon everybody could see the beautiful creatures galloping towards them, and then hear the clopping of their hoofs on the hard ground between some of the patches of grass.

The Silkie approached the travelers' camp. Up close, they struck Window as even more magnificent than they were from a distance. Three of the five had bright red fur, one of them with black streaks in the red. One Silkie had blue fur, and the other was light violet.

"Wow," thought Circles. "They have colors just like Woots!"

The Silkie slowed from their run and smoothly walked up to greet the travelers. They towered over everyone, even the massive Rings. All five stood in a straight row before the travelers.

Window spoke first, "Hello, Silkie. We are pleased to meet you. Would you join us for a while?"

The violet colored Silkie bowed her flowing neck towards Window, but didn't speak.

"Maybe they are not Talkers," Window said to Raine. "Can you try to speak with them?"

Before Raine could answer, the five creatures suddenly started to twist and turn, and sway their necks around in a wild looking fashion. They lifted each of their feet off of the ground and then stood still again.

"They are not Talkers," Raine told his friends, as he held his finger-rings up near his ear. "But Silkie are Dreamreaders. Circles, was it you that asked them to dance?"

"I was just wondering what they would look like dancing. I didn't know that they really would dance," explained the Woot.

"Dreamreaders are creatures that can tell what others are thinking, and these five danced for you as a gift of greeting. They know, Circles, that it was you who wished them here today. So we can all thank you for bringing them over to meet us."

This time, all five of the creatures bowed. Circles smiled, and bowed in return.

Panni walked up to the blue Silkie and held out her hand. The giant creature lowered his head down to her, so she could pet it and scratch his ears. The Silkie responded to the scratching with a whistling sound that rose and dropped in pitch several times.

"Well, Blue, here, just read my dream," Panni told her friends, as she gave the Silkie a name. "Thank you, Blue. You are very polite," she addressed to him.

Window spoke aloud to their visitors, but he hoped they could read what was in his head, as well. "Would you like to travel with us for a few days? We are going across the plains to the east?"

Violet whistled two quick times and bowed again. The travelers smiled, even Rings, as best he could. They knew that that meant the beautiful animals would keep them company for a while! The treasure hunters' adventure had just gotten even better that it had ever been.

Circles couldn't wait any longer. He approached the slightly smaller of the red creatures. *May I ride on your back for a ways?"* Circles thought to himself, but didn't speak aloud.

Little Red bowed politely and dropped to his knees. Window gave Circles a boost, and soon the Woot was galloping around the grasslands of the Northern Plains. He held on tightly to big handfuls of fur on the Silkie's back and neck.

Before two more minutes had passed, Panni was riding on Blue, Window was riding on Violet, and Raine was atop Red-Ears. Rings, of course, was too big to ride on Fireback.

Both the travelers and the Silkie had a wonderful time. They spent the entire afternoon, riding and jumping and racing.

Raine used his messenger-rings a bit, and really got to communicate with Red-Ears. Window enjoyed riding, but mostly liked watching the others.

Panni had ridden horses at the castle, and now she almost flew across the grass on Blue, as her long, golden-white hair trailed behind her in the wind. Panni's legs glowed in the sunlight, and her skirt flapped wildly around her, as she felt more free than perhaps she ever had. Window couldn't help but notice again how

beautiful she was. To him, Panni really did look like an Angel
riding upon a Silkie.

After a while, Rings said that he was missing his old racing
days, and that they should have a real race. So, Window on
Violet, and Raine on Red-Ears, rode out about a quarter of a mile
into the plain, where it was decided the race would finish.
Panni would ride on Blue and Circles would ride on Little Red.
Rings and Fireback would race along with the others.
The racers stood together at the edge of a big patch of sillow-
grass and waited for the start. Window shouted as loudly as he
could towards the starting line, "One, two, three – Now!"
The racers galloped across the grassland. All three Silkie and
Rings were very evenly matched. Dust and grass flew behind
them, as they seemed to sail over the plain. Silky fur and blonde
hair flew in the wind.
Rings and Fireback pulled ahead of the others. It was a very
close race between them. Rings' strength was able to keep his
shorter legs up with the Silkie's. At the end, it was a tie, both
racers crossing between Window and Raine at the same time.
Every Talker clapped, every Silkie whistled, and everyone
bowed to everyone else. Rings was even almost smiling. He had
really enjoyed the race, but he hadn't run in a while. So after they
had all walked back to the trees, Rings plopped down in the tall,
cool, grass and rested. The Silkie lay their bodies down on the
ground as well, and everyone enjoyed the shade.

Panni treated the Silkie to some berries as the breeze cooled
the racers. Raine shared with the others that Red-Ears told him
the Silkie would accompany them across the grasslands to the
Battleplain. This made everybody extremely happy, especially
Circles. He could not have thought of a better gift to receive. He
wondered if maybe today was his birthday.

Around the fire that night, the travelers led the singing and
were joined by the whistling of the Silkie. Circles said that any
creature with a neck that tall should really be good at whistling,
because the air had such a long throat in which to gain speed

before the whistle came out. And, he was right. The Silkie were very good whistlers.

The trip across the northern grasslands was a very enjoyable one. Window, Panni, Circles, and Raine were each invited to ride on the back of a Silkie. Rings was too big to ride, and could not walk as fast as the Silkie, so Fireback, very politely, walked more slowly, and kept Rings company. Rings tried to learn to whistle, but that didn't work. But Rings did figure out how to ask questions in his mind, and the Dreamreader would answer him with whistles or bobbing or shaking his head. In just a couple of days they became good friends. Fireback even agreed to visit the Deep Woods with Rings sometime.

On the third night, after supper, Raine decided to go for a little moonlit ride on Red-Ears. Circles watched as they rode out from the camp. Raine's blue glow shone in the moonlight, as he and his friend galloped across the night-time plain. And, just like Window thought of Panni a couple of days before, Circles thought that Raine really did look like an Angel riding a Silkie.

Circles walked over to Little Red, who was doing some late-night grazing in the sillow-grass, and asked him, *"Do Angels ever ride on Silkie in the moonlight?"*

Little Red answered with dream-thoughts into Circles' mind, *"I have heard those stories, too, Circles, from my mother-Silkie. They are stories from the very old days. But, I don't know if they are true. I have never seen an Angel."*

"Oh, well," Circles sighed. "Oh, well."

+++++++++

The travelers and their companions made a very striking sight as they continued across the plains to the east. Five gigantic, colorful Silkie and a massive Brarrie would have been almost impossible to miss, had anyone been watching, as they moved across the wide horizon.

The travelers pressed on. Panni loved that she didn't have to walk for a few days, and she especially enjoyed the freedom she

felt while riding. The Silkie moved smoothly, and riding on Blue
was very comfortable and pleasant.

By day, they sang and whistled. At night, they told stories.
They waded the Taesenne River when they reached it. Once it
rained a little, but nobody minded.

But at the middle of the fifth day together, they had reached
the end of their journey.

Window learned from Violet that the Battleplain was just over
the next long rise. The Silkie would go to the top of the rise but no
farther. This was the end of their Silkie-lands, and the end of
their journey with the treasure hunters.

The goodbyes were sad, but sweet. Everyone agreed that they
would meet again, and everyone really hoped that it would be
true.

Violet used her hoof to draw a map showing where the Silkie
dens were, so the travelers could easily find them next time.

Panni hugged Blue's neck so hard that he whistled when he
didn't mean to. There were tears and thanks and good wishes all
around.

The travelers left their grassland friends and continued down
the long slope to the Battleplain. They looked back to the hilltop
behind them one last time, and watched sadly as the beautiful
plains animals slowly turned, and galloped away.

At the bottom of the long sloping hill, the travelers entered the
Battleplain. It was once called Selle-Triefenne, after early
Freeland explorers, but was renamed in W.Y. 67 following the
battle there, between the Atland Army and the Northlands forces.
That battle was the largest and most decisive of the war in the
North.

Casualties were heavy on both sides. The Atland soldiers who
were killed were buried at the far eastern end of the plain in the
Battleplain Cemetery. The Battleplain itself was similar to the
rest of the Northern Plains. The travelers had no difficulty
continuing across it to the east.

The company of the Silkie had taken the minds of the treasure hunters off of the Freelands coins that they were looking for in the cemetery. But now, as they neared the site, they once again thought of finding the coin box left there by the Northlands Expedition.

The travelers had been through so much together, though, that looking for a few coins was not the grand treasure hunt that they felt it was a couple of months earlier. Still, Window wanted to see if they could find the coins, for his grandfather, and for Oldsmith.

As they approached the eastern edge of the plain, Window was well aware that his grandfather's expedition was attacked by wild hill people at the cemetery, as were Oldsmith and Revell, in that same part of Calisenne. He twice reminded everyone to keep their weapons near and their attention sharp.

By late the next afternoon, the travelers could see the gravestones of the cemetery in the distance. There were rows and rows of headstones, which had been quickly made from soft white-stone taken from the low hills a bit farther east.

The cemetery appeared to simply be settling back into the grass of the plains. There was no fence or gate or sign. There were only twenty rows of low headstones, partially hidden by the tall sillow-grass. Window's terrible thoughts of going to the cemetery, that he felt weeks before, didn't bother him at all.

It was a peaceful place, a quiet spot for those who had been killed so long before. And, about a half-mile to the south of the graves, they could see the Northway as it passed by to the west and east.

The treasure hunters pulled the harness from Rings' back, and he rested as the others walked through the rows of graves. The names of those buried at each site were roughly scratched into the stones. "Peller – Ames – Fasette – Olney," Window read aloud as he walked along past some of the stones.

It seemed so sad, and yet so long ago – eighty years. Window wondered if any of the dead soldiers' families ever thought about where their lost members were buried. Most of the Atland soldiers had come from the homeland across the ocean, so there was no way that any of their relatives could ever have come here to visit the graves, or even know much about where they were located.

Window looked back towards the others and noticed that Raine was silently sitting on a gravestone and looking up into the sky. He seemed lost in thought. Window walked back to him and sat down for a moment.

Window didn't say anything, but Raine did. "Last year," he began, in a very soft voice, "I was caught in a battle on a world called Kess-Gieal. I had delivered a message and was waiting for a reply when the opposing forces attacked. Because of my finger-rings, I survived the attack, but ten thousand Kessans did not. And because of what I saw, I will never be the same. Death and injury were everywhere. It will haunt me forever. Sometimes I cannot get the thoughts from my mind."

Window couldn't think of a single thing to say. He just sat quietly by Raine, until Circles came up to them and asked Window, "Okay, Mister Treasure-hunter, where is that gravestone we are looking for?"

Window got out his notebook to show Circles the name they wanted to find. It was written just as it had been in Grandfather's notebook back home.

Captain John Page – second row, third stone

"This should be really easy to find," Circles told the others. And he was right. The rows of stones ran parallel to the Northway, and the names on them faced the east. Circles ran to the beginning of the first row and, with great exaggeration, called out the rows as he pointed to them, "Row one, Row two." Then he counted down the second row, "One, two, three." He was pointing at the gravestone of Captain John Page.

The treasure hunters joined Circles at the stone. Rings came up closer so he could see, too.

"Well, there it is," Circles announced. Page's name was clearly scratched into the marker. Under his name, it also said, "W.Y. 38-67" and on a third line, "Atland Northlands Campaign."

"I guess that the officers got a little extra on their stones," Window spoke, mostly to himself.

Circles got down on his hands and knees and started pulling grass from behind the Page marker. "It looks like the ground here is pretty uneven," he unhappily announced to the others. "Maybe somebody has beaten us to the treasure."

Circles stood up and moved away from the stone, and Rings carefully stepped between the markers to replace him. And just as he had done at the cannon on the coast north of Meriselle, Rings dragged his long claws across the ground behind the stone. With just one scoop through the dirt, he easily uncovered what was left of the Great Freelands Coins Treasure – the empty, rusted, broken, metal box that had, at one time, held the coins. That was all that was there. The coins were gone. Someone else had found them!

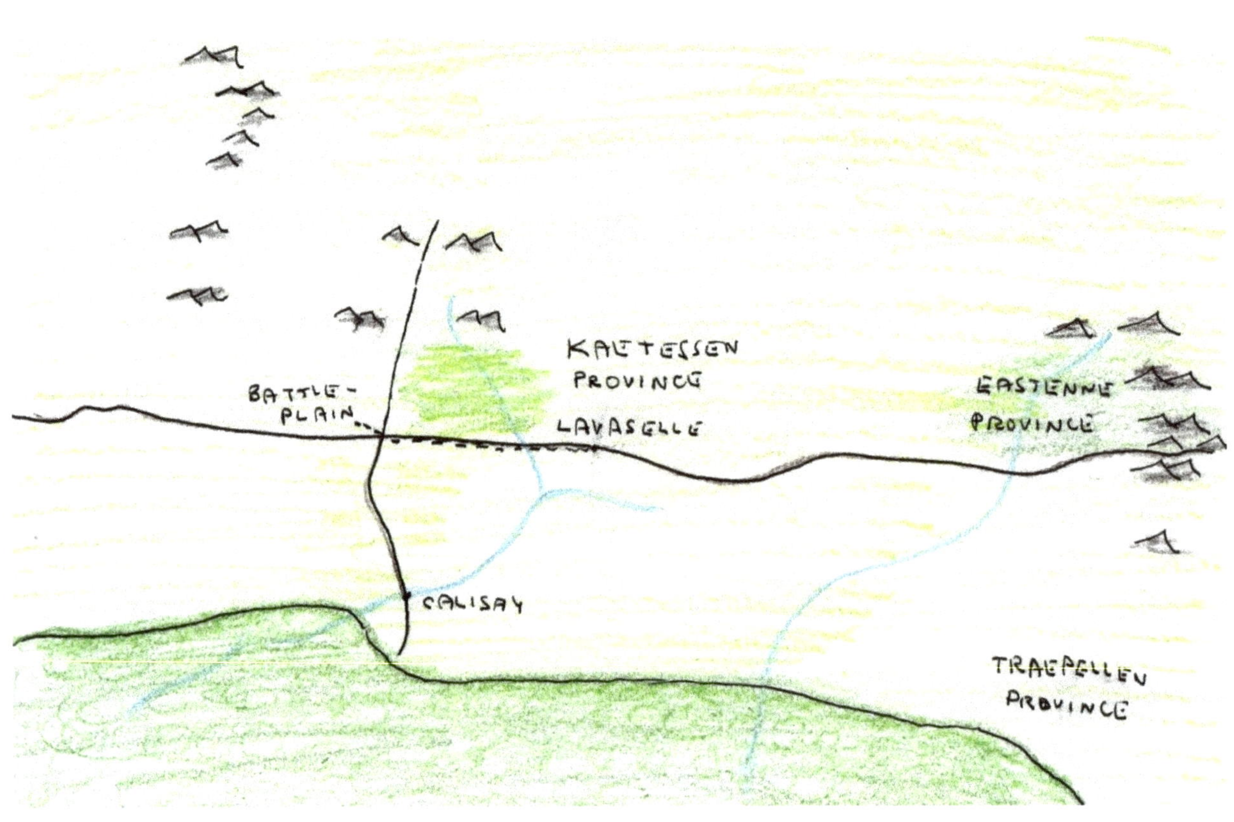

BATTLE-
PLAIN
KALTESSEN
PROVINCE
LAVASELLE
EASTENNE
PROVINCE
CALISAY
TRAEPELLEU
PROVINCE

CHAPTER FIFTEEN

AT THE LAVESELLE INN

To the east of the Battleplain Cemetery was the beginning of the Kaetessen Province. Kaetessen was a mostly forested land that extended towards the far eastern mountains, where the destroyed and lost mines of the Northlands Kingdom were located. Window and his band of unsuccessful treasure hunters would follow the Northway in that direction to the village of Laveselle, where Oldsmith's son, Dawson lived.

Dawson was the proprietor of the local inn, The East Road Inn, and the travelers could stay there while they decided what they would do next.

Rings was rather tired of traveling, but he loved the adventure and the friendship he had found. Raine and Panni had nowhere to go. Well, Panni could go to Calisay, and work with Sara in the bakery, but Panni was still exploring the world outside of Traepelle, and searching for where else life might take her. So for now, her love for Window would keep her with him as long as was possible.

Window and Circles didn't like to think about the end of their adventures together. Circles fur hadn't changed color yet, and he didn't want to go home until it did. Also, he kept reminding Window that they hadn't found any treasure, and so they had to keep looking. Each of the travelers had these things on their minds as they journeyed east.

"I want to take a hot bath," Panni announced as they talked about staying at the Inn.

"I want to lie in the shade – and get a new pair of boots – but not wear them for a while," came Window's wishes.

"Oh, I need shoes, too," Panni joined in. "Mine are almost worn through."

"I want to sit on the porch and drink lemon-tea," Circles declared.

"You don't even know what lemon-tea is, Circles," Panni reminded him.

"I don't care," came the response. "It sounds delicious. Plus, I know that while you are drinking it, you don't have to do anything else. So, I will be a Woot of leisure."

"Also," he continued thoughtfully, "I want to learn some more about reading and writing. I figure that Dawson will have some books that I can look at."

"How about you, Rings? What are you looking forward to?" Panni wanted to know.

"I want to take off my harness – and find a nice cool stream to sit in."

The friends looked towards Raine. There was a sad moment as they were reminded that he was completely lost from his world. At first he didn't say anything, but then he joined in with his wish, "I would like to sail to the Senestelle-Talavenne Stargate. From there I could be home in just a few days."

"That sounds nice, Raine," Circles replied, only understanding the part about sailing home. "I would go with you if I could."

"I would like that very much, Circles, I would like that very much."

The conversations continued as the miles passed beneath their feet.

The travelers reached the Calisay South Road in just one day, and then, just two more days brought them to the edge of Laveselle. They hadn't been in a village, or talked to many people, since they left Calisay weeks and weeks before.

"I hope that nobody here will be bothered by Deep Woods Talkers," Window expressed as they started up Laveselle's wide main street.

"Yeah, I wouldn't want to scare anybody," Circles thoughtfully spoke up.

Window went on, "Oldsmith said that the people here were very friendly, and would welcome anyone who was a friend of Dawson's – especially after they hear about how you were chased by Prince Martellan's soldiers. They don't like any of the soldiers from Calisay, who come this way occasionally, and cause trouble."

"Are there any soldiers in the Kaetessen Province, Window?" Panni wanted to know.

"There is one castle near Laveselle, but the castle noble is considered to be a fair and thoughtful man, who is generous with his servants. Dawson, and his daughter, even help cook for him on some special occasions, when there are many guests coming to the castle."

As the odd group of travelers walked into the shade of the tall oaks and elms that arched over the town's wide, tree-lined, main street, they each felt a comforting sense of calm. The buildings of Laveselle looked much newer and better kept than those in Calisay. Oldsmith had said that Laveselle was one of the few such remaining places in all of the North. The streets were clean and its many trees greatly added to the pleasantness of the village.

Some of the townspeople came out from their houses and shops and curiously watched the travelers pass. Two boys, who were playing with toy soldiers in the dirt and roots under an ancient oak tree, waved and Circles waved back. The boys abandoned their play and followed the travelers up the street, keeping what they thought was a safe distance from the strange group of visitors.

Dawson's place was easy to find, and soon the travelers were all lined up in the street in front of The East Road Inn. Window climbed the wide steps to the Inn's large porch and knocked at the door. Actually, they were heavy double doors that were now open to allow the breeze to come through the Inn's thin screen doors.

Dawson came out to greet his new guests, and sixteen diners, who were in the middle of lunch, some of whom had seen the strange group of travelers approaching through a window, pushed out onto the porch with him. When the travelers left Calisay, Oldsmith had sent Rook to tell Dawson to expect the visitors, but, of course, they were a couple of months later than expected.

Dawson was a tall man, like his father, and just as friendly. He was wearing a wide, white apron, since it was the middle of the midday lunch at the Inn, and a time when townsfolk, who were not guests at the Inn, would stop in for a well-cooked meal. Actually, there were seldom many guests staying at the Inn, since there were seldom many travelers on the Northway. So, The East Road Inn was really more of a restaurant than an inn. Fortunately, Dawson had learned to cook with his sister, Sara, when she and Oldsmith still lived in Laveselle, and he was quite talented in that regard.

Since Rings could not fit into the Inn, Dawson and his daughter, Mellie, brought food outside where the other travelers sat under a tree on some benches. Mellie was seventeen, with dark brown hair, cut above her shoulders, dark eyes, and an infectious smile. She helped a lot around the Inn, but would probably have rather been off with her friends somewhere, maybe swimming in the little lake south of town.

Window had grown pretty tired of eating berries and fruit on his trek through the Northlands, so he was very happy with the travelers' choices of bread and cheese and stew and milk that Dawson offered them. The curious Inn diners quickly tired of watching a group of travelers eating lunch, and soon went back inside to finish their own meals. A few of the children from town, who had gathered along the edge of the street, stared at Rings for a long time. But he didn't do much, so they, too, eventually tired of watching him and went back to their games.

When he had a chance, Dawson came back outside and visited with his father's friends. "Welcome to Laveselle, Weary Travelers. My father will be happy to hear that you are safe. I know that he has been extremely concerned."

"It is very generous of you to feed us, Dawson. Thank you for being so kind."

"You are all welcome, Window. I invite you to stay here and rest as long as you like."

Mellie was fascinated by the Deep Woods Talkers, and by the starman as well. Strangers rarely came to the Inn, and never odd strangers such as these. She skipped some of her kitchen duties and sat outside with the others.

Dawson had learned to speak some Atlandan from his father, but was not as fluent as Rook or Sara. Mellie could understand it fairly well, but was very slow at speaking. Now she wished that she had practiced more, when her grandfather had asked her to learn the language. She spoke to the travelers mostly in Freelandan.

The pleasant afternoon at the Inn turned into several pleasant days. They relaxed and rested and thought about what they would do next.

As the days went by, the wishes of most of the travelers came true. Panni got her bath and shoes and other new clothes as well. Window got his boots and shade to sit under. Rings found a stream in which to cool off, and Circles got to sit on the porch and drink lemon-tea – and he loved it. "I'll bet that Laveselle is the lemon-tea capital of the world," he declared, after a particularly satisfying glass of the sweet-sour drink.

The travelers each were given a room at the Inn, except for Rings, who picked a spot behind the woodshed that he could curl right into. Dawson sent a message to his father by one of the supply wagons that made regular trips to Calisay. It would be delivered to the Matenne Palace where one of Oldsmith's friends would receive it, and take it on to him.

Oldsmith had told Dawson that he would make the trip to Laveselle to see his traveling friends again, whenever they arrived. The journey by wagon from Calisay would probably take him two or three days.

Dawson's wife was an energetic, dark blonde-haired woman named Polla. She welcomed the visitors openly, and did all she could to make them comfortable. She did much of the work around the Inn, but just a little of the cooking. Cooking was Dawson's specialty.

Window felt badly that he had no Freeland money to help pay for their food and clothes and lodging, but Dawson didn't seem to mind, and never asked for payment. He had been to Calisay the month before, and learned all about how fond his father was of the travelers. He was happy to buy them a few things, and feed them for a while, as he enjoyed their company.

Panni offered to help Dawson and Mellie in the kitchen, and one afternoon she baked the bread for the evening meal. Another day, Window and Raine helped Dawson fix some torn shingles on the Inn roof, and repair a fence across a side of the property.

Other than that, it was as Circles had wished – a life of leisure. They all rested, and looked forward to the upcoming visit by Oldsmith – and his grandson, Rook, was coming too! Oldsmith's daughter, Sara, had to stay and work in her Calisay bakery, but would send some pies with her father.

Circles located Dawson's bookshelf and found a book he wanted to read from. It was a story about three friends who discovered a wild horse in the wilderness, and tried to train it to be a racing horse. Unfortunately, like all of Dawson's books, it was in Freelandan, which Circles didn't know how to read at all.

"Oh, well," Circles sighed, "Oh, well." Instead of reading, he had another glass of lemon-tea.

Panni found a spot on the back porch where she could sit in the sun without bothering anyone. Each afternoon she fed Dawson's chickens, and enjoyed talking to them. They always agreed with everything she said.

On the third day, as she was filling her feed apron, Panni looked out from the side of the Inn and down the street. Her heart froze. Soldiers were coming.

Five grey-clad soldiers, with swords at their sides, and light armor on their chests, were walking towards the front porch.

Panni didn't recognize their armor as any she had seen before. They wore only a simple star on their shoulders.

She thought, "Maybe they have heard that Rings is here and they are looking for him!"

Panni ran around to the back of the Inn and found Rings under the stand of willow trees. "Rings! Rings! Hide quickly. Soldiers are coming."

The big beast jumped up as best he could and hurried behind Dawson's barn. Panni ran back to the Inn. She climbed under a side railing on the front porch, and was sitting on that railing, leaning back against the Inn, as the men reached the steps.

"Fornae telenne tosaede?" one of them called to her.

"Na coesan forae naedesse," she answered slowly, making sure that she didn't accidentally say anything in Atlandan.

"San toolenne, baelenne," came the unhappy reply. The soldiers turned and walked back to the street and continued on their way.

Dawson came out from the front door as soon as they had gone.

"I told them that there were no rooms available, Dawson," Panni explained, breathing quickly. "I hope that you don't mind."

"That only saved me from doing it, Panni. The only soldiers I want staying here are those from the Pariselle castle. They are always welcome. The others are not."

Dawson and Panni went around to the back of the Inn and told Rings that he could come out of hiding.

"I don't know if those soldiers were from the Calisenne Province, or know that I am no longer welcome there," Rings said sadly, 'but I am sure that I can never go back to Calisay to race, ever again."

"That's too bad, Rings. I know how you love racing."

"It's a good thing that I love sleeping, too – and treasure hunting. Thanks, Panni, for keeping me safe," he added, and walked back to the shade of the willow trees.

The next day Oldsmith and Rook arrived by wagon from Calisay. Their reunion with the travelers was a joyous one, and their friendships were quickly renewed. Raine was immediately accepted as a member of Oldsmith's growing family, too, as the others had been in Calisay.

Oldsmith was disappointed that the cemetery coins were not found, and felt sadness for the deaths in the Woods, but was very happy that the travelers were safe. Most of their stories, however, had to wait until that evening, when the treasure hunters and their friends all gathered in the Inn's big dining room.

Dawson took the large table from the middle of the room and pushed it over by the east double window. Circles, Panni, Raine, Oldsmith, Dawson and Window all sat at the table. Rings sat on the grass, right outside of the window, where he could be part of the conversations. Polla, Mellie, and Rook pulled up chairs near the other end of the table, and everyone settled in for an evening of stories.

Window felt completely at home and comfortable with all of his friends. It was as though he was now part of a big new family. Polla and Mellie brought crackers, and cheese, and drinks for all, as the stories and conversation lasted long into the night.

Everyone had a guess as to who discovered the Freelands coins at the cemetery, and everyone's guess was the same. They were all sure that Revell had come back and found them. Other scenarios were suggested, but nobody really believed that they were true.

"I have told a few people here in town, over the years, about the coins, Dad," Dawson revealed to Oldsmith, but I don't think that any of them actually went looking for them. They could have, though, I guess."

"Do you still have Revell's key that I gave you, Window?" Oldsmith wanted to know.

"I do, Oldsmith, I do. And some day I hope to use it."

"Oldsmith," Panni wondered, "Did Revell leave any clues at all as to where he was going, or where he lived?"

"None that I remember, Panni — just that he always wanted to go east, to search for the lost Northlands mines."

No one had any other suggestions with regard to the Freelands coins, so the conversation turned farther west.

The travelers' story of the Silkie fascinated everyone. They all knew the rhymes and tales about the plains animals, but none of the Oldsmiths even knew of anyone who had ever seen one. Now both Mellie and Rook wanted to go to the Northern Plains, so they could see a Silkie, too.

Then the conversation turned to King Alezan's Treasures. All of the Oldsmiths were mesmerized by the search for the treasure in Meriselle and the coin found at the cannon. Circles ran to his room and retrieved the Amerand money-piece. He proudly showed it to everyone when he returned.

Oldsmith said that he knew that some Amerans had tried to settle in the Northlands, back in the days of the King, but were turned away.

"We think that one of those ships was sent away with a load of gold and silver coins," Panni reminded everyone.

"Where did the Amerans go, Grandpa?" Rook asked.

"I guess that they went farther south somewhere. I know that some went to the Windlands."

"Yeah, like my grandma's ancestors," Window added.

"Your grandma doesn't happen to have a barn full of Freeland gold and silver coins, does she, Window?" Dawson asked, only half kidding.

"No, but she has a springcookie board that seems to know something about the coins, and maybe the other King's Treasures as well. I can't explain it, but it seems to be true."

Window, with Circles helping, explained all about the springcookie clues that seemed to point to the King's Treasure that went to Meriselle. Everyone agreed that the cookies seemed to be related to the coins.

"Okay," Window led the conversation. "Let's think about the cookieboard clues we think might apply to the Calisay treasure of King Alezan. We have the kites, the bridge, the tower, and perhaps the shield. Three of those things are definitely in Calisay.

What about the shield? It had two crossed swords, or maybe
lances.”

“One thing to consider,” Oldsmith offered, “is that the Calisay
towers were each built for a different member of the original
Alezan Royal Family – a son or daughter or other relative. The
tower on the cookieboard, which is in the exact center of the
Calisay tower field, was built for the King’s oldest son, Cairiston.
He would have become ruler someday, had the kingdom survived.
In fact, it is called the Cairiston Tower.”

So, perhaps the board is telling us that the oldest son took his
part of the King’s treasure, and hid it in the tower. If his part was
the larger gold items, as you suspect, like the statues and large
castle ornaments, then it would take a lot of space to hide them –
a large secret room perhaps.

“Have you ever been in that tower, Grandpa?” Rook asked.

“I have been in several of the other towers, but never that one.
I don’t know if anyone is allowed in there.”

Rook knew that answer. “Grandpa, Prince Martellan’s soldiers
have their headquarters in the base building of Cairiston Tower. I
have been over there before. No one can get close to it, except the
soldiers.”

“Do you recall the symbol of a shield and swords anywhere on
the tower, or nearby?”

“Grandpa, I think that each of the twelve towers has a symbol
at its base. Circles and I saw two of them when we went exploring
by the towers, when he was in Calisay. The symbol on each tower
represents the particular family member the tower honors.

“King Alezan’s symbol was the crossed swords and sun,”
Oldsmith went on. “Since Cairiston was the oldest son, and first
in line to the throne, perhaps his symbol was taken from the
King’s symbol, and also included crossed swords, maybe with
something else instead of the sun.”

“I’ll bet that it is Cairiston’s shield on the cookie,” Circles got
into the conversation. Everyone else continued to listen intently.

Then Rook gave his assessment. “And, I think that Cairiston’s
part of the King’s Treasure is hidden in or near that middle tower
– and I want to find it.”

"I see that we now have another treasure hunter in the family," Oldsmith announced.

"Make that two more, Grandpa," Mellie spoke up. "I may want to go treasure hunting with Rook in Calisay." Then Mellie looked towards Panni, as if hoping for her support, and Panni smiled her approval.

Polla went and got more snacks, as the treasure talk continued.

"What about the four other cookie pictures, Window," Oldsmith wondered, "the ones that might point to the King's Treasure that was taken to the east? What were those pictures?"

"There was a windmill, a flag, some flowers, and an Angel. The flag had two designs on it – they looked like big stars twinkling – or something like that.

Dawson immediately recognized the description. "The Eastenne Province flag has two stars like that on it, Window, each made of a horizontal line crossing a vertical line, with shorter lines crossing the intersection of those two on the diagonals. In the early days, the Northlanders called gold and silver, the 'Stars of the East'."

Circles was so excited, he could hardly breathe.

"What were the flowers?" Oldsmith asked Window.

"The cookieboard flowers had pointed petals with pointed leaves that stood almost straight up into the air."

Then, Polla spoke up, "Those sound like they could be skyflowers. And, they are common in the eastern mountains."

"And the windmill?" Window went on, believing what he heard with great amazement. "Are there any windmills in the east?"

"Maybe they are windfans, Window," Dawson suggested. "The Eastenne mines had windmills above them that were attached to great fans deep under the ground. When the windmills turned, they turned the fans down in the mines, and that pulled fresh air down to the miners."

"That only leaves one, Window," Circles counted excitedly. "What about the Angel? Are there any stories of Angels in the east?"

"This is too easy, Window," Dawson kiddingly answered. "The next time you find some secret map, try to find one that is not so easy to figure out. The far eastern end of the Northway is called Eastpoint. At the very end of the road is a stone gateway called Eastpoint Gate. That gateway is also called the Gate To The Angels."

"Old stories tell that Angels lived out in the wild lands beyond Eastpoint Gate. That is why it was the Gate To The Angels. Nobody really knows what is out there."

"That's it," Circles almost shouted. "I told you that the cookieboard was a map to the King's Treasures! The third treasure is out by the Eastpoint Gate somewhere!"

Window smiled broadly at his friends. "My grandmother has a lot of explaining to do."

Window went on, "I have been trying to remember how the pictures carvings were arranged on my grandmother's cookieboard. I do remember that her board had three columns of four carvings each, and I am sure that the cannon was at the top of the column on the left, and the Angel was at the top of the board on the right. I suppose that if the rest of the carvings were arranged properly, each column could be like a map to one of the King's three treasures. The first column would lead to the Meriselle treasure, the middle column to the Calisay treasure, and the third column would be a map to the treasure in the east."

"Your grandmother is a smart lady," Circles concluded.

Mellie had been listening with the greatest interest. She spoke up for the first time that evening.

"I know a poem. My Grandma Oldsmith taught me a poem once – about Angels." Everyone looked towards Mellie and waited as she thought about the words she wanted to say.

"I can't say it in Atlandan, but part of the poem is about Angels who live under a lost moon. The poem says that they live beyond the Gate To The Angels in the land under the mountains of the moon, and they write their magic with Angel letters carved into stones. And also in the poem, some other Angels live in castles in the sky."

Circles didn't need to hear any more. "Let's go, Window. Let's go find the treasure under the mountains on the moon! Let's go find the Angels!"

Then he quickly added. "And what about the King's mines, Window? Let's go find the mines, too."

"But they were destroyed, Circles, or lost in the quakes."

"I'll bet that Revell found them," Circles offered. "So, we could find them too."

Window was thinking as fast as he could. "Were they all gold and silver mines, Oldsmith, or other mines, too?"

"There were at least four jewel mines as well – mines of blue-diamonds and rose-diamonds and skystars and light-stones. Those four gems are the stones that were on the royal crowns of the King and his family. Those are probably also the jewels that were taken back with the crowns to the east, and hidden as the third part of the King's Treasure."

"There was also a trillion mine," added Dawson, "and a vermillion mine, too. Those are colorful, sparkly minerals that flake into powder, and can be melted easily, and formed into beautiful, soft, colored-metal, for bracelets and neck jewels. The young women of the royal castles especially love them."

"Children's stories even tell that Pixie's use trillion and vermillion dust in their magic," Polla added. Circles eyes lit up again.

"What do you say, Window?" Circles asked with great enthusiasm. "Do we go on to the east and find more treasures? As Raine told me once, you can choose your future right now."

Window looked around the room at his friends. He didn't have to ask. He could tell what they wanted.

"We will have a fine time," Window answered. "Yes, Circles, we will go find treasure and Angels in the east."

Circles was so happy, he fell on his back and squealed.

+++++++++

Sally Breesian Resand turned the key of the front door lock and stepped inside. She knew the house well. Sally had lived there with her brother before she was married. Now, she hadn't seen Window in three months or so, and was concerned. But Grandpa Windowen said to not worry.

There really wasn't anything to do. The three rooms were just as neat and quiet as when she was there a month ago. She looked at the few things on the table, then noticed Window's bookcase on the south wall.

It was a light colored, wooden bookcase, that was low to the ground, and it held all of Window's books on two shelves. Many had been gifts to Window when he was a boy, a few he got from the Windtown School, and several were given to him by his parents, when they moved away to the Windcoast in W.Y. 142.

Sally sat down on the floor and started to look at the titles. They were mostly books about adventure and exploration. "No wonder Window wanted to go to the wilds," she thought to herself.

One by one, Sally pulled the books from the case. As was the custom in the Windlands, on the cover of many of them was a brief description of the book. She scanned each description as she looked at their covers.

> *On The Early Trails, by H. Cassidy: Adventure stories of the early days of Wind Lands settlers*
> *Tales Of The Wind Lands Riders, by R. Rogers: Stories of a band of riders who kept the roads open during the settlers' first years in the South and Middle Lands*
> *Stand By For Adventure, by T. Corbett: A fictionalized story of three men as first explorers of the far Inlands*
> *Danger In The Deep Woods, by T. Corbett: The story of three men forced to cross through part of the Deep Forest*

*The Settling Of The Wind Lands: A record of the first
    settlements on the Windcoast and Middlelands*
*Maps Of Ameran: Maps of the six Ameran states, the
    city of Greenport, and adjoining sea lanes*

"Dad got this on his first trip to Ameran in W.Y. 122,"
Sally remembered.

*Sailings To And From The West: Early Atlandic
    explorations of Wind Land's west coast and
    eastern South World*

"This was Dad's book when he was a kid," announced
Sally to herself.

*Captain Calette And The Pirates, by C. Rockwell: Sea
    adventures around the Cape Islands*
*Captain Calette And The War Of '49, by C. Rockwell:
    Adventures off the northern island channels and
    the frozen northern waters*
*The Blue Sea Island: The story of three boys
    shipwrecked for two years in the southern
    Atlandic*
*The Treasure City: A lost city of fabulous treasure is
    discovered in the jungle by two young adventurers*
*Detective In The City: A collection of short mysteries to
    be solved by the ingenious Mr. Dollar and his
    friend Mr. Drake in the fog-shrouded city of
    Briston*

"Window must have read this book twenty times when he
was in school."

*The Adventure Of The Secret Passage: Two schoolgirls
    solve a mystery involving a strange diary, a
    missing picture, and a moonlit night*
*Night Sky Stars: Star names and patterns in the
    northern skies*

*Numbers For The Millions: The standard school
mathematics book for the last year of study*

"I still have my copy of this book, too."

*Birds Of The Inlands: A field guide to birds of
Newlands farms, prairies, and forests*

*"Hey, that's my book!" Sally exclaimed to herself. "Mom
gave that to me!" She put the book down on the floor next to
her. "I'm taking it home with me."*

The books went on ...
The King Of Atland: The story of the founding of Atland
The Great Kingdom Wars: Early Old Countries History
*The Opening Of The Wilderness: The story of settling
near the Midlands River*
*The Story Of The Horselands: The discovery voyages of
the near south coast of the Newlands.*
The Building Of The Falls Canal
*Up The Opaline Trail: The story of the great cattle
drives from New South*
*The Northern Plains Campaigns: The story of the
Atlandan armies in the North, W.Y. 64 – W.Y. 68*
*The Battle Of Laws: The last great battle of the
Continent Wars*
*The Adventure Of Pertane: The story of how one man
helped to force Atland to forfeit its interest in the
Wind Lands at the end of the Continent Wars*

*Sally looked at the second shelf of books. "I'll save those
until the next time I come back," she thought, as she picked
up her newly discovered book about birds from the floor.*
*She glanced one last time at Window's bookcase, and
noticed something. "Now there is an empty spot, where I
pulled this book from. Maybe someday there will be a book,
in that spot, about what Window is doing now. Maybe it
could be called 'The Adventures Of Window Breesian'."*

She sighed, "Window, I hope you are okay. Take very good care of yourself."

Sally Breesian Resand put "Birds Of The Inlands" under her arm, and took the key from her pocket. She stepped out onto the porch and locked the door behind her. If she would ever see her brother again, she did not know.

+++++++++

The decision of the travelers to go on to the east was exciting for them all. But, the next morning, after a breakfast of eggs and bread and milk, Dawson had still another big surprise for Panni. He hadn't mentioned it before, but now that the group had made their plans he felt that the time was right to share it.

The week before the travelers arrived, a messenger had come to the Inn from the Pariselle castle. The castle noble was planning what was called a Palace Dance for those who lived in the castle, as well as guests from neighboring noble-lands. As he had been in the past, Dawson was asked to come join with the regular castle kitchen staff to prepare food for the visiting guests.

Also, because Noble Paris was such a generous man, he had again invited Dawson to extend the dance invitation to his daughter, if she had reached her eighteenth birthday. Mellie was not yet old enough to attend, so Dawson pulled Panni aside and asked her if she would like to attend in Mellie's place.

"Oh, Dawson, it would be lovely to go. I have missed my castle and the beautiful ceiling-high tapestries, the colorful carpets, and flowing dresses – and the dances." She became sad for a moment.

"What would I wear? Who would go with me?" Her heart jumped. "Could Window accompany me? Could he?"

"Yes, Window could go with you. And, as for your dress, Noble Paris understands that my family has no fancy ball gowns, so he will allow you to borrow gowns and shoes from the ladies' wardrobe at the castle. And, Mellie will be able to attend with you, as your lady-in-waiting. All the ladies at the dance will have someone to assist them, to help with their gowns and anything else they need."

Dawson went on, "Mellie has been disappointed before, because she was not old enough to be allowed to go to a dance there. This will give her the opportunity to attend, even though only as an observer."

Panni's head was spinning with thoughts and plans.

"If you are sure that you want to go," Dawson urged, "maybe you had better ask Window if he would like to go with you."

"Yes. Yes. Right away," responded Panni, as she quickly went looking for him. She found Window in the visiting-room with Raine, making a list of supplies the travelers would need on their journey to the east.

Panni asked Window to come out onto the back porch with her. She had never asked anyone to a dance before. She had never even been a guest at a dance, but she had served food and drinks at several at the Traepelle Castle. Panni loved the music and the beauty of the dancers as they circled the hall. She loved the clothes – the satins and silks and laces and jewels. But, this time she would be attending for real. She would be dancing. She wondered if Window liked to dance. Then she was afraid that he would say that he would not go with her.

Panni explained what Dawson had said to her. "Please, Window, will you please dance with me? I would so like you to."

"Panni, it would be wonderful," Window immediately answered her. "Certainly, I will go with you, but I don't know how to dance very well."

Panni almost laughed, as the biggest smile came to her face. "Don't worry, Window, I do."

The ball was to be held in two days, so the next day was full of dance preparations. Dawson took Polla to the castle and they returned with several gowns for Panni and Mellie to choose from. Mellie picked a dress of shimmering pink, with lace on the sides and the bodice front. Panni chose a long, sleek, light blue dress, with a very loose and flowing skirt, and a simple top that wrapped

tightly around her chest and tied across her back. The gowns
were both beautiful choices for the young women.

Panni and Window spent a couple of hours practicing each of
the next two afternoons. Although Panni had never danced with a
man at her castle, she knew every step and every turn and every
bow and curtsy. She coached Window, and he did his best to
learn. Finally, she told him, "We will be fine, Window, you are a
fine dancer, and I am, well..."

"A really, really fine dancer," Window broke into her comments.

"Why, thank you, Window. And you are a gentleman."

"And tomorrow night, you will be my lady."

The next evening, at sundown, since Dawson was already at
the castle cooking, Oldsmith prepared the Inn wagon and horses.
He put two extra benches across the back sidewalls of the wagon,
and pulled sitting blankets over them, so Panni and Mellie's
gowns would not be soiled as he drove them to the dance. Then he
waited at the front porch as the dancers readied themselves.

Window was wearing Dawson's best shirt and pants, and a
deep black evening jacket borrowed from the castle. Polla had
trimmed his hair so it waved behind his ears, but still fell over his
collar in back. His dark brown eyes stood out, in contrast with his
silver neckscarf, which he tied and pushed down beneath the front
of his jacket. Also, Dawson had given him a silver, star pin to
wear on his lapel.

Mellie's dark hair was pulled back on the sides, revealing her
simple, light-stone necklace. She was a very pretty girl, and very
excited. Of course, she had never worn such a fancy dress before,
and this would be her first trip ever to the castle.

Panni's hair was pulled back on just the left side of her face,
and held there with the rose-diamond comb Oldsmith had made
for her. Across her upper chest, she wore the open star necklace
that had once belonged to Oldsmith's wife. He was very pleased to
have Panni wear both of those pieces of jewelry.

Panni was stunning as she came down the stairs from her
room. Her gown moved easily with her dancer's body, and her
silky hair flowed down her back. It seemed to join as part of her
dress. As she came closer, Window noticed that the blue of her
dress perfectly matched the blue of her eyes.

"Good evening, My Lady," Window addressed her at the bottom
of the stairs.

"And, good evening to you, Sir," came her smiling reply.

"Hey, Window," interrupted Circles, who was there to help send
them off. "How long does the dance last?"

"It is over at midnight, Circles. We will be coming home then.
What are you going to do tonight?"

"Dawson found a story book that his father had given him
when he was a kid. It is written in Atlandan. Polla is going to
read it to me, and teach me words. Rings and Raine are going for
a long walk around town. They are both getting ready to become
travelers again."

"Me, too, Circles. I'll see you in the morning."

"Okay."

Window and Oldsmith helped Panni and Mellie into the Inn
wagon. Window and Panni rode together in the middle seat, and
Mellie sat in the back. She turned around and faced backwards,
watching the road pass behind them.

The Pariselle castle was a short ride out into the country. The
two Inn horses gently pulled the dancers, and the lady-in-waiting,
through the warm evening air, on the quiet Kaetessen Province
road.

As they passed the first mile, the castle tower bell struck nine
times. The clang of the hours sailed across the fields to them. In
the distance, they could see the lights of the castle.

"The dance has begun," Window spoke to Panni.

"My dance began the day I met you, Window," Panni replied.

The Palace Dance was beautiful and exciting. The ladies and
gentlemen shined and shimmered in their best outfits. The violins
and violettes, and tambourines and trumpets, filled the grand hall
with beautiful music. Mellie attended to Panni, and watched the

castle elegance with great wonder in her eyes. Window watched Panni, with the same wonder in his.

Window and Panni danced again and again. Panni held to his hand as they stepped and turned and spun. No one knew that she would sometimes gently push Window in the correct direction, or stop him a bit sooner than he planned.

They kept their eyes on each other, and their hands softly touching, as the night of music and dancing continued.

Panni's eyes glowed, and her heart soared, as she shared the night with Window. He held her close, and turned her with care and affection. As the evening came to a close, they shared a final close-waltz. Panni rested her head on his shoulder. It was a sweet ending to a wonderful night.

As they rode in the wagon back to the Inn, the castle tower bell rang the twelve hours of midnight. The sound sailed past them, and then echoed back from the buildings of Laveselle. The horses clopped on. The night air was cool and refreshing.

"Do you dance with your love, Mary, Window?" Panni quietly asked.

Window was surprised that Panni asked that question, but answered, "We have danced a few times, Panni, but never at a dance like this Palace Dance."

"Does she dance for just you, sometimes?"

Window didn't answer right away, so Panni continued, "I don't want to dance for many men – but I would dance for one man."

Panni was looking off into the distance, still speaking quietly, so only Window could hear her. "I want to find love, Window."

She paused for a long moment. "I found you, Window, in the forest. But, now I want to find love again. Where can I find love?"

"I think that maybe love is like a treasure, Panni. Sometimes you find it, and sometimes you don't – at least, not where you might expect to."

"Once, I was afraid that you didn't love me. But, you freed me from that fear.

"I have heard, Panni, that even in chains, we hold the key to our freedom. I am sure that you freed yourself. Maybe I just helped a little."

"For most of my life, Window, I was lonely – but now I am just wanting. And since love is like a treasure, I will go looking for it. I will find it. Love will be my greatest treasure."

Panni looked softly into Window's eyes. "Thank you for coming with me tonight, Window. I will never forget it."

The wagon reached the Inn. Window and Panni's evening together was ending. She held his arm as he walked her up the front steps. Then, she gently kissed him on the cheek and curtseyed to him one last time before she turned to climb the stairs to her room.

+++++++++

For the next three afternoons, Mellie hurried with her kitchen chores, and then sat on the side porch, carving a springcookie board. Dawson had found her a soft piece of wood and a tiny carving knife. She wanted to try to make some of the cookies to send with the travelers. She said that as long as she wasn't going, at least she could send something of hers along.

Mellie's cookieboard turned out quite nicely. She carved eight different pictures on it – including a tree, a sun, a bird that she said was a willowix, which was her favorite bird, and her best carving, a swan.

When she showed the board to Window, he remarked that he didn't know that there were any willowix in the Northlands. Mellie explained that she had only ever seen one, but it was beautiful as it soared across the fields behind the Inn.

"To what treasure is this board the map?" Window asked with a grin.

"None, yet, Window," was her serious answer. "But if I ever have a treasure to hide, I will follow my cookieboard clues and hide it wherever I end up!"

Window told Mellie the springcookie recipe, as well as he could remember, and she baked for several evenings. After the first few

cookie batches didn't turn out very well, Mellie started to make up
her own recipes. By the time she was finished baking, she had
made hundreds of cookies, using scores of different recipes. There
were sweet springcookies, and salty ones, and soft cookies, and
hard cookies, and spiced cookies, and rye cookies, and cookies with
nuts in them, and cookies with dried fruit. And, most of the
cookies had a raised picture on them! The travelers would have
enough cookies to last through months of adventures.

Dawson packed just as much food as he could spare, and some
that he couldn't. He sent bread and crackers and fruit and meat
and cheese and peas and beans and potatoes and salt and sugar
and oil and two pots to cook in. Rings would have plenty to carry.
They would leave in five days.

As the travelers spent their final days preparing for their
journey to the east, they spent their final nights in the inn dining
room, playing cards. Everybody played. Circles and Panni and
Rings and Window and Raine and Oldsmith and Dawson and
Polla and Mellie and Rook all took turns in wild and happy
matches of Northdraw.

As in Calisay, Circles held the cards for Rings, who sat just
outside the big window. Raine said that he had played cards on
twelve different worlds, so he didn't have any trouble quickly
learning the game. He didn't win, though. Mellie was the
champion one night, and Oldsmith was the winner the next.
Dawson and Window also won. Rings really enjoyed the game
now, and said that after he helped his friends find some treasure,
he would be coming back to play again. And, this time he would
win, he promised Dawson.

As they played, Polla and Mellie brought snacks of crackers
and cheese and salt-sticks and lemon-tea for everyone. The fun
lasted long into the night. They were a very happy family of
friends, sharing their precious time together.

On the fifth day, the travelers were up before the sun, packing
and making final preparations for their journey to the east. At
last, everything was ready.

The travelers and their friends gathered on the grass in front of
the Inn. There were goodbyes and thanks and promises and
wishes from everyone.

Mellie looked on sadly. She had initially wanted to go with
Panni and the others, but changed her mind. Still, she would miss
them. She had never before met anyone like the travelers. They
had given her a new idea of what was in the world, and, what
someday, she could find for herself. Her eyes were bright, as, after
saying her goodbyes, she sat on the edge of the porch, and quietly
watched from a distance.

Raine tied the last pack strap on Rings' harness. Circles hung
his bow from a harness side-hook. Panni gave Window a glance of
readiness. Window checked – he still had the medallion in his
pocket. They took one last look at their friends, and started up
the road to the east. The sky was clear and the air was warm.
The sun would soon be overhead.

It was a perfect day for an adventure.

KAETESSEN
PROVINCE
LAVASELLE
CALISAY
EASTENNE
PROVINCE
EAST-
POINT
TRAEPELLEN
PROVINCE

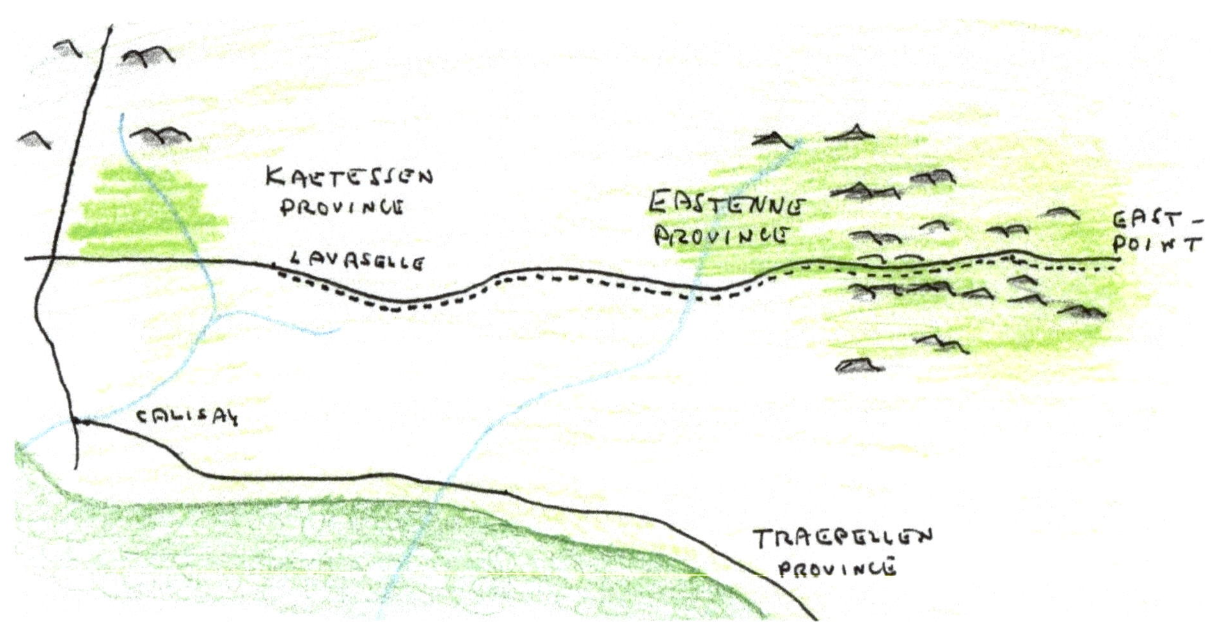

122

CHAPTER SIXTEEN

TO THE EASTERN MOUNTAINS

Window looked ahead to the east. The mountains were not yet visible, but he knew that, somewhere in those mountains, at the end of the Northway, he and his friends hoped to find the third treasure of King Alezan.

Circles slid down from his spot on Rings' back and walked alongside Window. "Hey, Window, how come Dawson's place was called The East Road Inn? I thought that this road was the Northway."

"Well, it is the Northway, but this last section that goes from here to the mountains is called the East Road by the people who live along it. It runs from Laveselle to its end at Eastpoint."

Panni joined the conversation. "How long will it take us, Window, to reach the part of mountains where we think the mines might be?"

"About a week, Panni, but the road goes the whole way, so it shouldn't be difficult."

Window went on, "You should know though, Panni, that by tomorrow, we will be at the northern edge of the Traepellen Province. So, we will not be too far from your home."

"I wonder if I will ever be able to go back, Window. I miss my family so. By now, my mother and my sisters must have given up on ever seeing me again. And, as much as I hated the castle, I miss my friends there terribly. Sometimes I imagine what they must be doing. Right now, it is the time that the kitchen servants would be preparing a mid-day meal for the nobleman. The castle servants would be cleaning, and the dancers would be resting and reading in the shade on the castle veranda, after a morning of light exercise and practice."

Window saw a stone lying in the road ahead. As he walked up to it, he kicked it, and watched it roll out in front of him. His memory flashed back to when his whole adventure started. He knew that his medallion was in his pocket. He didn't know if he would even find out where it came from, or what lie ahead for the treasure hunters.

They passed many farms and fields and several villages. But by the third day of their travels, the lands became much less populated. They would soon be in the Eastenne Province, an area of few people and little else, except low mountains and rough-lands. How they might find the Northlands mines, Window didn't know. Their only hope was to find some clues of some kind, to help point the way.

Raine continued to be a quiet partner to the rest of them. At night, he would usually just sit by their fire and look to the stars. Sometimes, though, he would tell an exciting story of one of the faraway worlds he had visited. That seemed to cheer him up for a while. It certainly cheered up Circles, who loved to hear his adventures.

Circles still practiced his archery skills every day. When he was in Laveselle, Oldsmith had bought him some extra arrows, and now Circles had plenty. His padded fingers gripped the bow very tightly, so it never slipped as he was shooting. But, of course, when he was practicing, he still only shot where he could retrieve the arrows. He had no idea when he might be able to get more.

After a few days, the Eastenne mountains began to appear on the far horizon, and the skyflowers, from the cookieboard, began to appear along the side of the road. The skyflower blossoms were mostly colored white, but a few were soft yellow. Just as Polla had described, their petals and light green leaves pointed to the sky.

Panni thought that they looked like the flowers were saluting the travelers as they walked by.

"Remember to be aware of any possible dangers in the mountains," Window reminded everyone. But, no one needed to be reminded.

As they neared the mountain foothills, the treasure hunters came upon groups of long-abandoned cabins, broken wagons, and other evidence of the miners that were common in the mountains before the Northern Wars. There had apparently been whole communities of workers who lived there and worked the mines.

The Northway wound on through the hills, with branches and smaller side-roads sometimes splitting off to the side.

"It would take us years to follow all of those roads to see where they go," Window disappointedly announced. He looked over at Raine, but the starman kept his thoughts to himself.

The main road curled through a low pass between the mountains and they followed it on.

On their second day into the mountains, Circles was riding on Rings' back and looking around with his far-scope. As they came over a small rise, he excitedly announced, "I see one! I see a windfan on the side of that big hill! There is a mine over there!"

Down a short side road, they could see the windmill blades, sagging and broken, hanging from a leaning blade-tower. They hurried to the spot. Below the mill blades was what had once obviously been a mine site.

There were collapsed buildings, abandoned equipment, and rotting timbers scattered everywhere. The windmill was half way up the hillside, above the collapsed entrance to the mine itself. Most of what they saw was overgrown with weeds and bushes. It was a terrible mess of broken lumber and wrecked equipment.

It was impossible to tell if the mine had been destroyed by the Atland army, or a ground-quake. Either way, it was damaged beyond anything the travelers could do to recover it.

"Well, we have found our first mine. Now what are we going to do?" Panni asked. It really looked like a hopeless task to find anything of value there – if there was something to find.

"I guess that to get anything out of this mine, we would need to be miners," she went on.

Circles surveyed the area from the top of a mound of dirt at the edge of the mine grounds. "Rings would have to dig for weeks to uncover anything beneath this rock and dirt. Even trying to reopen the mine entrance would take a long, long time."

Everyone just stood and looked at the mine ruins, extremely disappointed.

"Let's have lunch," Panni suggested. Everyone agreed.

Over an East Road Inn meal of bread and meat and peaches, the treasure hunters realized that finding any gold or silver at any of the King's mines was probably an impossible task. It would take hundreds of workers, tons of equipment, and months of work. Now they could see why the mines had remained abandoned. They could probably find more of the mines, but they still wouldn't be able to retrieve anything from them.

As they were finishing their lunch, Window asked what everyone thought they should do next.

"Let's forget about looking for anymore mines," Rings suggested. We could search around these mountains for years and not find anything more than we did today. It makes me tired just thinking about it."

"Yeah," Circles agreed. "Let's let somebody else dig for the gold. Let's go find the King's Treasure instead. At least it's probably not buried under tons and tons of rock."

Window looked at Panni. She nodded her agreement. Raine did the same.

"Okay," Window announced. "We'll do that. We will go on to Eastpoint and look for the King's hidden treasure of jewels."

Circles smiled.

"But, first," Window suggested, "let's have some sugar-sticks for desert."

Circles' face widened into a big smile. They all joined him.

After lunch, the disappointed treasure hunters were feeling a
little better. At least, the mine had been so easy to find, that they
really hadn't spent any time looking for it.

They returned to the road through the mountains, and pressed
on towards the east. Circles kept his bow over his shoulder, and
everyone continued to scan the mountainsides for any unwelcome
company.

As they walked, Circles decided to make up a song about "The
Great Northlands Treasure Hunters," as he started to kiddingly
call their group. After about an hour, he sang it for everyone. It
was fun and silly, and lifted their spirits as he sang it. Before the
afternoon was over, everyone was happily joining in on the chorus.

"Empty your wagons, empty your barns
 For wonders to behold
 The Great Northlands Treasure Hunters
 Need a place to store their gold!"

The East Road continued to wind between the low peaks of the
eastern mountains. As they pressed on, they passed more side
roads and forks that could have lead them to more mines, but they
kept on the main road. No particular dangers came up, and the
journey was enjoyable. Their thoughts turned to finding the
hidden King's Treasure.

That night, after their supper, the travelers decided to play
Panni's guessing game. Rings was becoming more and more
interested in campfire games, as he called them, because he still
loved to compete. Tonight, he won three matches in a row, and
was feeling pretty happy about it. Then he made a mistake. He
challenged Raine to a match, and the others just watched and
listened as the two friends quizzed each other with impossible
questions, about things of which the other knew nothing. So, it
became an entertaining game to see who could make up the most
ridiculous answer. It got so everyone laughed with every answer.
Raine hadn't had so much fun since he had become lost from his
ship and his world.

Finally, when Raine answered a question with the guess "Three Brarries sitting in your soup," Rings started laughing so hard that he started coughing – and couldn't stop.

Then the others noticed that Raine was laughing so hard that his face had turned a brighter shade of blue. Nobody knew if that was a good thing or a bad thing.

Panni had to intervene and call the match a draw. Then she got out some of Mellie's sweet picture-cookies and passed them around. That seemed to quiet everybody down.

Soon the Eastenne moon rose over the trees and the fire flickered and faded into the breeze. Each of the happy travelers lay down for a summer night's rest. The moon looked over them as, one by one, they fell asleep.

"Window, Window, wake up. Would you please talk with me for a while?" Panni had gone to where Window was sleeping on his blanket and was gently touching his arm.

"Window, will you talk with me?"

"Panni – Yes, what is it?"

"Window, I am sorry to wake you, but I have had a dream that is troubling me. I can't get it from my mind. If we could talk for a short time, I would feel so much better."

"Here, lie down by me. Tell me about it."

Panni curled close to him. She lay her face on her hands as she spoke. She closed her eyes.

"I have been dreaming. I dreamt that we came across a young girl who was lost in the forest and was looking for her way home. She was wearing blue-diamonds in her hair, and she had no shoes."

Panni relaxed a bit as she went on, "The girl was crying and could not stop. I wanted to help her, but I didn't know where she lived. The harder I tried, the less I felt I could do for her. Then, in my dream, she ran away into the woods."

Panni pushed closer against Window. "I felt so helpless."

Window pressed his hand against her shoulder. Panni let out a sigh and relaxed some more.

After a moment, Panni spoke again. "When I was at the castle, I used to dream a lot. Usually it was a dream of being free. Sometimes I would ride away on a great horse, or sail away on a great ship. Since I have been free from the castle, now I sometimes dream of going back there. I don't want to go back, but I do miss my friends. The dancers were my family. We shared our joys and our sorrows – and our hopes."

Panni continued to speak of her life at the castle. As she did, she became more and more settled and comfortable. Window listened attentively, but with his eyes closed as well.

"When I told my dancer friends that I was going to run away, they were very concerned for me. Several of them wanted to come with me, but were too afraid. Now I think about them a lot. I wish that I could free all of them who wish to leave."

Then Panni realized she was feeling much better, but also how much she had been talking. She thought that it was Window's turn to share something.

"Were you dreaming, too, Window?" she quietly asked him.

"Yes, I was dreaming, too, Panni. In my dream, we met a rider from the far Eastlands. He told me that there is a new world to explore beyond the Gate To The Angels. I asked him what we might find there, and just as he was about to tell me, this traveling companion of mine woke me up. I never found out what is out there."

Panni smiled. "You are my friend, Window, my very good friend."

"Go to sleep, Panni, you are my friend, too."

Panni let her eyes close even more tightly, and took a deep breath. That was the last thing she remembered.

+++++++++

The next day found the travelers almost all of the way through the mountains. At lunchtime, they stopped to eat at a spot that had many large rocks among the trees. Raine opened some food packs as Panni went ahead on the road a bit to fill the water tins from a stream. She came running back to the others.

"I have found something!" she excitedly told her friends.

She led them to the spot. Off in the grass to the side of the
road was a big light-colored rock, with a flat side that faced the
road. Cut into the rock, were ten curved symbols, like fancy
letters, each about as big as her hand. They seemed to form two
words.

"Does anyone recognize those letters?" Panni asked her friends.
At first, no one said anything.

Then Circles spoke up, "I bet that they are Angel letters – like
in Mellie's poem! You have found Angel letters, Panni!"

No one had a better answer as to what the carvings were.

"How about you, Raine, can you read them?" asked Rings.

"I can't read them, Rings," he answered, as he touched the
stone with a finger-ring. "But I can tell you that they are very old.
These carvings have been here for many, many years."

"But look how sharp and fresh the cuts look," Panni observed.

"I am sure that they have been here for more than a hundred
years – maybe much longer."

"Do you think that they were put here by Angels?" Rings asked
hopefully.

"I don't know, Rings. I don't know anything about Angels."

Window offered, "We don't know what ancient people may have
lived here. I supposed that the letters could have been carved by
someone else, a long time ago."

Panni looked again at the swirling letters cut in the rock.
Angel letters or not, they were very pretty designs, and very
smoothly cut into the stone.

"If I were an Angel, these are the letters that I would use,"
Panni concluded. "I wonder what they say."

"Maybe they say that this is where the Angels used to live,"
Circles guessed.

As the travelers continued on their way after lunch, they all
searched for more Angel letters on the rocks they passed. When
the group stopped for a short rest, Circles ran ahead of them to
continue his searching. He stopped at the top of a small rise and
climbed onto a large stone that lay by the side of the road. After
he had looked around and convinced himself that there were no

letters cut into any nearby rocks, or treasures sitting in the middle of the road ahead, he climbed down from the stone.

Something felt odd on the bottom of his feet. Circles glanced down. Below his feet was a patch of dirt, but instead of being dark, it was bright. And, it wasn't just bright, it was sparkling bright. Circles was standing in a patch of sparkling, silver, dirt.

"Window," he called back to towards the others, "look at this. What is it?"

Window caught up with the Woot. "Hey, Circles, this is great. I think that you have found trillion – or maybe vermillion. I don't know which one."

"Wow! Is it valuable, Window, like gold?"

"Dawson said that it can be made into bracelets and other jewelry, so I guess that it is."

"I wonder where it came from."

"It comes from under the ground – from a mine. Somebody must have lost it here."

"Wow! I wonder who could have lost it."

"Let's try to pick it up. You start trying to collect it and I'll get something to put it in."

Window returned to the others.

"Hey, everybody, I have a surprise for you. Circles has found some sparkling dust. It could be trillion. We are going collect it and save it.

They all hurried ahead to the spot, excitedly, to where Circles was scraping the glittering dust into a pile. He held up a sparkling handful of it to show everybody. The sunlight reflected from the tiny, sparkling metal pieces, and scattered silver sunrays in every direction.

"That's really pretty!" Panni exclaimed.

"Congratulations, Circle," Window offered. "Once again you are the best treasure hunter of us all."

"That's a really little pile of treasure!" observed Rings.

So, the group of treasure hunters finally had their treasure – well, at least some kind of treasure. Panni remembered that vermillion was multi-colored, so Circles must have found trillion. They collected as much as they could, put it in a towel, and poured water over it to wash it. The dirt washed away and the trillion remained. When they had finished, they had what seemed to be about a cupful of the dust. And once it was clean, it sparkled and reflected much more than before.

Each of the travelers took turns letting the trillion run between their fingers. Even Raine found it delightful to play with. Panni did it over and over again.

"It is kind of hypnotic," she observed. "I just want to keep doing this."

The trillion was truly fascinating to see, and to hold. After everyone had their turn playing with the silver dust, Panni poured it into an empty berry tin and snapped the lid closed.

"Someone must know where the trillion mine that Dawson mentioned is located," Window commented to the others. "And that someone must have been here in the past couple of weeks, or that dust would have all been washed away by the rain by now."

"I wonder who it could have been," Panni spoke to no one in particular.

"Maybe I am going to find my mysterious traveler at last," Window offered.

"Maybe it was Revell," Panni guessed

"Maybe it was the Angels," Circles added.

The wondering travelers returned to the road.

That evening, as they camped, Window checked a map Dawson had drawn for him. "We are sure to reach Eastpoint tomorrow," he told everyone.

"And find the King's Treasure," Circles reminded him.

"Maybe, Circles, maybe."

As the stars filled the sky overhead, Panni sat by the fire and played with the trillion. She had taken the tin of dust out from its place in a harness pack and was pouring its fascinating contents between her fingers. The firelight reflecting from the dust made it look as though she was pouring a sparkling liquid from one hand to the other. As she poured, some of the dust leaked through her fingers, but she caught it on her skirt.

Window came and sat next to her.

"Did any of the dancers at Traepelle have any jewelry made from trillion or vermillion, Panni?"

"No, I had never heard of it before, Window, before Dawson told us about it.

"Neither had I. But Polla said that she knew stories of Pixies using trillion dust in their magic."

Panni went on, "When I was a little girl, my mother would tell my sisters and me stories about the how the magic Pixies would come and ask for bread with sugar or honey spread on it. My mom said that the Pixies came from beyond the mountains. We never thought that there really were Pixies, though. We knew that they were just stories."

Panni thought for a moment, then admitted, "It would be fun, though, to really meet a Pixie."

She continued, as Window watched the dust pour between her fingers. "In one of the dances I learned at the castle, I was supposed to be a Pixie. I was working on it with my dancing partner when I ran away. The other girls had different dances they were working on, like being birds, or swans, or cats."

"How many dancers were at the Traepelle Castle, Panni?"

"I was to be number twelve."

She poured the glimmering trillion dust into Window's hand. He played with it, as she went on.

"We each had a regular partner we danced with. My partner was named Katice. The others of the dancers were Alysse and Amarie, Avelle and Lisette, Caprice and Collette, Jannice and Jannia, and Feather and April. Feather and April were my best friends there, at the castle. We spent many nights on the evening porch together, talking. I do miss them so. I wonder what they are doing right now. I wonder if they are dancing tonight.

Panni closed her eyes, and tried to imagine how a pair of well-trained, castle dancers would be spending a warm summer evening.

+++++++++

Feather Blonde and April Moon finished dressing. Feather pulled her cream-colored, silken blouse over her head and gracefully moved her shoulders as it fell into place. April wrapped a shimmering, half-skirt around her waist and fastened it loosely with its bright, red ribbon tie. They loved the clothes. And, they loved the music. They loved being dancers at the Traepelle Castle.

They were both twenty-one years old, and, unlike many of the other dancers at the court of the Prince of Traepelle, they were not there because they were from poor, servant families and were forced to dance. They were there because they loved to dance. They loved to sing. And, they loved to wear the fine silks, laces, and jewels of the Province noblehouse.

Feather Blonde and April Moon were the best of all the dancers. Their form and style and movement made them the center of attention whenever they were performing. Their grace and beauty were compelling. When they were on stage, it was impossible to watch anyone else. They were very beautiful young women.

Feather was the slightly taller of the two, and a bit more slender than April. Feather's face was a little thinner and her legs a bit longer.

April had the more dramatic features – her body less subtle, and her eyes unbelievably piercing. Even a brief glance from her could be hypnotic.

Feather and April were the perfect pair of performers. As dancers, they were stunning. And, when they sang, their voices blended with ease, and complemented each other exactly.

But this time it was a little different. Tonight they were not dancing. They were not singing. They were again trying their way at acting. The year before, they had parts in the castle play, and this year, along with several of the other dancers, they had again been chosen for the cast. They were on their way to their second night of rehearsals for a comedy called "The Last Knight Of The Day."

"Come on, Feather. Hurry or we'll be late again," April called to her suitemate, who was just finishing brushing her hair. But brushing her hair didn't do Feather much good, because Feather's hair would never do anything except what it wanted to do.

Feather's hair was brilliant white-blonde and cut in different lengths down the sides of her face from her bangs to her shoulders. It was mostly straight, but soft and fluffy, and seemed to float out from her head and flutter. It gave Feather a very wild but compelling and captivating look that was like no one else's. "Just because you don't have to try very hard to look fancy, doesn't mean I can't take all of the time I want," Feather retorted.

April's hair was longer than Feather's, and much better behaved. It fell in gentle waves past her shoulders, and was, like her name, bright golden-orange. It reflected warmly in the light of the dressing room's wall candles and framed her face perfectly. April put the final touch to her look by sliding a long, multi-jeweled hairpin into the smooth waves just above her left ear.

"What's it matter if we are a little late, Moonie?" Feather continued, as she fought with another runaway patch of feathery hair. She always called April, "Moonie." April never liked it much, but they had become so close in their two years dancing together that she really didn't mind anymore.

There were a few other things on which the girls didn't agree. April was organized and conscientious – never late – and always finished all of her work. She kept her clothes and bed and other things neat while Feather's were often a mess.

Feather was sometimes flighty, and always happy about something, or you might say, happy about nothing. This

*made her carefree, which often got her into trouble, because
she rarely finished her chores or her studies. April often had
to come to Feather's rescue, and help her get out of some
problem or other.*

*"You are always late, Feather. I get tired of waiting for
you. Besides, if we are late for rehearsal tonight we will get
in trouble again. This play means a lot to me. The Prince
and Princess will both be in attendance this year."*
*"How come you got all of the good lines this time?"
Feather responded. "Last year, I had as many lines as you
did."*
*"Maybe it is because, last year, you didn't <u>learn</u> your
lines, and you didn't practice. Maybe it was because you left
your costume in our room, and held up the entire
performance while you went back looking for it."*
*"And, Feather, it was so embarrassing last year, when
you forgot your lines during the performance, and we had to
make up part of the play as we went along."*
*"Oh, come on, Moonie. That was fun. And, that play was
a little boring anyway. It was all about real people doing
real things. Well, except for the scary parts. It was too scary
for me."*
"Well, I like scary stories," April responded.
*Feather continued. "Besides, this year we get to wear
those new gowns that Madam Trelesse brought from
Calisay! The brocade and see-through laces are fantastic!
And all of those ribbons across the open backs are
charming."*

*Suddenly, Feather put down her brush. "Hey, wait,
Moonie, I hear the Pixies again. You go ahead. I'll be there
in a few minutes."*
*"Oh Feather, why do you keep saying that you see
Pixies? You know that there aren't such things. Come on!"*
*"Oh yeah? That's what you said about Owts – until one
showed up at the castle last year."*

"I know – but that was different. Owts are real animals. Pixies are, well – magic."

"So, don't you believe in magic, Moonie? Like the magic of the sun on your face, or the magic of a soft, late-evening breeze on your bare skin as we sit on the night porch?"

"Sure, I do – but I don't believe in Pixies. You can stay here and pretend to talk to them. I'm going to rehearsal."

"Wait, Moonie, before you go. May I please borrow that book you were reading last week – the one about the evil queen and her dark adventures? These Pixies love to read, but they find my books about love and luck a little too tame. You know, Pixies like to cause trouble whenever they can, and they don't much enjoy reading about nice people doing nice things."

"Oh, Feather, quit it! There are no Pixies – especially book-reading Pixies! Now, come on! We are gonna be late again!"

April started out the door from their evening room – but stopped suddenly. From behind her, to her right, in the direction of the stained-glass side-window that opened into the garden, she heard a slight tapping sound. She listened, and then it came again. She rushed to the window and swung it out and open. There, standing on nothing but the warm night air, were two sparkling Pixie girls, just as Feather had described them to her last week. They were only about eight inches tall, and surrounded by glowing light and twinkling dust that swirled all around them. One of the Pixies was covered in pink light and pink dust, and the other in silver. Their faces were silky smooth and they had very small, pointy noses. Both tiny girls were dressed in thin, lacy, overshirts, and glittering, bouncy, playskirts. They wore soft looking shoes – April thought that they looked like dancer's shoes.

"This one is named Pinkie, and this one is called Kisses," Feather introduced. At the sound of their names, the Pixies spun around and turned flips in the air, sending a

shower of sparkling pink and sliver dust everywhere. Feather caught some in her hand and blew on it, sending it swirling back into the air.

"Hello, Feather. Hello, April." Their small, bright voices rang in perfect unison.

"H...hello, Pinkie. Hello, Kisses. I...it is so nice to meet you," April stammered. In her complete surprise, she could think of nothing else to say. She just stared at them in disbelief, as the light of the Pixies reflected in her own bright eyes.

"Guess why I am called Pinkie," the more colorful of the two Pixies laughingly asked April.

"Is it because you are pink?" replied April, immediately smiling at the joy of the happy little being.

"And, how do you think that Kisses got her name?" Feather broke in.

"I have no idea," laughed April, as the cute, little, silver creature flew up and brushed her tiny lips against April's face, just below her eye. A tiny, sparkling kissprint was left to mark the spot.

Then April noticed something. "I thought that Pixies had wings," she wondered out loud.

"Oh, we do have wings," answered Kisses for the two of them – and then they finished together, "We just left them at home!" They squealed with delight at their joke, and flipped in the air, sending more sparkling dust flying everywhere.

"Thank you for letting us borrow your book, April," they both said, again speaking exactly together. Pinkie continued, "I hope that there are some wicked things in it that we might learn."

Kisses jumped back into the conversation, her high voice almost squeaking with excitement. "We are visiting the Traepelle City soon and want to try some new tricks on the people there. And, Pinkie wants to scare some dogs and cats on this trip." Her tiny voice was oddly exciting and soothing at the same time. Both tiny girls shook with glee, again

*sending sparkling dust flying out and settling on the
windowsill.*

*"You are very welcome," replied April, with a smile. "I
am always happy to add to the evil in the world – especially
if it is performed by such sweet creatures as you two seem to
be."*

The two Pixies smiled again and politely bowed in reply.

*"Here it is!" Feather called out from behind April. She
had quickly gone into their sleeping room and retrieved the
book from April's bedstand.*

*As April took the book from her, she gave Feather a little
nod of regret for doubting her, and asked, "How do you think
little Pixies carry books like this? It is as big as they are."*

*"Gee, I don't know, Moonie," Feather replied with a wry
smile. "I guess that they use magic!"*

+++++++++

The treasure hunters were again up with the sun. They would
be through the mountains by noon, and reach Eastpoint soon after
that.

"Keep searching for clues as we go along." Circles reminded
everyone. Of course, no one needed reminding.

And, no one wanted to take the time to stop and eat, so at
lunchtime, they just pressed on. Some clouds drifted overhead
and blocked the sun for a while, but nothing could darken the
travelers' spirits. And, before they were on the road much longer,
out ahead of them, they could see the end of the Northway, and
Eastpoint Gate – The Gate To The Angels!

Well, the Gate To The Angels wasn't really a gate, but a
gateway. The gateway was marked, on each side of the road, by a
wide, stone pillar. There may have been a gate between the
pillars at one time, but now only the pillars remained.

The road went right up to the pillars and stopped.
Immediately on the other side of the gateway, was the edge of a

tall, steep hillside that fell down before them, towards the east. At the bottom of the slope, the ground flattened out, and grasslands continued out as far as they could see.

The excited travelers hurried to the gate. The pillars were not plain stone, but were carved with very intricate designs. There were lots of swirling and curling patterns cut into the rock. The pillars also held picture carvings of flowers and birds, and the sun and the moon.

"Look everyone," Panni exclaimed, "more Angel letters! They are wrapped around the base of this column." The softly curving letters were beautiful to look at, as they curled their way up between other designs.

"Hey," Circles pointed so everyone could see. "Here is a carving of those stars on the Eastenne Province flag."

"Dawson said that they represented gold and silver, the 'stars of the east'," Panni remembered.

"Raine," Window asked, "are these carving also very old?"

"Yes, Window," answered the starman, as he examined the cuts in the stone with his rings. "Just like the letters Panni found carved into the rock back in the mountains, these carvings could be hundreds of years old. Certainly they were put here before the Northlands were settled."

"Well then, these carvings were here long before the gold and silver mines were even started, so the stars must stand for something else." Window continued. "I wonder what those two ancient stars stand for."

Circles had an idea. "Maybe they are the symbols for two Angels, Window."

"What two Angels?" Window replied.

"The two Angels that have stars for their symbols."

"Oh, those two Angels."

"Looks like this really is the Gate To The Angels, Window," Panni spoke up, as she smiled at him.

Rings finished the speculation. "Maybe they are just what they are – two stars."

Circles had already forgotten about the Angels. "What about the King's Treasure? Let's find it!"

"Let's find it after we have something to eat," Panni suggested.

"Oh, alright," Circles reluctantly agreed.

Window unhooked the packs and bags from Rings' harness, and then pulled it off of his back. Usually, at lunchtime, they left the harness on, but everyone assumed that they would be staying here for a while.

Raine got out some bread and cheese and apples. Panni poured some lemon-tea for everyone to celebrate their reaching the end of the Northway. While they were eating, everyone's thoughts were on the King's Treasure.

Window was thinking aloud. "Since this is the treasure of the King's crowns and chains and jewels, it should be, by far, the smallest of the three treasures. So, it could just be buried around here somewhere. It wouldn't have to be in a big cave, or anything like that."

Circles had had enough lunch. "Okay, let's find some treasure."

Window agreed that it was time. "We need some clues. Let's start looking."

The treasure hunters lived up to their name and started searching all around the Gate, and off to the sides of the road in the trees. They checked the road for anything unusual, and overturned rocks half buried in the grass. Raine carefully searched the carvings on the pillars for more clues.

"Maybe the jewels are buried right between the pillars, in the middle of the road," Panni suggested.

"Maybe they are buried right next to the pillars, like the treasure that was next to the cannon," Rings guessed, "or beneath those big rocks over there."

"Maybe the jewels are buried between these two trees that have stars carved into them," Circles called over to the others.

Circles had done it again! About thirty feet from the road, off to the north, were two very tall, very old-looking trees. On the sides of each of the huge trees that were facing the road, the bark had been peeled away a couple of feet from the ground.

And, almost completely hidden by years of the weathering of rain and sun and snow, were two faint, but recognizable, Eastenne

Province stars. One star was carved into each tree. Each star was formed of a horizontal line crossing a vertical line, with two shorter lines crossing each of those at the diagonals. There could be no doubt. The stars had been carved into those trees many years before.

The travelers stood and looked at each other. Buried between the trees could be a treasure they had been searching so long to find. Nobody seemed to want to move. They each were afraid that they would be disappointed again. Even Circles was reluctant.

Finally, Window spoke up, "Who wants to be the one to dig?"

No one answered. Everyone waited for someone else to volunteer.

Panni couldn't wait any longer. "Let's decide with the guessing game. I'll give the first clue."

She smiled as she asked the guessing question. "Who's the treasure hunter with the biggest claws, and the same name as some of the treasure he might dig up?"

"Rings!" everybody else loudly answered together.

The big animal grinned, as best he could, and did just as he had before. He walked between the two trees, and dragged his claws across the ground. He pulled up a giant pawful of dirt and pushed it to one side. There was no treasure.

Circles' heart sank.

He pulled a second giant pawful of dirt from the ground. There was no treasure.

Panni's heart sank.

Rings pulled a third giant pawful of dirt from the spot, and there it was – the top of a large, heavy, wooden chest, with metal straps around its edges to give it strength. Everyone stared without saying anything. They could hardly believe it.

Rings uncovered more of his find as the travelers watched in wonder. Then he hooked the claws of one paw into a large handle-ring that hung from one end of the chest, and slowly pulled it from the dirt. The chest slid up onto the grass and sat there, quietly staring back at the stunned treasure hunters. It was a massive chest – it's lid almost as high off of the ground as Window's waist.

But it was true! They had done it! They had found the King's
Treasure! They had found one of the treasures of King Alezan!

Panni's heart was beating wildly. Circles grabbed on to
Window's leg and squeezed it tightly. Window couldn't stop
smiling. Raine gave Rings a big friendly slap on his leg, as Rings
growled his approval.

"Well, who wants to open the chest?" Window asked his friends.

No one spoke up. Raine glanced at Rings and they nodded to
each other. Raine gathered Circles and Window and Panni
together, and gently guided them up to the front of the chest.

There was a very rusted lock on the lid of the chest. Panni took
out her dagger, and, sticking the blade inside the loop of the lock,
easily broke it open. She returned the dagger to her waist, and
took Window's hand. Then she and Window and Circles slowly
raised the lid of the chest.

Just as the lid came open, the sunlight broke through the
branches of the trees and landed on the chest. The treasure
hunters' eyes were filled with the sparkling and shining and
glittering and reflecting of a chest filled with jewels!

There were white-diamonds and blue-diamonds and rose-
diamonds and skystars and light-stones, rubies and sand-gems
and silver glass-sparks, all reflecting the sun into their eyes. And
partially buried by the jewels, they could see golden, jeweled
crowns and silver, jeweled crowns. Scattered across the jewels
and crowns, were bright chains and shining rings! There were
brilliant greens and blues and reds of every shade. The colors of
the jewels seemed to fly into the air.

No one moved for a moment. They were all entranced by the
beauty before them. Panni ran her fingertips along the front edge
of the open chest but didn't touch any of the treasure. Then
Window reached into the chest and pulled out a crown from
among the jewels.

"Here you go, Circles. You are now king of the treasure
hunters." He tried to set the crown on Circles' head.

The multi-jeweled crown was so big that it slipped over Circles'
head and down to his shoulders. Circles laughed, and bowed to
Window in reply. Window dug around in the chest, and found a

ksmaller crown, perhaps one that was worn by a young prince. This time the crown fit Circles perfectly. Circles beamed, as his treasure hunting subjects honored him with applause.

"As my first official decision, I think that each of us should take something from the treasure, right now," King Circles announced to his friends. "We have searched and worked for a long time to find it."

Everyone nodded agreement.

The chest contained at least six crowns of the Northlands Kingdom. Even the King's crown was there. Each was beautifully covered with jewels and intricate designs of gleaming precious metals. And, buried among the jewels, along with the crowns, there were neck chains and pins and rings and bracelets and jewelry of every kind. There was so much treasure, that they couldn't possibly search all the way to the bottom of the chest. There were simply too many jewels to dig through.

Window and Panni stood before the chest of dazzling treasures. Panni gave Window's hand a squeeze. He returned the gesture, sharing in her happiness. Then Window reached in to the chest, and looking through the treasure, chose a gold and silver bracelet. The flat silver band was covered in a very intricate design and was wrapped in thin gold wire around the band in several places.

"This would look very good on you, Panni."

"Oh, thank you, Window. It is perfect. I am really happy to have it. I will wear it to remind me of you."

Panni slipped the bracelet on her left wrist. It was beautiful against the glow of her skin.

"You look like a princess, wearing that bracelet, Panni."

"I feel like a princess, Window."

Then Panni searched through the sea of jewels and chains before her. She found a small jeweled case and opened it. Inside was a simple, wide, silver hairpin, with a single rose-diamond embedded in it. It was very similar in appearance to the silver hair comb Oldsmith had made for her.

"My dear, Window," she said with a smile. "Let's see if this will fit on your shirt."

Panni took the pin, and spreading its two clasping fingers, slid it onto the low, rounded neckband of Window's overshirt, just above his heart.

"Wear this when you need to be close to me. I will be right there with you."

Window squeezed her hand again.

Then Circles took his turn. He dug around inside the chest for a long time, and finally announced, "I can't decide. I'll just pick something later."

Rings decided the same thing. But Circles kiddingly reminded him that when he joined their group, he had said that he didn't really want any treasure, anyway.

So, Rings jokingly informed Circles that he had decided to charge them for carrying the treasure back home, and so he would reluctantly take a couple of jewels as payment.

Circles responded to his friend, "Oh just take whatever you want. You have earned it ten times over."

Next, Raine searched through the chest. He chose a beautiful blue-diamond neck chain.

"Do you have someone in mind to wear that, Raine?" Panni asked him.

"Yes I do, Panni, and I dream that I will have a chance to give it to her." He carefully slid the chain into his pocket.

So ended the happy travelers' fantastically successful day of treasure hunting. That evening around the campfire, everyone was still too excited to eat much, so Panni and Circles poured the last of the lemon-tea for everyone. As they toasted each other again and again, Circles announced that the tea had never tasted so good. It was the perfect way to celebrate their wonderful adventure.

Then, as the sun disappeared beyond the trees, their campfire flickered high into the sky. Circles stood in front of the fire and led his friends in another couple of verses of his treasure hunters'

song. This time when they reached the chorus, they really had
something to sing about.

"Empty your wagons, empty your barns
 For wonders to behold
 The Great Northlands Treasure Hunters"

And everyone shouted the last line together.

"Need a place to store their gold!"

EASTENNE
PROVINCE
EASTPOINT
ANCIENT
LANDS

CHAPTER SEVENTEEN

INTO THE ANCIENT LANDS

The early morning sun seemed a bit brighter than usual to the treasure hunters. As they sat on some large rocks under the trees, and had bread and fruit for breakfast, they could look over and see the open chest of jewels, quietly sitting and waiting for them.

They were all still excited and happy about their discovery, but it was, also, an odd feeling for them. They had prepared for weeks and weeks of searching in the east, but had found the treasure quickly – almost too quickly. No one knew what to do, now that they really did have a chest containing a kingdom's worth of jewels.

None of them talked about what they would do next. They spent the entire morning sitting in the shade, or looking through the chest, or looking out through the Gate to the east. Past the Gate, at the bottom of the steep hillside, the grasslands spread to the horizon. There was no hint of what lay beyond.

Circles dug through the chest again and uncovered a silver pin with a bright red gem in the middle of it. He pinned it to the side of his arrow quiver, and said that it made him look like a king's archer.

As Rings pawed through the jewels, he again said that he would take something from the chest later. "I want to see the expression on Dawson's face when he asks if I would like to place a little bet on a hand of Northdraw, and I plop down a couple of these big red ones."

Window thought about what special thing he could choose from the chest to give to Mary. He decided to pick something after they got back to Dawson's, when he could more easily spend time making the decision. He glanced around at his friends. They were all just sitting quietly, as if they were waiting for something to happen, or something to do.

Window left the others and walked up between the Gate pillars. For a long time, he looked out to the east. He had found his treasure, but the unknowns of the far east were still calling to him. "I wonder what's out there?" He couldn't shake the question from his mind.

When Window returned to the others, they all looked at him as though it was time to make the decision to go home. Nobody seemed too happy about it. He sat down by his friends, but didn't know what to say.

"Well, let's get going," Circles at last spoke up. "I'll help Panni pack things up, and you guys can bury the chest again."

Window was confused. "What do you mean, Circles, bury the chest?"

"Well we can't just leave it sitting here. Somebody might come along and find it. Just put it back in the same hole, and we will pick it up on our way back."

"On our way back from where?"

"On our way back from finding the Angels, of course."

The others all suddenly sat up straight and looked at Window with bright eyes. Window's spirits lifted, too.

"That's right, Window," Panni happily reminded him, "We have found the treasure. Now we have to go and find the Angels."

Rings didn't wait to hear anything more. He jumped up from where he was lying on the ground. "Come on, Raine. You can close the chest and make sure it is ready to be reburied, while I clear some more of the dirt out of the hole. We'll put it back in the ground, right where it was, and pick it up later."

Answering with a smile, the starman hurried to help the Brarrie.

It had happened so quickly that Window was shocked. But it was that good kind of shock that is so welcome. Then, just as quickly, Window realized that it was exactly what he should have expected from his friends. They were all too close to each other, and too close to having still more adventure that, of course, none of them wanted it to end. And he felt exactly the same way.

"Okay, Circles," Window happily agreed. "You bring the treats."

"Would it be okay if Rings brings the treats?"

"That would be fine with me – just as long as you are with us."

"I am sticking with you, Window. We are a team."

"Yes, we are, Circles. Yes, we are."

It didn't take long before the King's chest of treasure was once again in its resting place under the dirt at Eastpoint. When it was completely covered, Rings stomped around on the dirt to flatten the ground. Then, he flopped on his belly and rolled around on the spot for a while, to completely hide any sign that the ground there had been disturbed.

"One rain shower, to finish the job, and no one will ever suspect that something has been buried here," Rings reported to Window.

"I'd like to mark this spot, though," Window responded. "Just so, someday, someone else might come along here and see it, and wonder who was here before them."

He pulled his boot knife from its sheath, and walked over near the pillars, to a tree that had smooth, thin bark.

"Besides, I haven't been able to find my medallion anywhere on my journeys, so I will put it here myself. Then, when we return, I will at last find it, here on this tree."

He carved the stripes and star into the bark, rubbed the cuts, and slid the knife back into his boot.

The others were ready to begin the next part of their adventure. Panni and Raine hooked Rings' harness straps together, and loaded their packs. Everyone felt renewed and excited to go on.

Panni was overjoyed to have her life with Window and the others continue. Window and Circles stood at the Gate and looked out to the east. Window's heart and mind were once again filled with the happy desire to travel to an unknown destination, searching for whatever they might find.

"I wonder what's out there, Circles."

"Let's go find out."

Together, the five treasure finders climbed down the embankment beyond the Gate To The Angels and walked out onto the wide grassland. Then, with the sun overhead and a bright feeling in their hearts they continued straight to the east.

+++++++++

It was a warm summer day on the eastern prairie. There were few trees and fewer hills, just a flat land of grass. That evening the travelers stopped and set up their camp as usual. But, not as usual, there were no trees to provide firewood. They burned some dry prairie bushes, but the fire didn't last very long, so they simply lay down on the grass next to Rings.

Panni looked up to the night sky, and watched the star pictures as they moved across the expanse above her. She found the one star that Raine had said was on the way to his home world. It silently blinked at her. She wondered if she would ever go on a journey to the stars.

By the middle of the next day, the travelers could look to the eastern horizon and see a massive hill of grass far ahead of them. When they finally reached it, they realized that it was the western end of a high, wide mound that just continued off to the farther east, as far as they could see.

They climbed the forty or fifty steps up the grassy slope and stepped on to what Circles named the "Highway."

The Highway was a massive hill with a flat top that was about thirty feet wide and edges that sloped down to the prairie. The odd hill appeared to be miles and miles long. When they reached the top, they continued their journey, walking right down the middle of the Highway. It proceeded to the east without any curves or turns or rises. It was just a raised, straight, grass-covered path to some unknown destination.

"This had to be built long before the Frees settled the Northlands," Panni offered.

"I don't think that we are in the Northlands, anymore," Window responded. "We are somewhere else, but I don't know what to call it."

"Maybe we are in the land of the Angels," Circles spoke up.

"Maybe we are, Circles, but I don't see any Angels around here."

They followed the Highway on across the grasslands. It was fun to walk above the rest of the world for a while. They could look out and see far into the distance, but there wasn't anything to see – just more grass.

After a few hours, they came upon a small stone watchtower, built right on the top of the Highway where they were walking.

Circles climbed the twenty steps to its top, and used his far-scope to scan the distant horizon.

"What do you see, Circles?" Panni called to him.

"Grass!" came his one word response.

They spent another evening without a fire and all hoped that they would soon reach a tree or a stream or something.

The middle of the next afternoon, the travelers got their wish. The Highway ended briefly, as a small river cut across its path. There was a wooden bridge across the river, joining the two parts of the Highway.

"Hey, look at this." Circles pointed to a design carved into a bridge side-support beam. "This doesn't look quite the same as the Angel letters."

Panni examined the curved cuts in the wood. "These cuts look pretty new to me."

Raine nodded in agreement.

They crossed the bridge and continued on to the east.

Early the next morning, in the far distance, they could see the edge of a forest. As they got within a couple of miles of the forest, the Highway began to slant down to the level of the rest of the grasslands, and before long, they were again walking on the open prairie.

The travelers noticed that the grass began to look dry and sparse. The air became extremely warm, and they walked on in discomfort.

"I can't wait to get into the shade of those trees," Panni expressed. Then she added, "Hey, there's a fence up there!"

What looked like a fence from a distance was really more of a low, stone wall. It was about two feet high, and crossed from their left to their right in front of them. It was built of dirt with stones placed into it, forming a wall that extended in each direction as far as they could see. The top of the short wall-fence was flat, and smooth.

The most amazing thing about the stone fence was that, just on the other side of it, the grass looked green and healthy, unlike the grass they were standing in at the moment. Also, on the other side, there were big clumps of colorful flowers scattered about, growing in the grass. It was as though two different parts of the world had been joined together at the fence.

The travelers approached the stone barrier, but couldn't see a gate or opening in it anywhere. Circles jumped up and ran along its top for a short way, then called to the others, "There are more Angel letters carved into the top of the fence over here."

Window, Panni, and Raine climbed up on the fence and sat down. "I see some here, too," Panni observed.

"Look at that!" Circles called to them, with surprise in his voice.

About fifty feet into the green grass on the other side of the fence, there were rabbits – a score of rabbits – rabbits with unusually tall, pointed ears, all sitting side by side in a straight line. The rabbits just sat quietly in a perfect row, a few feet apart from each other, as though they were watching the travelers.

"Hello, Rabbits," Panni called to them. The rabbits broke into a run and scurried into the woods behind them.

"Who do you think built this fence, Window?" Circles wanted to know.

"The same people who trained those rabbits," was Window's answer, since, of course, he had no idea.

"Let's go on into the woods and look for Angels or somebody," Circles proposed to his companions.

Rings stepped over the fence, and the others hopped down into the greener grass on the other side.

Panni was the first to notice, "The air is so cool, it is like we are in a different part of the world."

She was right. The air on the far side of the fence was cool and pleasant. Panni stuck her hand back across the fence to where they had just been. The air on that side was very hot, as it had been before. "This is a curious place," Panni stated the obvious to herself.

As they neared the forest, they all just stopped and stared in amazement at the trees. Window didn't recognize any of them. The trees were all different from the trees he knew. Their shapes were different – their leaves were different. Some were very tall with exceedingly thin branches. Some were wide, with wispy leaves. Some were intertwined with each other, with leaves that had very rough edges. There were trees with crooked trunks and trees with slick bark. Some trees seemed to be part of the same plant, with their branches looking like arms that were growing together.

Many of the trees had flowers – some had red flowers, others had blue or yellow. Some had tendrils that fell from their branches to the ground. It was like an exotic forest from a different world.

"Raine, you should feel right at home here," Window suggested to the starman.

Raine answered with a quiet, understanding nod.

The travelers walked up to the edge of the forest. They immediately found the beginning of a dirt path that wound off under the trees between some odd looking flowering bushes. It was as though the path was there waiting for them.

"Okay, here we go," Window announced. He led the way, as they stepped into the strange woods.

The explorers followed the path for about a half an hour as it wound through the extraordinary forest. They saw brightly colored birds, and more-brightly colored bugs. Then they came upon a spot where the trees thinned out a bit, and a small stream crossed the path.

"Let's fill our water tins," Panni suggested.

Raine got out their three metal water-tins and unscrewed the caps. He handed one of them to Panni and she knelt down by the flowing water. As she had done hundreds of times before, she dunked the tin down into the water so it would flow into the tin. But, unlike the hundreds of other times she had done this, it didn't turn out the same.

As a bit of the water would start to flow into the tin, all of a sudden, it would jump back out again. She tried again and again – the water wouldn't stay in the tin! It was as though the water was alive and was refusing to go in.

"This is a very curious place," Panni said, again mostly to herself.

Then Raine tried, but the water would not go into the tin.

"Wow, that is really strange," Rings offered.

"That's not all." Circles had noticed something even more odd to report. "Do you see that high spot of ground that the stream is flowing over – and the low spot over here? Look what the water is doing – the water is running the wrong way. The water is running uphill!"

It was true. The water in the stream was flowing from the lower ground to the higher ground!

"I wonder if the Angels had anything to do with this," Circles wanted to know.

Panni cupped her hands together and dipped them into the stream. When she pulled them out, instead of having water cupped in her hands, she had bubbles. And, not little bubbles, but the water in her hands had separated into ten or twenty wet, jumping, bouncing, bubbles of water that moved as if they were alive. They seemed to be little water bubble creatures.

As the bubbles settled down and reconnected with each other, they joined back together just as normal looking water bubbles would do.

Some of the bubble creatures leaped from her hands and splashed back into the stream. A few of those bubbles, that missed the steam, scooted along the ground of the path and then jumped into the water.

"Looks like we will have to fill our water tins someplace else," said Window, with an astonished look on his face.

Raine spoke up and made a rare comment. "Well, I have been to maybe a thousand worlds, but I have never seen anything like this before."

Circles offered his observations, "Well I have been to only one world, and I have never seen anything like this before either."

"Who wants to go swimming?" Panni smiled at the others.

Rings had an idea. He walked into the stream and started stomping as hard as he could. Water and water bubble creatures of all sizes went flying into the air. He kicked some of the water with his giant foot, and more bubbles landed on the trees and bushes nearby.

There was a mad scramble as hundreds and hundreds of lively, squirming bubbles made their way back to the stream. They made dripping, splashing sound as the rejoined the rest of the water. In about a minute, they had all returned to the stream, and it was as before – flowing water – but still flowing uphill.

The travelers didn't know what to think. And, there really wasn't much to say. They slowly waded through the stream, and, as they did, the water seemed to try to move out of their way.

As they continued on the forest path, Circles had the only comment to share. "I wouldn't want any lemon-tea made with any of that water."

Panni and Window smiled at each other.

After a couple of more miles into the woods, the path widened and became more of a narrow road. They followed the road until it came to a fork. Both branches of the road looked similar, so there was no way to make a choice as to which might be the best way to go. But, since they didn't know where they were going, it didn't seem to matter anyway.

"Circles, as our best treasure hunter," Window asked, "would you like to pick which road we take?"

Circles was reminded again of what Raine had told him about choosing one's future. "Okay, Raine," he asked his friend. "How do I make this choice as to which way we should go?"

"This is not a true choice, Circles. Choice involves assessing your values and your desires. Since you have no way of assessing either of those things here, it is not a choice."

"What is it then?"

Raine paused before answering. "It is an adventure."

"You just made that up. It is so a choice."

"Then it is a choice, and you do control your future."

"I don't want to decide. I want someone else to decide."

"Then you have just made your choice. Either way you chose your future."

"Hey, Panni and Rings," Window broke in to the conversation, "While those two prepare their next philosophy book, do either of you have a pick as to which road we follow?"

Circles spoke up, "Oh, alright, I will decide." He thought a moment. "Since my arrows have points on them, I will let the arrows choose, and point our direction. I don't know how many arrows are in my quiver right now, but if it is an odd number, we will take the left fork, if it is an even number, we will take the right."

Panni stepped behind Circles, and counted his arrows. "Eleven," she announced.

"Okay, I choose to take the left road," Circles declared.

"You did not choose – the arrows chose," Raine argued.

"We treasure hunters know how to do these things, Raine. Someday, when you are older, you will understand," Circles kidded him.

Then something else jumped into Circles' mind, and he asked, "How old are you, Raine?"

"One hundred and twenty."

"Wow! Are you really?"

"Do you choose to believe me?"

The discussion went on and on, as they took the left fork.

The left road turned out to not be a very successful choice. After about an hour of walking, the forest started to become misty, and they had difficulty seeing much that was ahead of them. Soon the mist turned to fog, and before they realized it, they were completely surrounded by thick grey haze they could not see through at all.

"This is creepy," Circles shared. "We can't see where we are going or anything."

Window noted, "It will be dark soon. We'd better get out of this fog."

Circles offered his solution. "If I have eight toes, we will turn around and go back."

Panni spoke next, "I don't even know how many toes you have, Circles. Since your feet are covered with fur, I have never noticed. Do you know how many you have, or do I need to count them?"

"I have eight!" the Woot answered, with great self-assurance.

The travelers turned around, and slowly worked their way back through the fog, in the direction they had come.

As they walked on, the fog faded, and soon the air was clear and pleasant again. When they finally reached the spot where the road had split, Circles pointed the direction he had not picked before, and announced, "I choose this way."

"A fine choice, Circles," Raine assured him.

They followed the right road farther into the forest of fantastic trees.

As the sky darkened above them, the travelers camped for the night. Strangely shaped firewood was plentiful, and the evening was warm and comfortable. The cries of far-away birds kept them company.

Around the fire that night, as the travelers rested, the full moon was overhead. Circles and Raine were sitting together, off to one side of the others. Circles looked up at the moon for a while, and then asked Raine, "Does the moon seem different tonight?"

Raine gazed up and considered the question, "It looks the same to me, Circles. Does it look different to you?"

"I don't know. Something just seems changed somehow."

"Do you hear that?" Circles asked his friend.

"It sounds like voices floating in the air, or someone singing far away," Raine answered.

"There it is again. Hey, maybe it's Angel voices," Circles hoped aloud.

"Maybe it's just the wind blowing through these odd trees."

"Yeah, maybe."

They listened, but the sounds didn't return.

Later, just as everyone was getting ready to sleep, Raine searched out Window. "Window, there is something you should know. The power of my finger-rings is quickly fading. I cannot make them strong again. In a few weeks, or maybe sooner, their power will fade completely. Then, I will never be able to use them."

"I wish that I could help you, Raine. Is there anything at all we could do to fix them?"

"I don't think so, Window. The metals and materials that are needed do not exist on this world. Besides, the equipment on my ship is damaged. And my ship is lost to me, anyway."

Raine went on, his voice getting softer, "I have been trying to get used to the idea of spending the rest of my life here, but it is a difficult thought for me. I so love my own world."

"Is anyone waiting for you to return – any one you really care about – like the someone you had in mind when you choose the necklace from the treasure chest?"

"Her name is Nikee. She has waited for me before, but before, I always returned to her. As much as I miss her, I hate even more the thought of how her heart must be slowly breaking as she waits for me now. I love her beyond the stars."

Raine spoke even more quietly. "I want to see her one last time, before my rings fade completely. And, I would like you to meet her, Window. I want you to know her, even if just for a moment."

Raine raised both of his hands in front of his chest and slowly opened them, away from him, with the palms facing out. He touched his thumbs together. Clear, white light shone from the tiny jewels on each of his rings.

The rays of light moved slowly out from his fingers and blended together about ten feet in front of Raine and his friend. Then the lights swirled together and a colorless picture appeared.

It was a life-sized picture of a beautiful, young woman, standing in the air, looking back at them. The woman's hair was long and white. Her clothes were short and thin.

Then the picture came alive for a moment. The woman smiled at Raine, and spoke to him. The sound of her voice came to them from the talking image. It was a soft voice. It was a happy voice. *"Tae quwe-an resae. Jae tou-en."*

Raine looked at the image with a deep sadness in his eyes. The woman seemed to look right back at him.

The picture began to flicker. Raine closed his fingers together, and the lights all vanished. The jewels on his finger-rings were very dim. His rings were fading. He could not keep the picture alive any longer.

The light of the moon shone on Raine's face. The glow of his skin was only very faint, but the moonlight reflected his soft blue color.

Without saying anything, Window left Raine to his thoughts and went back to the others by the fire. Raine looked up to the moon, and then beyond. Then he lowered his head, and closed his eyes.

++++++++++

[TO THE EDGE OF THE LIGHTWOOD FOREST]

Ten thousand worlds away, Nikee Like opened her eyes. They were bright blue and sparkled against perfect white. She reached for her message slate. It was empty.

She rose from her bed – her body tall and compelling – her legs long and thin. Her skin was slick and smooth – shining almost as blue as her eyes. Her hair shone sleek and silver – intense against her chest, her shoulders, and her partially hidden face. She had not slept. Her heart could not rest.

Nikee dressed without caring – her shorts tight and thin – her shirt loose and open. Her thoughts were lonely – her days long and difficult – her nights long and restless. Her message slate was empty. Her picture screen was dark.

Nikee's mouth was straight and her lips tight and silent. Her heart was unsure. It had been too long. He was weeks overdue. He was lost or captured or in hiding. He was broken. He was beyond the edge.

She looked out of her window-wall. The towers and spires of Kalesse were glowing as usual. They didn't know. They didn't care. The air cars sailed past her as they always did – the buildings below opening up to receive them.

She looked again. Her message slate was empty. He was lost. He was captured. He was unable to reply. Her picture screen was dark. Her mind was stumbling.

She had missed him as she always did – and so anticipated the excitement of ending her aloneness. She had gotten new clothes to celebrate his return – a playful dress and the tallest shoes. Now that didn't seem so important.

She wrote still another thought letter and watched as it disappeared into the sky. He was late. Where could he be? Why did he not reply? Her heart could not breathe.

She glanced about for a moment, quickly tracing and retracing her memories. She saw herself in the mirror. She couldn't wait here any longer. She had to get closer to him. She picked up her personal case and stepped into the blue-grey ray of light. Her apartment flickered and was gone.

Nikee Like opened her eyes. They were bright blue and sparkled against perfect white. They were trying to see beyond her tears. She stepped onto the walkway and followed it to the gate. One more step and she was there. She would wait here – at Moonfarm.

She would walk beneath the trees and feel the air on her face once again. She would watch the day sky and the night stars just as they had together – and relive each moment. And, she would look again into his eyes as he promised to return to her. She would remember the flash of the sun's reflection on its great sails, as The Star Journey lifted through the clouds at Starport.

And then each day, as she watched each cloud and each star, she would be reminded. The lightwood ships are sleek and fast. Their pilots are smart and smooth. Their finger-rings are powerful and precise.

Nikee stepped from the porch. She sat under the shading trees and listened to the whisper of the leaves as they had done so many times. She imagined his quiet voice against her cheek. A brandi-bird lit on a branch above her. It flitted a moment, seemed to look down at her, and flew away. The world was simple here. Her vision was clear.

The day-clouds faded. It was getting late. The sun disappeared and was replaced by the first moon. The moonlight reflected in her eyes. Her heart traveled up past the moon and on and on beyond moons and suns far away. Her eyes were blue diamonds – her face blue evening sky.

She opened her hand and looked at the bright silver ring on her finger. He had given it to her. It was still glowing. She sighed with ease and almost smiled. Her thoughts slipped from between her lips, "I love this place."

Then Nikee Like closed her eyes. She would wait here. She would wait for ten thousand years. She would wait here. She would be here when he returned.

+++++++++

The next morning, the travelers continued their march deeper into the odd forest. More strange flowers appeared, and many animals that lived among the trees. There were bright red squirrels, and huge owls, and tiny tree lizards of wild colors. There were ground-bears and silver rakes, and little wiggling leaf-bugs. They also came upon more tall-eared rabbits along the road. The animals seemed to stop whatever they were doing, and just watch, as the explorers walked by.

Later in the day, the trees thinned out a bit, and the sun was able to break through the leaves in many places. Then between an opening in the trees, they could see something ahead on the curving road. It was large, and light brown in color. Pushing ahead, they entered a wide clearing in the trees, and soon discovered what it was.

What they came upon were the partial ruins of a large stone castle or building of some sort. Some of the walls still stood, but many were fallen, and lay scattered on the ground in front of them. The stone of the ruins looked even older than any they had seen anywhere in the Northlands.

The castle-ruins appeared to have been abandoned for many years. It seemed quiet – and then they heard something.

Circles took his bow from his shoulder and notched an arrow on the bowstring. Window pulled his longsword from the harness. They scanned the ruins for any sign of danger. They watched and waited.

A voice – the clear voice of a young man, broke the silence. "Welcome, Travelers."

The welcome travelers turned about searching for the source of the greeting. The voice seemed to have come from a spot just off to their left, but there was no one there – just a fallen tree trunk that was lying in the sun to the side of the road. Again, the voice addressed them – a voice in Atlandan.

"My name is Arrow – and this is Cadence. Welcome to our home."

Window answered for his group. "Please come out so we can greet you. Where are you?"

"Well, on this log, of course."

The travelers all just stared at the log. They could not see anyone. Just then, high above, a cloud drifted over the clearing and briefly blocked the sun.

Then they saw their greeters – two little men, or maybe they were boys, were standing on the log, looking at them. One was dressed in a light green overshirt and pants, and had a small bow and a full quiver of short wood-darts over his shoulder. The other one wore a tan colored tunic, and a belt with a knife, and several odd-shaped devices dangling from it. The creatures were taller than Circles, but not as tall as Panni.

And, actually, they were not standing on the log. They were standing above the log, a few inches into the air – above the fallen tree trunk! Before Window could say anything, the overhead clouds drifted beyond the clearing, and as the reappearing sunlight struck the creatures, they disappeared.

The travelers heard a voice again. "They can't see us, Arrow. Let's go under the trees, in the shade."

A moment later, the men reappeared in the shade of a large, crooked-looking tree, near the castle ruins.

As the travelers saw the beings more clearly, they could see that the strangers looked a lot like young men, but their faces looked somewhat like cat faces. They had cat-looking eyes, and long, thin, cat-looking whiskers, that stuck out from the side of their faces. Also, on their faces, just below their eyes, and on their hands, there was what seemed to be light fur. Their bodies were slight, and their shaggy hair was smooth. Arrow's hair was dark, and longer than his friend's. Cadence's hair was grey. Their ears stuck through their hair. There was fur on the tops of their ears, too.

"Are you Angels?" Circles called to the two beings.

"There are no Angels here," Cadence, the shorter creature, in the tunic, replied.

"We are keepers," added Arrow.

"Are you sure that you are not Angels?" Circles repeated his question.

"No, we are just the keepers here," Arrow assured him.

"What do you keep?"

"We keep secrets."

"What secrets?" Circles pressed on with questions.

"The secrets of the world. They are buried in the ruins here."

Circles had one particular secret in mind. "Do you know where the Angels live?"

Arrow continued his answers, "We know many things, but we cannot say. It is a secret."

Cadence explained, "Keepers are not allowed to tell anyone about their secrets."

"How did you know our language?"

"We know many things," the two odd young men answered together. "We have been here a long time."

Circles was fascinated, and walked closer to the two cat-like men, as the others just listened, and let him do all of the talking.

"How do you do that? How can you float above the ground like you do? Is it science, or magic?"

"We don't know much about science," Cadence answered, this time.

"Then is it magic?" Circles wanted to know.

Arrow answered, "It's a secret."

Then Arrow asked a similar question of Circles. "How do <u>you</u> make your feet <u>stay</u> on the ground?"

"Magic," answered Circles, as he sat down on a tree stump. Window was proud of his friend's response.

Circles thought for a moment. "What can you tell us that is not a secret?"

Cadence answered, "These are the lands where the world was born. These are the ancient lands that were here before all of the others. And, we are the guardians of the steps to the world."

Circles didn't understand that answer. "What happened to your castle?"

"Many years ago, a powerful ground-quake shook the ancient lands, and destroyed much of it. We were picked to stay here, as the guardians. Everyone else left and went to other places."

"What other places?"

"It's a secret," they answered together.

Just then, three of the tall-eared rabbits ran up next to the two secret keepers and sat down in the grass.

"I guess that you talk to rabbits, huh?" Circles went on.

"It gets a bit lonely out here, sometimes. Can you stay awhile and visit?" asked Arrow, his bright cat-eyes looking at Circles hopefully.

Circles looked back to his friends for their agreement. "Sure, we would like that."

The strange secret keepers led the travelers in among the castle ruins to a large open courtyard. There were colorful flowers around the edges of the yard, and stone tables and benches in the center. Everyone was introduced, and everyone found a place to sit. The Cat-eyes, as Circles stared calling the two castle creatures, sat in the shade against a wall, so they wouldn't keep disappearing when the sun struck them.

Circles' curiosity continued. "Arrow, if you live here all of the time, why don't you try to fix your castle?"

"Sometimes we use trillion to fix it, but then the quakes just come again and knock it down, so now we mostly just let it go.

"Were you at Eastpoint recently?" Circles guessed.

"How did you know that?"

"It's a secret," Circles wryly answered.

Window joined the conversation. "We found some trillion that someone spilled near there."

"Cadence, I told you to be careful."

"I was careful, but I maybe did drop a little while I was playing with it."

Circles spoke again, "What do you do with the trillion, Cadence – magic?"

"It's a secret, Circles."

As the conversation continued, Raine pulled Window aside. "My rings tell me that there will soon be another quake here. It could be dangerous."

"Okay, Raine, I understand. I'll tell the others when I have a chance."

"I have a bow, too, Circles," Arrow offered. "Would you like to shoot at my practice target with me?"

"Let's have some cookies first," suggested Cadence. He went through a small doorway, into a part of the castle that was still standing, and quickly returned with a dish of light brown cookies.

"I baked these myself," he announced.

The travelers could hardly believe what they saw. They were picture-cookies! This was going to be a very interesting visit, indeed.

The visiting with the Cat-eyes went on far into the night. Arrow declined to talk about why he and his friend disappeared in the sunlight. Cadence explained how he loved to carve things, and he loved to bake, so he sometimes carved designs into a board and used the board to press cookies.

"We have cookies like that in the Windlands, too," Window reported. No one bothered to mention the King's Treasure they left buried back at Eastpoint.

"I guess that we have our secrets, too," Panni whispered in Window's ear.

After they finished the cookies, Window and Raine built a fire, and the travelers shared some of Dawson's berries and apples with their forest-castle hosts.

Panni explained about where she came from in the Northlands. Rings told of the creatures in the Deep Woods. "We have heard of some of them," Arrow responded.

Raine didn't feel like talking about where he came from, so he just told the Cat-eyes that he came from "far away." Then he didn't speak at all for the rest of the night. He seemed to be not feeling very well. Panni went to sit by him.

The late-night moon drifted into the sky above them. "I have an idea," offered Arrow. He left the group, and went back into his castle room, and returned with a stringed instrument that Window thought looked a bit like a small Freeland board-harp.

As Arrow gently plucked on the instrument strings, Cadence stood up by the fire and sang for everyone. His song had a magical sounding melody, and was about a place called the Moonlands, where "the sun hides in the night."

"I bet that is where the Angels live – like Mellie's poem said," Circles quietly mentioned to Window.

Next, Circles sang for everyone. His sweet song was the perfect ending to the evening. It was very late, and time to sleep.

"Do you two sleep, or is that a secret?" Circles asked Cadence.

"Yes, we do sleep, Circles. But, not every night. Sometimes we sleep in the daytime."

"Me, too," Circles replied. "Me, too."

The Cat-eyes politely offered a room inside the castle in which the travelers could sleep, but it was such a nice night, that, after a brief discussion, it was decided that everyone would sleep outside.

The travelers were tired. Three of them quietly slipped into their blankets. Circles lay down against Rings, and closed his eyes.

Window lay awake for a while, listening to the sound of forest insects singing in the night, and watching the moon until it drifted out of sight.

Just as he was about to fall asleep, Window heard a new sound. At first, he couldn't figure out just what he was hearing. Then he realized that the sound was coming from the stone benches where the Cat-eyes had curled up for the night. Cadence and Arrow had fallen asleep. They were purring!

Window smiled to himself as he closed his eyes. It was a very pleasant night in the Ancient Lands.

ANCIENT LANDS
MOONLANDS

CHAPTER EIGHTEEN

TO THE MOONLANDS

Window woke with a start. The ground was shaking! The whole world was shaking! He tried to hold on to the ground as he looked around. Panni was trying to sit up. Circles had grabbed on to the fur on Rings' side.

Raine was standing at a nearby tree and was hanging on to a lower branch. He was unable to keep his balance. They could all see each other, but no one said anything. Window had warned the others of what Raine had told him, but knowing what was happening didn't make it any less frightening.

After about a minute the tremor stopped. Everyone let out a sigh of relief and gathered together by their fire pit. Panni hugged Window and Circles kept hold of Rings.

"What do you think, Raine? Will there be more tremors, or a large quake soon?"

"I believe that we are safe for a while, Window. I don't expect another episode for several days. As to how dangerous they might be, I cannot say." He sat down on a large piece of a fallen stone wall. There seemed to be no new damage to the castle.

Cadence and Arrow came running out from a big arched doorway. "Is everyone alright?" Arrow asked.

"We are fine," answered Window. "Does this happen often?"

"After having no quakes for many years, we have had many tremors lately. The quakes do not bother Cadence and me, but we feel that it not be safe for you here. It may be best if you go on from the Ancient Lands."

"Thanks, Arrow. We'll talk it over during breakfast."

The travelers opened some tins of peaches and sat down to eat. Raine said that he wasn't hungry. The others all noticed that he just sat with his head down and his eyes closed. They could see that he was not well.

It was quickly agreed to travel on through the forest, to the lands on the other side. Arrow had told them that it would take about three days, and that then they would reach another ancient forest called the Moonlands. Circles was about to ask why they were called that, but stopped himself, just in time, to avoid hearing someone tell him "It's a secret."

Cadence and Arrow would go along with the travelers for one day, then return to the castle. After packing up their supplies, everyone was ready to go. They followed the road as it left the castle clearing to the east. Window noticed that there were also roads leading to the north and to the south.

As the, now, really odd-looking group of travelers walked along through the forest, Circles got into a conversation with Cadence about secrets. Then Circles offered to trade some secrets with the Cat-eyes man.

"If you will tell me where the Angels are, I will tell you something that you don't know, like where the Silkie live," he offered.

"Arrow, do we know where the Silkie live?" Cadence asked his friend.

"No, Cadence, we used to know, but like so many other creatures, they have moved since we last saw them. The world used to be a simpler place. Now it has gotten very unsettled."

"What do you mean, Arrow?" Panni asked. Arrow didn't answer.

The trek along the forest road was an easy one. Raine, though, was obviously having difficulty keeping up. After they stopped for a quick lunch, he asked Rings if he could ride on his back, along with his harness.

"I know that you are already carrying a lot, but it would help me if I could ride for a while."

The Brarrie continued being very generous to his friends, "It will be fine, Raine. Have Window help you up."

As Window assisted Raine in climbing up the harness straps, Raine spoke quietly to him. "I didn't realize that as my finger-rings faded, that it would affect me so. I don't know how much longer I can go on with you."

"We will take you with us no matter what, Raine. We will never leave you alone."

Raine squeezed Window's arm and lay forward onto Rings' neck. Raine's finger-jewels were very pale, and flickering.

"What can we do, Window?" Panni asked, as they discussed their dear friend's worsening condition.

"I don't have any ideas, Panni. I wonder if Arrow could help."

"We'd better not wait. I will ask him right now."

Panni walked on ahead to catch up with Arrow. Just as she reached him, Arrow turned, and yelled to everyone, "Follow me, quickly! There are Mist-Taggers in the trees!"

At the same time, Arrow and Cadence both pulled their bows from their shoulders, and fixed a wood-dart to the string.

Window and the others were confused. They couldn't see any danger. Cadence tugged on Rings' harness and pulled him under the branches of a big tree. The others followed and stood by him.

Window slid his sword from its sheath. Panni drew her dagger. Circles armed his bow. Raine slid down from Rings' back and leaned against the tree. Rings held up his right paw and exposed his claws. They were as ready as they could be, to fight off an attacker.

"What is it?" Window asked Cadence, who had remained by him.

"The ground tremors have driven creatures down from the mists in the north. It has happened once before this year. They are very dangerous – they have great fangs that are filled with poison. Taggers are deadly with one bite – just one bite!"

Cadence spoke quickly, "I must join Arrow. Stay under these tree limbs. The Taggers run through the trees, but will have difficulty getting between these close branches to attack you."

The Cat-eyes creature ran back up the road to where Arrow was waiting. Then the two secret-keepers amazed the travelers in a totally unexpected way.

First Arrow, and then Cadence, just walked on the air, up into the trees! It was as though they were stepping on an invisible set of stairs that led up to a branch high above the road. Arrow continued on, and walked over, through the air, to a different tree. Then they readied their dart-bows and waited.

Suddenly, six long-armed, long-legged creatures leaped at them from higher above in the trees. The attackers were a bit smaller than the Cat-eyes, and were very skinny and covered in dark brown hair. Their long fingers and longer toes gripped around branches and swung them from branch to branch and from tree to tree with startling quickness. They had two long, yellow fangs that curved out from their mouths. They showed no fear, as they descended upon Arrow from the higher branches.

Both Arrow and Cadence began shooting their darts, as quickly as they could rearm their bows from their quivers. Their accuracy was lethal. With a lively "zip" and a sickening "thud," the darts found their marks. Four, then five, then six Taggers fell from the trees and bounced from lower branches as they tumbled to the ground dead, darts protruding from their silent remains.

Immediately, more Taggers came after the Cat-eyes, and several were in the trees above the travelers. Circles let loose an arrow at one, but the attacker moved too quickly. The arrow missed its mark. Circles shot another with the same result.

Four Taggers worked their way down the tree towards the somewhat sheltered travelers. Panni grabbed Raine's arm and held him with her as she pushed her back against the rough tree trunk. She would protect him as best she could. Rings was such a big target that Window assumed that he would be attacked first. Window was determined to keep the Taggers from Rings' back.

A Tagger leaped at Arrow, but the Cat-eyes ran to a limb in another tree. As the attacker turned to jump again, he was met by a deadly, metal-tipped dart, buried in his chest.

Window and the others waited, knowing that in only moments the Taggers would be upon them. Panni's eyes met Window's for an instant. There wasn't time for anything more than that.

Cadence jumped down from his high perch in only two mid-air steps and ran above the road towards the travelers. As he did, the sun suddenly broke through the clouds above the battle and bathed the road in sunlight. Then, as Cadence ran, he came out from the shade of the trees and disappeared into the patch of sunlight.

It was as though he had melted away, into nothing, except that he had not melted away. He was hidden from the view of friend and enemy alike. Window heard the zip of two more darts. He heard the thud of those darts as they struck Taggers close above him.

Arrow ran to join his friend in the sunlight. Two more Taggers fell to the grass below the travelers' tree. Then, as quickly as they had come, the attackers fled, back into the forest.

For the moment they were safe, but Arrow explained the Taggers would return when the sun was down and it became dark. And, Taggers could see very well in just a bit of light, like the light from the moon.

The sun flickered in and out from behind the clouds for the rest of the day. Arrow was sure that the Taggers would attack when it became dark. The only way to chase off the Taggers was to kill as many of them as they could. Their only hope to do that was to find a spot that might offer some protection when the attack came in the night.

The Cat-eyes led the travelers farther along the road to where it passed through a wide clearing, with no trees, except a single large Sage-tree in the center of the open space along the side of the road. They would set up their defense here. Window and

Panni gathered as much firewood as they could and prepared a huge bonfire to keep burning throughout the night.

The Taggers would have to cross the open space to get to them, and then the travelers would still be somewhat protected by the tree they would stand against.

Slowly, afternoon turned to evening, and the evening to night. As the darkness descended on their camp, Window lit the bonfire. The flames roared high into the darkening sky. The moon was low in the east and would soon give the Taggers plenty of light to attack by.

It was a very difficult time, waiting for what was sure to come. The travelers spoke to each other in low tones, and spoke of nothing in particular. Rings would fight with his claws. Circles counted his arrows. Panni would use Window's sword, and Window would hold Oldsmith's spear. They had to keep the Taggers' fangs from making even the smallest cut in their skin.

Raine could now only stand with great difficulty, and so he sat against the tree and waited with the others. He seemed to be deteriorating even more.

By midnight, the moon was high over the clearing. Cadence and Arrow paced around the tree, knowing that the attack could come from any side, at any time.

Another hour passed. Then they came. With cries of horror screaming from their throats, the Mist-Taggers attacked.

Thirty or forty of the terrible creatures ran from the forest, on their hands and feet, towards the single tree of the travelers and their protectors.

Darts and arrows shot out across the clearing, over and over again. Creature after creature fell to the ground in piles of ragged-fur bodies. One Tagger reached the tree. Window buried his spear deep into the ugly creature's belly. Its fangs dripped deadly poison as it cried out. Window fought to pull the spear free to use again.

The attackers were driven off – then again they came. Circles' arrows felled two, then three, of the beasts. Then his arrows were gone. The Cat-eyes were each down to a single dart.

Panni and Window waited for the final assault. Rings was ready. He would not go down easily.

Circles saw one of his spent arrows sticking in the ground about half way to the treeline. He had to try to retrieve it. He would have to take the chance.

Without warning the others, Circles jumped out from his place under the tree. He raced to the arrow and, as he leaned down to pull it from the dirt, a Tagger started from the trees towards him. Circles turned to run. The creature was amazingly quick. He would catch Circles before he could reach the safety of the Sage-tree.

Circles ran – the Tagger ran faster. The creature was sure to catch the fleeing Woot. He was sure to sink his jagged fangs into Circles' back. Under the tree, behind Panni, Raine struggled to his feet. Circles raced towards the tree. Raine opened his hands towards the Tagger.

The creature would catch Circles in three steps. Raine crossed his thumbs. "Circles!" Panni screamed to him. One – two – "Circles!" – the Tagger leaped in the air after Circles. In a fraction of a second he would bury his poison into the back of the little Woot. But something else happened instead.

Raine's fingers seemed to explode. A blinding flash of lightning crossed the clearing. A deafening crash of sound knocked everyone off their feet. The jagged, crackling, lightning bolt struck the Tagger as he flew through the air, and melted him – as it sent him flying back to the treeline. A sparkling array of colored light bounced off of the trees on the far side of the clearing and echoed back to where the travelers lay on the ground. A tree on the edge of the clearing was on fire.

The few remaining Taggers fled deep into the woods. The travelers picked themselves up from the ground, and rubbed their eyes and heads. Circles held his ears, trying to recover from the explosion of power that had cut across the clearing.

Window's vision cleared a bit. Through the echo of light in his eyes, he turned to his right and saw Panni. She was kneeling over Raine who had crumpled to the ground at her feet.

Panni turned to Window and frantically told him, "I think that Raine is dying! Look! His finger-rings have died. They have no light or colors at all. His face has no glow! He is dying!"

Raine had used the very last power in his finger-rings to save Circles. Now he was quietly gasping for air. He could hardly breathe. He could not speak. He could not move.
8   Circles ran to his friend from the stars, and broke into tears when he saw him. "Rainie! Rainie!" There was no answer.
"Cadence!" Arrow yelled, throwing down his bow. "Quickly, the vermillion!"
Window hadn't noticed the little silver-colored containers before. In the moonlight and firelight, he watched as Cadence reached to his belt and removed a small metal cylinder, similar to one hanging next to it.
"How much do you need?" Cadence asked, as he tried to calm his breathing.
"I don't know!" Arrow answered. He pulled the top from the container and poured a small pile of the multicolored dust into his open hand.

Raine was lying on his back. "Cover his eyes," Arrow instructed Cadence as they knelt down next to him.
Arrow gently blew into his hand, and about half of the vermillion dust flew onto Raine's face. The vermillion sparkled and glittered, and wildly reflected the fire and moonlight. Raine did not respond. He seemed to stop breathing completely.
"It's not working, Arrow!" Cadence cried out. "It's not working!"
"Try his rings!" Circles desperately yelled to the Cat-eyes. "Try his finger-rings!"
So Arrow did just that. Panni dropped to her knees next to Raine and lifted his right hand and opened his fingers towards Arrow. Arrow carefully blew vermillion from his hand onto Raine's hand and finger-rings.
Raine's hand came alive! It lifted itself from Panni's grasp and rose about a foot into the air. His hand opened upward. Color returned to the jewels in the rings on that hand. Light started to faintly spark from them, then grew brighter. Suddenly, five

colorful rays of light shot from Raine's finger-rings. There was no sound, just five bright rays of red, green, blue, orange, and silver coming from the jewels on his raised hand.

The light beams went straight up into the air, between the tree branches, and on up into the night sky – past the clouds, and on and on.

"It looks as though they are just going to keep on past the moon," Circles said, excitedly.

Then, the light rays faded from Raine's rings, and his hand fell to the ground. Raine opened his eyes, and moved his mouth, as if to say something, but was unable to speak.

With tears running down her face, Panni gently cupped her hands around Raine's face. Where her hands touched his cheeks, the pale blue of his skin darkened a bit. His eyes were clear and breathing was calm and steady.

"He is better! He seems better!" Panni happily spoke to both of the secret keepers, as, still kneeling, she hugged Arrow, and Circles hugged Cadence. "Thank you, thank you, for saving our friend." And then, speaking mostly to herself, she added, "He is so important to us."

Panni looked towards Window, feeling a need for comfort from him. He nodded to her with a reassuring smile. The Cat-eyes lowered their eyes, and their heads, in a slight bow of honor. Arrow spoke, "And we thank him, for saving us all."

The travelers decided to remain in the clearing for a few days, to give Raine, and everyone else, a chance to recover from the terrible attack of the Taggers. Panni stayed by Raine and tended to him. He remained very weak, still unable to speak. Arrow tried using a bit of trillion, to give him strength, but was unsuccessful.

Rings dragged the Tagger bodies to the woods and buried them under the trees. Before he covered the last one, Cadence also had an unpleasant chore to perform.

"Arrow and I are interested in everything in the forest," Cadence told Window, as he pulled a small glass vial from his belt pack. "So, I collect different flower petals, and bugs, and things to learn all we can. Now, I need to collect some of the venom from this Tagger. Maybe we can discover how to defeat its poison."

Cadence used a dart point to cut into the creature's mouth. Then he carefully filled the vial with the yellow-green liquid that oozed out from the venom pouch.

Later that night, during a quiet time, Circles asked Arrow about the Taggers.

Arrow answered as best he could. "There is evil in the world, Circles. It has been here as long as we have. Perhaps, someday, it will go away. But, for now, we need to do the best we can to defeat it."

On the second day after the attack, there were again tremors in the forest. Arrow warned that there could be a large quake at any time, but there really wasn't anything they could do about it, so they just tried to think of other things.

Circles retrieved as many of his arrows as he could. Cadence returned to the castle and brought more darts for himself and his Cat-eyes friend. Arrow felt that the Taggers would not return, so all attention focused upon Raine.

Raines's finger-rings flickered faintly, as both he, and his rings, remained very weak. Raine seemed to be in a partial sleep. He could look out at his friends, but not react to them. Panni fed him hot broth that he was able to swallow.

A third day came. There was no improvement in Raine's condition. The travelers discussed building a device from tree limbs and blankets that Rings could use to transport him back to Dawson's. It would be a long and difficult trip.

"I'm not sure Raine will live long enough to make the trip," Window confided to Panni. "He is so very weak."

The disheartened travelers sat in the sun by the road through the clearing and finished a lunch of meat and cheese. The Cat-eyes were nowhere to be seen, but every once in a while, there were a few less pieces of cheese than there were before.

Suddenly, without any warning, a man appeared, standing just a short distance from the travelers as they ate. It was such a quiet surprise that everyone was startled. No one moved for a moment. Window heard a wood-dart being fixed to a bow in the empty air next to him.

The man was tall and slightly built, and his skin was completely white – as white as a summer moon. He had silver-g8rey hair and a very angular face. His shirt and pants were light grey, smooth and simple, like those that Raine was wearing when they first met him. He wore a belt that seemed to be made of metallic sections, hooked together. Immediately, everyone happily realized that this visitor must be from Raine's world, too. The searchers had found him! They had come for him!

The man walked right up to the group and addressed them in Atlandan.

"Greetings from Tessimaysan. I am Starfin-Faeranon. I am looking for Messenger Raenedejjreonne. Could you please tell me where he is?"

Panni jumped up to greet the man. "Yes, yes! You have found him! He is here! Raine is right here! He is right here!"

Panni was thrilled to see the man but tried to calm herself as he spoke again.

"We read his signal near Traejena-Reyesse three days ago," explained the starman. "It was very powerful. I don't understand how he was able to signal us. Now his rings are so depleted that I cannot detect them."

"Science got a little help from magic, I think," Circles started to explain. Just then, he felt a slightly furry, but invisible, hand, gently cover his mouth.

"Oh, yeah," Circles said to himself, and didn't have anything more to offer.

The joyful Panni led the white starman to where Raine was lying under the tree. Starfin touched his finger-rings to Raine's hands and Raine's ring jewels sparkled. Raine opened his eyes, but didn't say anything. Starfin held one set of his finger-rings to Raine's forehead, and seemed to be listening to something.

Circles went over to Starfin and asked what they all wanted to know. "Can you help him? Will he recover? Will he be alright?"

"Yes, he will recover. By the time we reach Tessimaysan, he should be well again. It will take time, but he will be alright."

That was wonderfully happy news for all of them. Then came unwelcome news.

"But, I must return Raine to my ship, very soon. He needs to be attended to by our physicians at Toure-Daeren. We will also tow his damaged ship so it can someday be returned to him."

The sadness of parting hit the travelers. A few minutes before, they were concerned for Raine's life. Now, so very quickly, although he was alive, they felt the pain of just saying goodbye to him – especially a goodbye that was so sudden and complete. Certainly, they wanted Raine healthy, and able to return to his own world, but it would be a very difficult goodbye.

"Can he hear us, and see us?" Panni asked the starman.

'Yes, he can, Panni. And, Raine has stored his goodbye thoughts and wishes in his memory ring, so he can say goodbye to you, too. But first, I have read Raine's thoughts, and, as part of those thoughts, he has something for me to give you,"

Starfin explained to the travelers, "While Raine was with you, he often wanted to help you with things, but was not allowed to. But, as your messenger, he is allowed to give you gifts of parting. His thoughts have told me what those gifts will be."

"Rings, Raine's gift to you is the gift of forgetfulness – not for your memory, but for that of others who would harm you. You will be able to return to Calisay, without being hunted or bothered by the Prince's soldiers. Once you look into their eyes, the soldiers will not remember that they have been ordered to arrest and imprison you. They will seem to forget that you are even there. So you can visit Oldsmith, and race in Calisay again, without worry."

Rings' mouth couldn't smile, but there was a smile in his eyes.

"Just make sure that you don't get into trouble again," added Starfin.

"Panni, your gift is the gift of trust-seeing. You will be able to see inside the heart of anyone you meet, and tell if they are worthy of your trust and caring."

Panni looked down at Raine with fondness for him, and thankfulness for <u>his</u> caring.

"Window, Raine has chosen for you the gift of language. Like him, you will be able to understand and speak any language of the humans in your world."

Window was stunned by what he heard.

"Circles, Raine has seen part of your future, and knows that someday you will need to talk to the birds. So, your dream will come true now. You will be able to understand the birds and they will understand you."

The little Woot was thrilled beyond words. He squeezed the starman's hand and could only say, "Oh, Rainie."

The travelers were all in awe of Raine's gifts. Each felt a great gratitude towards their departing friend. They were wonderful gifts. Panni looked towards Raine and started to cry.

"Also, before I go on," Starfin added, "please tell your invisible friends that we thank them for their help, as well."

Panni wiped her tears, and smiled at Window. In the shade of the Sage-tree, two cat-eyed creatures appeared, and bowed to Raine's rescuer from the stars.

"I will need to use Raine's finger-rings," Starfin went on. "I am not a messenger, so the gifts he has chosen are not within my rings."

Starfin knelt down and gently took Raine's hands and lay them open on the ground at his sides. Then he asked the travelers to stand together about fifteen feet away from their friend.

Starfin raised his hands and directed light from his rings towards the rings on Raine's hands. The silver light from Starfin's fingertips flew into Raine's ring-jewels and came back out – colorful, sparkling, jumping, glittering. The powerful new light shot out towards the group of travelers, and surrounded them. Lights of different colors bathed each of them, some with red, some with blue, some with green, each with multiple colors of different shades. The lights danced around the travelers and brought to each of them the gifts Raine had chosen.

Just as Starfin was finishing, and the jewel-lights started to fade, there was a loud crack of sound from Raine's right hand. A bright beam of yellow light shot from one of his finger-jewels and bathed the travelers in a flash of yellow. Then all of the lights faded.

Starfin was concerned. "One of Raine's ring-jewels has split apart. It must have been damaged when he saved you from the Tagger. I am sorry. His gifts to you may have been affected."

"What do you mean?" Circles asked immediately.

"The yellow light may have added energy in an uncertain fashion. I expect that your gifts will usually work exactly as Raine desired, but it could be that at some rare times, they may not. They may act in an unexpected way. Again, I am sorry if you have any difficulties because of them. Raine would be disappointed, I am sure."

"We are all thrilled to have our gifts," Window spoke up. "Even if they might be a bit unpredictable at times."

Suddenly, Panni got an idea, and whispered in Window's ear.
"Yes!" he quickly answered.

Window took Arrow and Cadence aside and spoke to them. Cadence opened his small belt pack and dug into it. Then he unhooked the two metal dust cylinders from his belt. In a minute, Window returned to the others, with two tiny glass vials – one of trillion and one of vermillion.

"These are our gifts to Raine," Panni explained. "Please tell him to use them, if ever all else fails."

Starfin nodded.

"Before we go, Raine would like to speak to you one last time."

Starfin opened his hands and touched his thumbs together. Flashing rays of white shot out from his fingertips and swirled together in front of the travelers. Suddenly, Raine's image was standing before them.

Raine looked at them, from the swirling light, as he spoke. His eyes revealed the sorrow that he, too, felt at his leaving.

"You have been the best friends on any world, warm or cold or far away. You have given me a home and kept me safe. If ever I can return to see you again, I will do it happily. Please all take care of yourselves, and find your dreams. You deserve all the treasures of life."

Panni's face was wet with tears. Circles sadly tugged on Rings' fur.

"My memory ring is filled with thoughts of everything we have shared – and those memories are my treasure. I will keep you all very close to me, wherever I may go – even to the farthest star. I give you my thanks and my love."

Raine's image was flickering. He looked at each of them and gave his final goodbye.

> "Past the moon and past the stars
> The treasure we will find
> The treasure shared within our hearts
> Beyond the end of time"

The light faded and the image disappeared. The starman's friends lowered their heads in sadness.

At Starfin's request, the travelers carried Raine out from under the tree and lay him in the open. Each of the travelers stood by him for a moment, and took his hand and squeezed it one last time, as they quietly told him their goodbyes. Raine's tired eyes looked back into theirs, and he was able to softly squeeze each of their hands. Rings nuzzled against his arm.

The travelers stepped away from Raine and held on to each other. Starfin lifted his open hands out over Raine and himself. A blue-grey colored light shot from his rings, and sparkled around the two men. Starfin disappeared in a flicker of light. Then, in another instant, their dear friend, Raine, the man from the stars, was gone from their world, and their lives.

+++++++++

It was a quiet group of travelers that packed up their supplies that afternoon. They would go on, but without Raine, it would be terribly lonely for a while.

Cadence had given Window directions for reaching the Moonlands. Arrow had at first thought that those directions should be kept secret, but Cadence had made a good argument to tell them.

"Aren't we supposed to be here to help people? Isn't that why Arcadia and Alana were here?"

"You are right, Cadence. You are right. We see so few people that I had forgotten. I guess that someday you and I will just fade away like the others. Our secrets will do us no good then."

"I don't want to fade away, Arrow. I like it here."

"Me, too, Cadence, me, too."

Before the travelers started on their way, the Cat-eyes <u>also</u> had a gift for them. Although the travelers still had the trillion that they had found at Eastpoint, Cadence shared his vermillion with them, too.

Circles asked, "What will vermillion do for us, Cadence?"

He answered, "It may answer your questions, Circles, or show you the way, or help you in times of danger – or do anything – if you believe that it will."

"It may?" Circles wondered.

"Pixie dust is hard to predict."

"So it <u>is</u> Pixie dust!"

Cadence just smiled at the little Woot.

So, they now had a berry tin of silver trillion and a matches tin of multi-colored vermillion. Circles carefully put the containers in a harness side-pack for "when we need it," if ever that might be. Of course, it was uncertain what the dust might do in the hands of the travelers.

There were soon more goodbyes for the travelers. The Cat-eyes were returning to their castle ruins, and to keeping their secrets there. Window and his friends were going on to the east, to search for whatever they might find. Circles still wanted to find the

Angels, but, like that of the others, his enthusiasm had waned somewhat.

But, now, it was time for the Cat-eyes to start their journey home. The travelers thanked them again for their friendship and help. Cadence and Arrow nodded goodbye to each of them. Then, one at a time, Cadence and Arrow walked out from under the Sage-tree and disappeared into the sunlight.

The four Angel hunters started once again to the east. Each of them kept their thoughts to themselves as they followed the Ancient Lands road towards the Moonlands. The afternoon went quickly and by the time the evening was upon them they had reached the edge of the ancient forest.

Their camp that night was a sad one without Raine, but Window had been saving a surprise and decided that it was time to share it. He dug to the bottom of his pack and pulled out a deck of cards.

"Who's in for Northdraw?" he called to the others.

"Window, you brought cards!" Panni responded happily.

Rings immediately stood up and walked over to the fire. "Circles, will you hold for me?" he asked his sure-handed friend.

"Sure, I guess so," answered Circles, somewhat reluctantly.

"Will you play, too, Panni?" Window asked.

"Of course, Window, I could use a little diversion."

Window brought a couple of the food packs over near the fire, laid them down, next to each other, and opened an eating cloth over them, to form a table.

Rings lay down facing the table, and Circles sat in front of him, on Rings' paws. Panni tucked her skirt under her legs and sat back on them, across from him.

Window joined them, and as the firelight flickered, he dealt out the first hand. Before long, their spirits were much improved. They laughed, and reminded each other of funny things that had happened when they were playing cards back at Dawson's. By the time they finished the game, the friends were reconnected with each other and ready for a restful night's sleep. It was just what they all needed.

In the morning, breakfast was a very quiet meal. No one could think of much to say. It was difficult for each of them, without Raine being there, and it was about to get even more difficult for Window. Just as they were finishing eating, Panni spoke quietly to him. She didn't really want to, but she needed to tell him her thoughts.

"Window, I do think of returning home. With the King's Treasure, I can buy the freedom of my friends who are held as servants at the Traepelle Castle. I am sure that Dawson or Oldsmith will help me. And, I am looking forward to seeing my family – and being free. My life looks so wonderful ahead. Maybe after we explore the Moonlands we should go back."

She looked into his eyes to see his reaction. Window didn't want to think about it. He didn't want to talk about it. He just nodded "yes" without saying anything.

Panni sat by him for a minute, wondering what else to say. It had been a terrible decision for her. It had almost broken her heart to tell him. Then Window spoke to her.

"It will be a wonderful thing, Panni, to see your family, and free your friends. And, just think, with all of the Royal Treasure you will have, you will certainly become a princess."

"I don't need to be a princess, Window. I just need someone to treat me like a princess, once in a while – like you have done."

Window looked at her and then dropped his eyes as he spoke. "You <u>are</u> a princess to me, Panni."

+++++++++

[IN THE CASTLE OF THE HEARTS]

Across the lands far to the east, and farther to the south, Anna Bliss opened her eyes. The early morning sun was shining brightly on her face, but she didn't care. Today was the day. It was her seventeenth birthday. Today was the day she would become a true Princess of the Hearts.

Today she would cast off her children's clothes, and her children's duties. Today she would become a woman of the Palace Court, and, most importantly – today, she would get her horse!

Anna tossed back her satin sheets and lace-quilted blanket. She threw her sleeping skirt onto the floor, and ran her fingers through her golden-brown hair. She slipped into a fresh, bright red, tunic-dress, and looked out the window down to the outer courtyard, towards the stables.   Barely taking time to tie her riding shoes' straps around her legs, she rushed out into the upper hallway.

"Good morning, Princess," the bedroom maid politely addressed her, as Anna hurried by.

Anna liked the sound of the greeting. It was, of course, the very first time she had ever been greeted as "Princess." "I guess I'd better get used to it," she thought to herself.

"Good morning, Sevy. Have you seen him yet?"

"No, Miss, but I know that Catcher brought him here yesterday."

Anna smiled and quickly looked over the balcony railing, down to the grand castle day-chamber.

"Ma-Ma!" She yelled down to the family-table. Her mother was there, waiting for a fresh breakfast from the kitchen staff.

"Good Morning, Princess. Come join me!"

"Is he here?"

"Yes, Dear, he is here."

Anna descended the curved, marble staircase with less dignity than, perhaps, she should have – her skirt flying as though there was a breeze blowing up the steps to greet her.

"Happy Birthday, Dear Daughter," her mother wished her, as the young woman reached her mother's outstretched arms. "Here, I brought your headband. I knew that you would forget."

Anna <u>had</u> forgotten. Now she would wear the clothes and jewels of a princess – the jeweled headband, the sheer arm scarves, and bracelets. And, now, she would use a full-sized bow – and, she would become a Captain of the Horsemen.

Anna would ride with the Guard to the farthest outlands of Heart. She would begin, in a few days, by leading her horsemen to the river at the western edge of the kingdom. She had studied and trained for months. It would be her first duty as Princess.

Princess Anna hugged her mother. Then, she straightened her tunic skirt and walked to the side archway. She could see him – out in the stable yard, by the far fence. He was standing there, waiting for her. Catcher already had him saddled. Anna wouldn't be riding Cameo anymore. Now, she would ride Mystic. Because, today, Anna Bliss became Princess of the Hearts!

+++++++++

"Hey, Panni, say something to me in Freelandan," Window requested of his friend. They had already been on their way through some lowlands for several hours. "I want to try my messenger skills."

"Tereial sae tousee?" she immediately shot back at him. But what Window heard in his mind was, *"How much longer until lunch?"*

"Wow! That is something! *Desatae naden?"*

"How about now?" she responded, again in Freelandan. Window was thrilled. He understood her completely!

Now it's your turn, Circles. See if you can get a bird to talk to you," Window suggested.

"What bird? There doesn't seem to be any around here."

"Well, say something in bird-talk. Maybe one will come find you."

"*Se-fae-oh, Se-fae-oh.*" Circles half whistled into some nearby trees. In about a minute, a little grey-dove kind of bird flew up and landed on Circles' shoulder.

"It worked! It worked!" he shouted, and scared the bird away.

"Guess that bird prefers quiet talk," Circles happily continued. And, he was right. Before long, another grey-dove was on his shoulder, and stayed there for several minutes, as they walked along conversing.

"This is fantastic," Circles shared with his friends. "I will appreciate Raine's gift forever."

"I appreciate his gift to me, too," spoke up Panni, winking at Circles. "Right now I can sense what an uncaring, untrustworthy man Window is."

"Looks like your gift is broken already, Panni," added Circles. "You left out 'devious'."

"And, I'm going to leave you both out of supper tonight," smiled Window.

All three of them laughed. Rings just shook his head. He still didn't understand jokes sometimes. "Especially when they are not funny," he usually explained.

The rest of the day went on in the same cheerful manner. The travelers' joy of each other's company was returning. Their joy of sharing the road, and their adventure, was returning. They walked on, happily, together.

And then, in just two more days on the road, the four Angel hunters reached the edge of the Moonlands forest – except it wasn't a forest of trees – it was a forest of flowers!

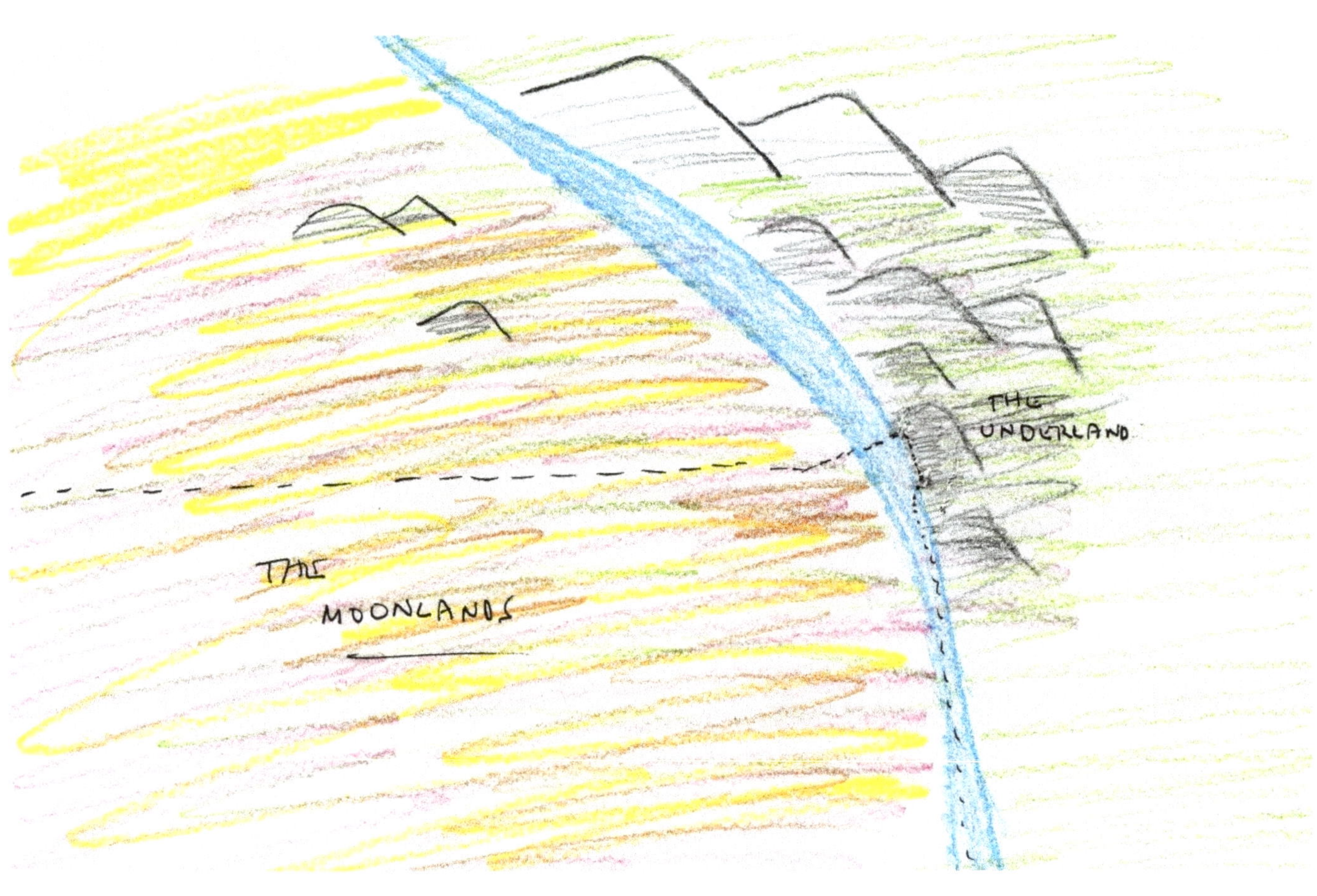

THE
UNDERLAND
THE
MOONLANDS

CHAPTER NINETEEN

THROUGH THE UNDERLAND

"Hey, this looks like someplace that an Angel might live," Circles shared with his friends, as they surveyed the Moonlands forest. "Of course, it also looks like a place where giant bugs might live."

As the travelers left the rolling grasslands and stepped into the forest, it was as though they were stepping into a beautiful garden of giant flowers. The flowers grew as tall as trees and lofted over their heads with giant blossoms of color. Some flower stems were smooth and light green. Some were rough with hundreds of wavy leaves sticking out. Many of the plants were tilted to one side and drooping enormous flowers of every description. There were fuzzy flowers and puffy flowers and twisted flowers and tall, skinny flowers. Some of the plants had exotic-looking fruit hanging from them.

"You are right, Circles," Window answered him. "I wouldn't be surprised if there were insects the size of these flowers, living in here. We should continue to be careful, and keep watch for anything dangerous."

"Which way should we go, Window?" Panni asked. "I don't see any paths or trails."

"Let's just keep heading east," he replied, and then added, "I wish that Arrow would have told us something about this place. We need to make sure that we don't get lost in here."

They pushed into the forest, between gigantic plants that reminded Window of trail-roses. The air became instantly much cooler and the light very subdued as it filtered through the overhanging leaves. Rings had to push his way between and over flower-stalks as they went. He knocked down and crushed many, many plants.

"We need a plan," Window admitted. "We could walk in this forest forever and never find anything. Does anyone have an idea?"

"I have an idea that we should leave that caterpillar alone," Circles suggested, as he pointed to a foot-long, crawling worm-creature that was climbing up the side of a flower stem.

"We have no way of knowing which direction to travel, Window," Panni agreed. "I have only one idea."

Neither Window, nor Circles, nor Rings said anything. They all just looked at Panni and waited.

She shared her thoughts. "Maybe this is a time that we could get some help from the trillion or vermillion. Since we have pretty much of both, let's just see if a small bit of one of them would tell us which way to go. I don't know how it would work, but I can't think of anything else."

No one had any other idea, so they got out the tins of dust.

Panni shook a very small amount of trillion onto her open hand. "Okay, now what?" She asked. "Any thoughts?"

"Just throw it into the air," Circles suggested.

Panni tossed the glittering dust straight upward. The trillion acted like any other dust and quickly fell to the ground.

"Try the vermillion," Circles encouraged.

This time something unusual happened. The vermillion dust rose into the air about a foot, then started blowing to one side — except that there was no breeze to blow it.

"It looks like it knows where it is going!" Circles happily reported. "Let's follow it."

They walked after the sparkling dust as it slowly floated through the flowers towards the south-east. But, after a few minutes, like the trillion, the dust fell to the ground.

"I don't think that we should use any more of the vermillion. Let's just keep going in this direction," Window recommended – and they did.

The explorers continued on through the giant flowers. They encountered a few beautiful, hand-size butterflies, but nothing else.

"Hey, Circles," Rings called ahead to his friend. "There's a big red and white butterfly sitting on your head."

"I know, I know. I am training him," Circles called back.

"Training him to do what?"

"I am training him to sit on my head."

"Oh."

At lunchtime, the explorers decided to try some of the odd-looking Moonlands fruit.

Circles chose one of several giant, orange berries that grew in bunches near the ground. Panni choose a greenish fruit that broke into juicy sections. She easily picked it from an overhanging flower branch. Window decided on a long, twisted fruit-pod, and Rings ate the thick leaves from a flat-looking flower stem.

"Start with just a small bite, everybody," Window warned. We don't want to get sick if these things are not good to eat.

Window bit into his selection. Its texture reminded him of the apple slices his Grandmother Breesian used to cut for him. It was a delicious treat with a sweet and a tart taste mixed together.

'This is really good," Circles announced after his first few bites. The others felt the same way about their choices. They were all convinced that the fruit was not harmful, and soon, they were sharing with each other.

The Moonlands lunch was a success. But then, shortly after the explorers started walking again there was another ground tremor. The flower plants shook and flower-fruit of all sizes and shapes fell to the ground.

"Hey, it's raining lunch," Circles called out. He was now getting used to the tremors and wasn't bothered by them so much anymore.

"Do you think that there will be a big quake, Window?" Circles wanted to know. "Will the ground swallow us up?"

"I don't know, Circles. It could happen, I suppose."

"Well, it better not," replied Circles. He didn't really like Window's answer and looked like he wanted to say more, but he couldn't think of anything else to say.

They continued to the south-east for the rest of the day. After a few hours, they used another very small amount of vermillion that sent them in the same direction. Eventually, the flower forest thinned out somewhat, and they were able to travel more easily across the partially open ground.

By nightfall, they arrived at the bank of a small river. Along the other side of the river, was a flat area of higher ground, and, beyond that, much higher ground, like a range of very small, but rugged, mountains.

They could tell that the river had been disturbed by the recent quakes. There were areas exposed that had obviously been under water before, and places where the river now flowed through sections of flowers, that used to be on dry land. They could also see, on the small mountains beyond the river, landslide debris that had recently come down the mountainside.

"Let's camp here for the night," Window suggested. "The water doesn't look too deep, so tomorrow we can ford the river and look for a way past those hills."

"I'll get started setting things up," answered Panni, as she loosened the straps on Rings' harness. She found a giant flower plant nearby that had long, thick, spikes growing out from its stem.

"I'll just hang our packs on these," she announced.

As the sun completely disappeared below the forest behind them they sat and ate a brief meal. The moon rose from beyond the mountains across the river and lighted their camp.

"Hey, Window," Circles wanted to know. "Do you think that there are mountains on the moon?"

"Look up there, Circles. Those rough parts on the moon look like mountains to me."

"I wonder if those are the mountains on the moon that Mellie's poem mentioned." Then Circles added, "I wonder if there are any Angels around here."

"I don't see any."

"Hey, Window, the moon looks different to me. Has it changed somehow?"

"I couldn't say, Circles. It looks the same to me. What do you think, Panni?"

"It looks closer to me."

"The Moonlands must have gotten its name from something," Circles offered. That got everyone thinking.

Before lying down to sleep, they stayed up for a while and watched the moon silently move across the sky. Circles wondered if there were any Angels on the moon. Rings wondered if there was anything to eat on the moon. Panni missed the warm summer nights she had spent with her friends on the Traepelle Castle evening-porch. Window thought of Mary. That night, they all slept with moonlight in their eyes.

+++++++++

[NEAR THE HARBOR AT BRECEENE]

Far, far, beyond the land of the Hearts, Captain Reed Cardette reeled in the mainsail rope, and tied it to the mast pegs. The Seaflyer had been skimming across the water, chasing the moon ahead of it, but now had slowed to almost a standstill near the northern Longsea coastline. In the moonlight he could see the lights of Breceene and he wanted to make sure that he approached the harbor from a position very close to the shore. He certainly didn't want the lookouts on the Pik ship to see him.

If his guess was right, the Pik frigate, Brance, was docked at that moment in the harbor at Breceene. His plan tonight was the same as at Kinast. Cardette would quietly sail his windflyer into the harbor and hide it among the many larger merchant and passenger ships. Then, wearing the belt that held his heavy wrench, pry bar, and breathing tube, he would lower himself into the water and work his way to the Brance.

If he was successful, when the Vox Kingdom frigate Universa reached the port tomorrow afternoon, the Brance would be unable to steer its way out of the harbor and would be trapped by the bigger guns of the Universa. The Brance captain would be rather unhappy, attempting to pilot a ship without a complete rudder.

This was the third Pik ship Cardette had followed across the Very East this summer. It would not be his last. The Pik Kingdom ships, from the very south of Oceania, had been raiding and robbing the people and villages of the Middle Kingdoms for years, but since last spring he had thought of nothing else.

Pik pirates had come in the night, killed his parents, and burned their oceanside home. Then they stole his family's beautiful Valdress horses and sailed away. He could never forgive them. He could never forget. Now his life had only one meaning – destroy the murderous Piks, and their murderous ships.

Cardette quietly piloted his ship along the shoreline to the harbor entrance. Then he let the Seaflyer slip between two North Kingdom schooners, and tied it securely to an empty docking post.

Looking across the harbor, through the scores of empty masts of sleeping ships, he noticed that there was a light burning in the Captain's cabin of the Brance. Maybe he could do more than temporarily cripple a Pik vessel tonight. Maybe he could catch the Captain alone, if, somehow, he could silence the ship's night-guards.

Cardette hooked his equipment belt around his waist and then added his scall-blade to the belt. He had better be ready for anything.

The moon was now directly overhead. It was time. He took a deep breath. Then Reed Cardette lowered himself into the quiet, cold water of Breceene Harbor.

+++++++++

The ground seemed to explode under them! Window was rolled from his blanket and sent several feet across the camp. The others, also, were tossed from their sleep by the quaking land. And, this time, it was a much stronger tremor than the others they had experienced.

The moon had long passed overhead. It was very dark. They couldn't see any stars because thick rain clouds filled the sky. Not only had there been another quake, but it would probably storm soon.

Window could hardly see the river in the darkness, but he could hear the water shaking and splashing as the tremors continued.

"Let's all sit together," Panni requested. "It would make me feel better to be close to you."

"Okay," Circles agreed, as everyone, without discussion, moved and sat against Rings.

"Wow! That was something!" Circles offered, as the tremors finally subsided completely.

They pushed against their huge, furry friend and tried to relax. Then, on the other side of the river and downstream a bit on the higher rocky ground, Circles suddenly saw a bright flickering light.

"Window, there is a fire in that rocky area across the river. It looks like a campfire. Someone must be over there."

Window peered out into the darkness towards the fire. "Let's be careful, and try to find out who it is before we approach them."

"Okay. Hey, I'll get my scope."

Circle went to his harness pack and pulled out his far-scope. He quickly scanned across the river to the spot of the campfire.

"Window, there is something odd about that campfire."

"What is that, Circles?"

"It's not a campfire."

"What is it?"

"I don't know. It's just a glowing light of some kind. Maybe it belongs to the Angels," Circles said hopefully.

"Yeah, maybe," Window answered, but he had no better guess.

They decided to check out the fire right away. Rings would carry the others across the river on his back.

"Let's put Rings' harness on him, so we can hang onto it, and we won't fall off," Window suggested. "If there is another tremor, anything could happen."

Panni retrieved the harness, and also brought Window's sword, in its belted sheath, and handed it to him. "Just in case," she told him.

The four of them slowly made their way in the dark to the edge of the river. Soon, the others climbed on Rings' back, and he carefully carried them into the water. They hung on to his harness as he fought against the flowing current. The water was deeper than they had expected. It eventually reached the bottom of Rings' neck, so they all got completely wet. Rings slipped a few times but they made it safely across.

As Rings climbed up the bank on the other side of the river they could see the light more clearly. It was bright like a fire, but the light rays seemed to shoot up into the air, rather than rise, as a flame would do. They couldn't see any people or animals around the light.

202

As they worked their way to its source, Circles made the discovery, "The light is coming from under the ground!"

The ground the explorers were on was rocky and rough. From several small cracks in the ground, between some of the rocks, there were bright light rays shooting out and up into the sky. The rays were silver with smaller blue rays within the silver.

"The dirt around these rocks looks as if it had been disturbed lately," Window observed. "I'll bet that the quake split the ground open and allowed this light to shine through." I wonder what could be down there making the light."

His eyes followed the light out of the ground and up into the night sky. The light rays reminded Window of the rays from Raine's finger-jewels.

"I'll bet these are Angel lights!" Circles hopefully announced. Then he went looking around the area for more of the lights.

Panni put her hand into the blue-silver ray. Her hand lit up brightly. "How can we get down there to see where this light is coming from? Maybe Rings could dig a hole in these rocks."

Just then, her question was answered by Circles. "Window! Window! There is a crack in the hillside over here. I can see more lights!"

The little Woot treasure hunter had done it again! Circles had found a crack between two sections of mountainside that were mostly covered with rocks of various sizes. A space between several of the larger rocks was an opening just large enough for him to slip through. Window could tell that the fissure had only recently been opened. From within, came a dull glow. It appeared to be a way into the underground of light.

Somewhere above the explorers, the sun was rising behind the clouds. An early morning storm would soon be upon them.

"If we are going to explore this opening, we had better do it right away," Window warned. "This looks like a serious storm coming. A rainstorm could easily close this entrance again. Look at all of the loose dirt and rock up there, above us."

It was quickly decided. Window and Circles would go through the fissure. Rings and Panni would wait outside.

Rings hooked his claws behind one of the big stones at the fissure and pulled it slightly away from the hillside. It made an opening just large enough for Window to slide through.

"We will try to not stay underground too long," Window assured Panni.

"Window, what if we get trapped in there?" Circles wanted to know.

"I hope that Rings has a lot of digging energy."

"Me, too."

"Okay, Circles, let's go."

Circles easily slid between the rocks, but Window had to slowly work his way in. After Window was inside, Panni reached her arm through the opening, and grabbed his hand for a moment.

"Please, please, be careful, Window. I couldn't bear it if you were hurt."

"I'll be back as soon as I can," he assured her.

Above them, the clouds continued to build.

Inside the mountain, the explorers found themselves in a narrow, cave-like passageway. Imbedded in the ceiling, walls, and floor, were many smooth, clear, oval stones. Some were about the size of Circles' fist, and others were smaller. At the center of each of the crystals was a dimly glowing light – most were glowing blue but others green or red or silver. The stones gave off enough light so that it was easy to see down the passageway.

Circles and Window worked their way along the passage as quickly as they could. The ground beneath them was very uneven and their way was sometimes partially blocked with rocks and mounds of dirt they had to step over. And Window had to duck his head often, to avoid hitting it on the low ceiling.

The passageway began to slope downward. The explorers climbed over more rough stones and dirt as they made their way deeper under the ground.

Still there was enough light from the glowing stones to show them the way. Deeper and deeper they descended, and as the passageway grew a bit taller, Window no longer had to bend over to walk. After about ten minutes, the passage leveled out and widened even more.

"Look at that, Window," Circles quietly spoke to his friend. The ground before them held five or six small holes, obviously dug in the dirt by an animal of some kind. "Looks like we are not alone down here."

"What animal would live down here, Window?" Circles asked.

"Something small and friendly, I hope," came Window's cautious reply.

The explorers carefully continued their search through the wondrous underland. Then, after just a few more minutes, they could see a very bright light from farther down the passage. They hurried towards it. Soon they were at the entrance of a large cavern. They stopped and stared in amazement at the fantastic sight before them.

Inside, the ground was scattered with beautiful lighted crystals. There were thousands of them. Some were smooth and oval. Others had the look of a cut diamond, with flat angular sides that split the stone's light into separate rays of color. It appeared as though each crystal had a glowing light inside – light that shot in every direction, and reflected across the cavern and back again. The high ceiling and walls were also alive with the colored light-stones. Most of the light-stones were rather faint, but together they lit the entire room as brightly as sunlight on a sunny day.

They stepped into the crystal-lit cavern.

"Look, Window," Circles noticed, "It's very bright in here, but light is coming from every direction, so I don't have a shadow."

Window realized that his friend was right. They were in the middle of an underground world of light.

"I wonder if the Angels live down here," Circles said to himself, refusing to give up his search.

He picked a stone, shining faintly with a white glow inside, and held it up to examine it, to try to discover the source of its light.

As he raised it in front of his face, the pure white of the light inside changed to a soft blue, then flickered, and faded completely.

"Hey, Window, this light just died or something."

"They all seem to be fading, Circles. Some of these stones don't have any light at all. Only a few of them have a very bright light inside."

One stone, in particular, caught Window's eye. It was a bright blue, diamond-like crystal, about the size of a walnut, half buried beneath several faded-color stones. Just as Window noticed it the light inside flashed even more brightly a few times. Window walked over and picked it up. The light-stone glowed brilliantly blue in his hand. Window slid the crystal into his pocket.

"Window, there's another passageway over there."

They walked unsteadily across the crystalline stone floor to an opening on the other side. They entered the passage, which was, like the first tunnel they had been in, small and dimly lit. Before long, they were in a section of tunnel with very few lighted stones to guide them. In a few more minutes, they were walking in near darkness.

Then they heard a very surprising sound – the sound of someone walking on dry, crackling leaves – and it was them! Beneath their feet, the tunnel floor was covered with dry, long-dead leaves. The explorers shuffled along, kicking the leaves out of their way, sending them flying through the air, just as Window loved to do back home in Windtown when the autumn leaves were on the ground.

But, then Window and Circles heard a sound much more surprising than crunching leaves. Coming from farther down the passageway, Window heard what he could not believe. He heard an orchestra playing!

"Window, listen to that!" Circles whispered.

They stopped walking for a moment. There was no mistake. Coming from somewhere ahead, was the music of stringed instruments. Window heard violins and violettes, the cellos and the basses. It was confusing and amazing.

"It's the Angels!" Circles quietly called to him. "The Angels are playing their beautiful music!"

Window had no better explanation.

The Angels' music was hypnotic. The melodies soared and captured the two listeners, as the dynamics thrilled them with syncopated rhythms.

"Let's go, Window. Let's go see."

The two explorers slowly made their way to the end of the tunnel and stepped into another underground cavern, this one perhaps as large as three or four cattle barns together.

As in the passageway, the walls and ceiling were embedded with faintly glowing stones, mostly of white light, but a few shone with color as well. The stones in the ceiling gave the impression of a star-filled sky overhead.

In the center of the cavern was the orchestra, making the music that was echoing down the passageway. But, it was not an orchestra of Angels. It was an orchestra of plants! – giant towering plants!

The underland plants were all dull green in color and stood about twice as tall as Window. Each had a single main stem and several branch-like arms extending to their sides. The plants were topped with large green-white blossoms that looked more like heads than flowers. Petals stuck out from each side of their heads, and, to the front, they had a flower-like extension that gave the impression of being a mouth. This made the plants look like giant plant creatures. All of the creatures were joined together by long, curly, intertwining tendrils. It seemed that the flower-plants were really just all one big connected being.

Surrounding the orchestra of plants, the cavern floor was covered with dry, brown, leaves and plant remains. Obviously, many plants had died there, and were still where they fell to the ground.

Window and Circles just watched and listened in amazement, as the beautiful music continued. It was being made, not by instruments, but by the plants' own branches and leaves! Each of the plant creatures was rubbing two or three of its flexible arm-

branches across some of the stiff leaves on other branches. The
leaves were vibrating and producing the beautiful sounds of a
string orchestra. Skinny leaves produced the high tones and
thick, fat leaves made the low sounds.

The plants waved back and forth as their arms rubbed across
each other. Their flower-heads waved above it all, as the music
went on for several minutes. It was music as beautiful as Window
had ever heard. "It almost sounds familiar," he thought to
himself. "I wonder if I could have ever heard it before."

Just as in a human orchestra piece, as the melody came to an
end, the plant musicians held out the final sweet note until the
sound echoes faded in the cavern. Then the giant plants lowered
their arms and stopped moving. Now they just looked like giant
people-plants silently standing, perhaps sleeping.

"Welcome, Dear Visitors." A nearly-whispered voice jumped
into Window's head. He searched for the source of the greeting,
but could see none.

"We have been waiting a long time for you," the voice came once
more.

Window again tried to see who was speaking. It was a feeble
sounding voice, like that of a very old man.

"You play beautiful music," Window spoke into the standing
group of plants.

*"Thank you, Kind Masters. We are pleased that you enjoyed it.
We have waited many years for someone to play for. We have
thought that, perhaps, no one would ever hear us play again."*

"Who speaks for you?" Window asked.

"I do. I am Moonbow," the voice came.

Then Window realized that he was not hearing the whispering
voice in his ears. He was hearing it in his head.

"Circles, we are hearing their thoughts, like the Silkie
dreamreaders!" Circles nodded. He was hearing the voice, too.

Then, one of the plants nearest them, the plant called
Moonbow, lowered his head down to the level of the visitors, and
seemed to be looking at them. The petals that stuck out from the

side of his head looked a bit like eyes, but Window couldn't really be sure if they were.

"*Have you all returned?*" Moonbow quietly asked inside of Window's head.

"It is just us two. I am Window, and this is Circles."

Circles bowed to the giant plant. Moonbow returned the bow. Window noticed the plant-creature's twisted roots, sticking into the hard, dry ground beneath him.

"*Have you come here to return us to the surface?*" Moonbow asked.

"I am afraid not, Moonbow. What is it that has happened to you?"

"*Ever since the world was new, we have been keepers of the moonstones. About two hundred years ago, a great quake broke up the lands, and the ground swallowed our cave and all of the stones. We have been lost here under the mountain, waiting for all of these years, trying to keep the stones safe. But many of them have faded away.*"

"*We Moonplants are so very, very old, and our seeds will not grow without the moonlight. And now, since the tremors of the past weeks, the world has changed again, and our stream has dried up completely. Water no longer comes to our home. I am sure that we cannot survive much longer.*"

Over near one wall of the cavern, Window could see a small dried-up streambed.

"I am sorry, Moonbow. We cannot help bring water to you. It is too large a task."

"*Only one Moonplant seed remains,*" the flower-being explained desperately. "*Will you help us? Kind Travelers, will you please help us survive?*"

"What can we do, Moonbow? What do you need?" Window asked the ancient plant.

"*Would you please take the last of our seeds and plant it in the world outside, on a night when the moon is high, perhaps on a hillside, where it will catch the rain and moonlight on its leaves as it grows?*"

"Certainly we will plant the seed for you," Window promised.

"We would appreciate that, Window. Then we could all meet again someday. Our thoughts will be a part of the new plant. Our memories of this visit will live on with it."

Moonbow extended a short branch-arm near his stem, and unrolled the leaf at its tip. He reached this leaf-hand under another of his leaves and gently pulled a small, green seed from his stem. He held the seed out to Window.

"Please protect it, Master Window. It is our very last hope of survival. If this seed dies, we will fade completely from this world."

"I promise to guard it, Moonbow. And, I will do my best to find a good spot to plant it."

Window carefully took the Moonplant seed, and put it in a small, flap-covered pouch inside his regular pocket. Moonbow reached out and touched Window's shoulder with one of his branch-arms, as a sign of thanks.

"Are you here all alone?" Circles asked.

"Oh, no. We have our Squibbles friends to keep us company. They were lost underground with us here, for all these years. They have survived because, although we have thousands of Moonstones, we do have a few Sunstones as well. Those stones help keep the Squibbles healthy. They eat our fruit-pods, and a few weeds and bugs, and once in a while they go outside through holes they have dug. So they have survived here as long as we have."

"And, the Squibbles are very helpful. They collected most of the Moonstones in the light cavern, and dug out fallen parts of the passageway you came through today. They love to go exploring, and have been deeper under the mountain. But, most of all, they are our friends."

"Where are they now?" Circles wanted to know.

"They are right here."

All together, the Moonplants, that had seemed to be sleeping, lifted their leafy, bottom branches. Immediately, hundreds of tiny, yipping, yapping, reddish-white, puppy-looking dogs jumped out from under the leaves and started running around. It was a happy, wild sight, as they wagged their stubby tails, flopped their floppy ears, and jumped around at nothing in particular.

The Squibbles were extremely small, each only a little bigger than an apple. The little dog-creatures ran and barked at each other, and chased each other under the plants and all around the cavern. As they ran, old, dry leaves and dust went flying in every direction. Some of the little creatures ran up the passageway, as their tiny barks echoed back to the plant cavern.

The Moonplants seemed to have awakened, and started to play with the tiny puppy-creatures. The plants dropped twisted tendrils down near the ground and the dogs would jump at them, and bark excitedly.

Then, a plant-creature picked up a Squibble in its leafy hand and threw it to another plant. Soon, dozens of little dog-creatures were being tossed back and forth, howling wildly. None were ever dropped, and all of them seemed to be having a grand time.

"Could you do that to me?" Circles wanted to know.

"Here," Moonbow responded. *"Come swing between us."*

Moonbow bent low towards Circles and drooped a thick, green tendril cord near him. It was joined between Moonbow and the plant-creature next to him. Circles sat on the tendril and held on as in a swing. Soon, Circles was swinging between the two plants, and smiling as he sailed high above Window.

Some of the Squibbles barked happily at Circles as he swung past them, over their heads. Circles squealed in delight. Then he decided to daringly let go of the tendrils with his hands and started to lose his balance. Just as he was about to fall from his seat, Moonbow caught him with one of his big leaf-arms and sat him safely in the tendril-swing again.

Then, as the Squibbles continued to yip at their new playmate, Moonbow and the other plant lowered Circles to the ground. The plants raised their bottom branches again, and the noisy red creatures all quickly ran back under them. Suddenly the cavern was quiet as before.

Just then, a brief ground tremor shook the cavern. Under the leaves, the Squibbles yipped and barked for a moment.

Moonbow lowered his head again towards Window and Circles. *"Perhaps you should go soon," he* whispered to them. *"But, before you go, may we please play for you one last time? It may be that we will never be able to play again."*

Window felt the sadness in the thought-voice of the ancient plant.

The moon-cavern plant creatures all lifted themselves up straight, and extended their many arms across each other. One started playing a soothing melody, and then they all joined in. Immediately the cavern was filled with music.

Circles listened for a moment, and started to sing with the melody of the leaves, making up Woot lyrics as he sang along. Whether or not the lyrics made any sense, no one will ever know. Window wondered if he would ever hear that melody again.

When the last of the soothing notes had faded away, Moonbow spoke with a voice sounding even more tired than before.

"The Squibbles will lead you to the top of the mountain. They have a way there, where you can quickly return to the surface."

"Pepper, Radish, Come here please. Kindly show these gentlemen to the stairs."

Two tiny, white-streaked, red puppies crawled out from under Moonbow's leaves. They each yapped once, and started off towards the far end of the plant cavern.

"Goodbye, Moonbow. I hope that we meet again." Window spoke quickly, as the two guide Squibbles scampered ahead, without waiting.

"Fare well, Kind Travelers. Think of us as you plant our seed. It is our life from now on."

Window looked back. Moonbow's head was drooping sadly.

"I will remember you always," Window called to him, but the plant creature seemed to already be sleeping.

The two explorers hurriedly followed the two Squibbles out of the cavern, and through a maze of tunnels and sharp turns. As they went along, there was sound from up ahead.

"Window, I can hear a storm outside. There is thunder – lots of thunder."

"Me, too, Circles. I hear it, too."

After about five minutes, the tiny Squibbles stopped at the base of a narrow, spiral passageway of rough steps that rose sharply upward. The sounds of a thunderstorm crashed down to them from above.

"Thanks, guys," Circles said as he looked down at Pepper and Radish.

After two yips, and a yap, the little guides turned and, wagging their tails behind them, scurried like leaves being blown by the wind, back towards the cavern.

Window and Circles quickly climbed the narrow, winding staircase. Within a minute, they were at its top, in a small cave-like room. And then, in that same minute, they burst through an opening between the rocks and into the storm outside.

The sky was alive. Lightning crashed again and again as torrents of rain soaked them in an instant. It seemed as if they were standing right inside of fighting storm clouds. The sun was up somewhere, but the sky was so dark that they could hardly see.

Behind them, the mountainous lands sloped upward to the sky. Before them was another steep slope they would have to climb down, to reach the level of the river below them.

"Can you see Rings and Panni?" Window yelled at Circles.

"They should be over there somewhere." Circles pointed below them and to their right.

Water was pouring down the slopes behind them as they searched for a safe way to get to the river. Chunks of rock and dirt rushed passed them, falling or being washed from higher above.

"Look out, Circles! Look out for those rocks!"

Circles turned and looked up the slope. The tremors had weakened the rocks and loosened the ground of the highlands above. The rain was bringing it all rushing down the steep hillside.

Circles yelled above the sound of the storm, "The mountain is falling!"

Window looked up again. Several hundred feet above them, the peak of the small mountain was collapsing! More rock and more water came pouring down the slope a little to their right.

Window looked down again, straining to see the river through the rain and darkness. It was out of its banks and flooding the entire valley below them. He and Circles quickly worked their way towards the spot where they had left Panni and Rings.

"Panni! Rings! Where are you?" Window screamed to himself.

All he could see of the spot where Panni and Rings had been was the rushing water of the river. He tried to use his hand to block the rain from his eyes as he searched the terrible scene below him.

Then he finally saw his two friends standing on a small island in the middle of the raging water. The swollen river had gone around the higher ground to which Rings and Panni had retreated, and trapped them between two violently rushing streams.

"Panni!" He screamed to her, as he and Circles slid down a slope of mud to the bank of the raging water. "Rings!"

Window tried to run along the rough ground to them. As he got closer he yelled again. "Panni!"

She heard him. She looked his direction.

"Window!" she frantically yelled back.

Another flood of rocks and water poured down the mountainside and into the flooding river. From the sky, the storm dumped more and more water on them. "Window!"

The river water was rising dramatically higher. It started to cover the low island Rings and Panni were on. She climbed up the harness onto Rings' back. In just a moment, the water was up to

Rings' ankles. "Window!" In another moment, the water was up to the middle of Rings' legs.

Rings could not fight the current! His feet slipped from the mud beneath him and the powerful raging water picked him up.

"Rings! Panni!"

Even the huge Rings could not fight the current. He and Panni were being carried away, along with the mud, the ripped-up flower-trees, and other debris the river had captured.

Panni was in the water, floating alongside Rings, still holding on to his harness. That was all she could do. The water pounded against her face and buried itself in her throat. Rings fought to keep his head above the water, but he could not swim – he could not keep the water from covering him.

"Window!" Panni screamed – then one last pleading time, "Window!" The wild river carried her and Rings swiftly out of his sight.

Window and Circles ran as best they could through the pouring rain and rocky mud along the edge of the raging water. Their friends would be lost. There was nothing they could do to save them. Window turned. He and Circles glanced at each other and grabbed each other's hand.

"Hold on! Don't let go!" Window yelled at Circles. Then, together, they jumped into the water. As the storm crashed around them, Window and Circles were swept, along with Panni and Rings, down the flooding river!

MIDDLE
SEA

CHAPTER TWENTY

TO THE MIDDLE SEA

"Rings! Rings!" Panni yelled through the thunder of the storm and the crashing of the water. He did not answer. She held on to the Brarrie's harness, determined to not let go, no matter what happened. The current carried them wildly along.

The flooding water took them far downstream. As Panni floated alongside him, Rings tried to swim, but his weight, and the weight of the water in his fur, pulled him down again and again. He had swallowed so much water that he could hardly breathe. Rings was drowning!

The river smashed them against rocks and standing flower-trees, and dragged them over rough ground. Rings was overcome by the water and could fight no more. He floated along with the current, completely without response, as Panni held to his side.

Finally, several miles from where they had been swept away, the rushing water slammed Rings and Panni against a low riverbank, and washed them over it. They floated across some higher ground and smashed roughly against a row of large rocks. They were left there, free from the worst of the raging river, but still in about six inches of water.

Panni and Rings were lost from Window and Circles. Panni's body was scraped and badly bruised, but she was otherwise all right. She would have to try to save Rings somehow.

Panni struggled to her feet and, pulling on Rings' harness, tried to drag him to higher ground. It was impossible. She could not move her huge friend. So, she lay down in the water next to him and wrapped herself around Rings' head to protect his face from the rain as best she could, as the storm subsided a bit

"Oh, Rings! Rings! Can you breathe? Can you breathe?"

Rings opened his eyes and looked at her. He tried to nod his head, but did not have the strength. Panni could see that his eyes were moving. He was still breathing.

She was thrilled to see that he was alive. "Oh, Rings, please be alright." She kissed the end of his nose and collapsed against him.

Then, the rain stopped as suddenly as it started. Panni used all of her strength to lift Rings' massive head into her lap. She wiped the fur from his eyes and rubbed his forehead.

Rings coughed and shook and coughed again. His breathing steadied somewhat. Rings was safe, but he was exhausted and injured. He had been thrown against the rocks and ground and pulled underwater again and again.

The strong wind that had brought the storm was carrying it away just as quickly. Panni and Rings lay on the riverbank and rested as a few rays of the sun briefly broke through the clouds above them.

Then Panni's spirits were happily lifted by the sound she wasn't sure she would ever hear again.

"Panni!" She heard Window's voice. She raised her head and saw both Window and Circles dragging themselves out of the water and up to the higher ground with her. "Panni!"

Window looked as fearful as she had ever seen him. Circles tried to run to get to her as quickly as he could. When they reached her, she and her friends hugged, again and again, with as much strength as they had left. Panni could see the tears in Window's eyes.

Window and Circles had had an easier time in the water than Panni and Rings. Window had been able to grab onto a giant flower stem in the river, and had been able to keep away from harm, as he and Circles followed their friends down the river. Circles had no trouble staying afloat, of course, so their trip in the raging water was not nearly as bad as it could have been.

Now their only concern was for Rings. Together, his three friends were able to pull one of his legs out from under him, so he could rest more comfortably. Rings coughed several more times and cleared more of the water from his lungs.

Window examined several cuts that Panni had on her legs. They seemed to not be too serious, and had stopped bleeding already.

The water in which Rings was lying soon drained away, leaving him in a massive patch of mud and rocks. His friends worked together lifting his legs and removing the sharpest rocks from under him.

Panni again rubbed Rings' face and head. He closed his eyes and seemed to sleep for a while. They watched over him as he rested. His breathing seemed fine so they felt much better about that. After about a half hour, Rings opened his eyes again and moved his head so he could see everyone better.

"Thank you, my Good Friends," Rings spoke with great difficulty. "I am so happy to see that you are all here. Is everyone alright?"

"We are okay, Rings, but we are worried about you," Panni answered him.

"I am very tired – and battered. My right foreleg feels terribly painful. I cannot tell how badly I am hurt. But, I am sure that it will take some time to recover. I am sorry to cause you distress."

"Oh, be quiet, Rings, or I will give you some distress," said Panni to him, almost crying with joy to see that he was awake and speaking.

"Yes, I will be quiet, Panni, for now." Rings closed his eyes again and slept.

The swollen river continued to rush past the travelers, but the sun broke completely from behind the clouds and shone down brightly on them.

Panni was concerned. "Window, what about our supplies and belongings? I so hope that they are not all lost."

"We will have to go back to our camp and look for them. And, that will probably take a while over this flooded ground. Rings will not be able to help, so it may take a couple of trips to bring it all here. We had better get started back there right away."

"I'll go back with you, Window," Circles offered.

Panni spoke up, "Circles, perhaps you should stay here with Rings. I will be able to carry more than you, I suppose."

"Okay, Panni, you go. I surely hope that our packs are not lost – and my bow and arrows."

"So do I, Circles. I would hate to lose my bracelet and other things – and for you and Window to lose your belongings as well."

"We'll be back as soon as we can, Circles. Watch Rings and keep him safe. Are you ready, Panni?"

"Yes, let's go."

Fortunately, the travelers had washed up on the same side of the river as their camp, so they didn't have to cross to the other side to return to look for their supplies. Window and Panni worked their way up the river's edge, through the mud and broken flower-trees.

They returned in several hours, each carrying two packs, with good news about the rest of their supplies. Their camp had been on high enough ground that all but one of their supply packs were still hanging from the flower spikes where they had left them.

The traveler's personal packs were wet, but okay. Circles bow and arrows were fine, but his kite was lost. Also missing were one pack of food and Oldsmith's spear.

In the other packs, some of the crackers and cookies were ruined, but all of the tins of food were fine. The trillion and vermillion were also safe. Panni opened her pack and took out the bracelet Window had given her and put it on. She had been so afraid that it was lost.

The explorers celebrated the good news concerning their belongings with a supper of berries and cheese. Rings didn't eat anything, but he sat up a bit and looked much better. They decided that, in the morning, Window and Circles would return up river to bring back the remaining supplies, including their blankets that had been left there because they were completely wet.

The travelers couldn't find any wood dry enough to burn so the night was a damp, uncomfortable one.

"I wish Raine was here," commented Circles, as he tried to get to sleep. "I'll bet he could get a fire started."

Happily, the next morning brought a sunny day. As the explorers sat together for a breakfast of dried meat and apples, Window and Circles finally had time to tell the others about what they had found in the Underland. Rings and Panni were fascinated by their tale of the light-crystals and the plant-creatures.

Window retrieved the blue-glowing stone he had taken and passed it around for everyone to look at. The glow inside seemed rather faint in the sunlight.

Then Window reached into his small inner pocket to retrieve the seed that he had promised Moonbow he would plant and carefully brought it out. He hadn't thought about drying it off after he climbed from the river. It had, of course, gotten completely wet, and, it had started to sprout!

As he showed it to the others, a small green tendril twisted from one end of the moon-seed. It was growing! He would have to plant it immediately.

"Wow, Window," Circles said to him. "You had better find a place to plant that right away."

"Okay, Circles. What do you say that you help me find a good spot?"

They looked around their camp and, after a short search, found a place to plant the seed. They choose the side of a slight hill where there was grass but not any large flower-plants that would shade it from the sun and moon.

"Window," Circles reminded him. "Moonbow said to plant it in the moonlight. Do you remember?"

"Oh, that's right. I guess that we had better wait until tonight to plant it. I'll keep it moist until then."

"I hope the moon is out tonight, Window."

"Me, too, Circles."

Rings sat up and moved his injured leg a bit. It was very sore. He would probably not be able to walk on it for a few days. He also had a lot of bruises, both on the outside of his body and on the inside. His muscles and organs had been battered severely.

So, as Rings rested, Window and Circles left to go back to their old campsite to get the rest of the supplies. Panni emptied all of their packs onto the grass, in the sun. Then, she carefully laid out their clothes and supplies to dry.

Panni retrieved Window's notebook from his pack. It had gotten wet in the flood. She carefully separated the pages from each other and laid it out in the sun with the rest of Window's belongings. The hot midday sun would soon dry the notebook pages, along with all of their other things.

Then, Panni sat herself in the sun, and let its warm rays wash over her. She closed her eyes and let her thoughts drift where they might. Her thoughts hadn't drifted very far before she fell asleep. She opened her eyes again in a few hours, carefully collected their belongings and returned them to the packs. She was feeling much drier – and better. Getting their clothes and supplies and herself dry, and repacking everything, had really lifted her spirits.

By the middle of the afternoon, Window and Circles were back with the last of their supplies. Together they emptied the remaining packs and sorted through everything.

The sky was still clear, as the sun went down that evening. The moon came up early, as they had hoped, so it was time to plant the moon-seed.

Window and Circles went to the hillside they had selected, and Circles dug a small hole in the dirt, under the grass. It was a place that was just as Moonbow had requested, where the moonlight, and the rain, would touch the plant's leaves.

Window held the sprouting seed up in the moonlight. The moonbeams reflected from it. He placed the moon-plant seed into the ground and gently covered it with dirt. Then he added a little bit of water just to keep it moist. Circles made a good luck wish over the spot, and they returned to their camp.

Later, in his notebook, Window drew a map of where they planted the seed, so he could find the spot again someday. Everyone agreed that they would love to talk to Moonbow when his thoughts were again alive in the new plant.

"These Moonlands are really something!" Circles shared with everyone. "They are really something."

+++++++++

The travelers spent four days and nights in their new camp along the river. On the second day, Rings tried to stand up, and discovered that, as he had feared, the muscles in his left front leg were injured. He unhappily sank back to the ground.

On the third day, Rings' could stand, and hold himself up. He even walked a bit, but it was painful.

On the fourth day, Rings' leg felt much better, and he could walk with a limp, He said that the pain was not too great. That was the day that Panni told Window of her decision.

It was the hardest thing Panni had ever had to do. She approached Window as he stood under a tree, looking out towards the east. As soon as he saw her, he knew what she was about to say. He didn't want to hear it, but knew that he must.

"Window," she began, with tears in her eyes. "It is time for me to go home. My heart remains with you, but it also pulls me to my family and friends and life in the Northlands."

"Rings is able to walk now, but he cannot go on farther. He too needs to return to his home and take time to fully recover."

"So, Rings and I will not be going on with you and Circles. In a few days, we will start on our way back, together. Rings will make sure that I get back to Dawson's safely, and I will make sure that he gets home to the Deep Woods, from there. He and I had talked about it before, but now that he is injured, we have agreed that the time is right."

Window listened to his friend with an overwhelming sadness.

"Rings is ready to go home because he has found his treasure. It is his friendship with us. And, he wants to see us all again as soon as you get back to Dawson's."

"And I have found the key to my chains, and my life. I have learned it from you. That is my treasure. I am now so rich, in so many ways."

"It breaks my heart, Window, but it is time." She broke down in tears and fell against his chest. Window held her tightly in his arms. He knew that it was the best decision, but he hated it.

Panni spoke, through her tears. "Will you come back with us, Window? Or will you go on?"

"I will talk to Circles, and we will decide together."

He pulled Panni close. "There is no reason to wait. I will ask him right now."

Window hugged her again and turned away. He couldn't look into her eyes just now. He went to find Circles. She went to tell Rings that she had told Window of their decision.

When Window found Circles, he couldn't think of an easy way to tell him of Panni and Rings' plans, so he just told him. "Circles, Panni and Rings have decided to return to the Northlands."

"Yeah, I was guessing that it was time," Circles calmly and quietly responded. "It will sure be fun to see them at Dawson's or Oldsmith's when we get back," he added, pushing his sorrow from his mind.

"So, you want us to go on exploring?"

Circles' big dark eyes looked at his great friend. "I want to see the ocean with you, Window."

"But, Circles, we have already seen the ocean."

"I mean the other ocean – the eastern ocean. There must be one out there somewhere."

Window's heart happily jumped a bit. He knew that he, too, still wanted to go on. He was not yet ready to end his adventure.

Window hugged the little Woot as he answered him.

"Okay, Circles, we will go see the other ocean. We will go to the eastern ocean together, and have lots of adventures."

"Let's make sure that we bring plenty of treats," Circles reminded him.

"Okay, Circles, I will carry the treats."

"And I will eat the treats. I want to make sure that I do my part."

"I can always count on you, Circles. You are very reliable."

"And, hungry," added Circles.

The travelers spent that evening, planning what to do about the treasure at Eastpoint. Because of his injuries, Rings would not be able to carry much of it, if he and Panni stopped there on their way home. Also, because of his injuries, they wanted to take the shortest possible route, as well as, avoid any trouble in the Ancient Lands.

So, Panni and Rings would travel directly home from where they were, passing to the south of the Ancient Lands, and return to the Northlands much farther south than the way they had come. They might even pass close by Panni's Traepelle Castle home on their way to Dawson's Inn on the Northway.

Although she refused it at first, Panni would take Window's sword to help keep them safe. She and Rings would also take some of the trillion and vermillion dust with them.

As the travelers planned the return of the treasure to Northlands, they realized that they were confronted with several major problems. Finding the treasure was difficult but bringing it back home, and using it, might be even harder.

First, they would have to return the treasure chest safely to Dawson's and then protect the treasure once they got it home.

They all agreed that the first use of the treasure would be to buy freedom for Panni and her servant friends at the Traepelle Castle. But, that could not be done without help from someone. If Panni showed up at the castle with a bunch of jewels, the nobles would simple take them from her and imprison her again.

Also, they couldn't just start trying to sell or spend all of the different treasure pieces. The hated Prince Martellan, in Calisay, was sure to hear about it and send soldiers to retake the treasure from them. It was obvious that the only way to use the treasure was to do it slowly and secretly.

The treasure finders had already decided, of course, to share the treasure with Dawson's and Oldsmith's families. Now they planned that Dawson and Oldsmith would enlist the help of Noble Paris, and Oldsmith's Matenne Palace horseman friends, who could assist Paris.

The horsemen could help Rings bring the treasure back to the Paris Castle. Then Noble Paris could slowly sell the treasure pieces without attracting any special attention. It would be Paris who would actually travel to Traepelle and buy the dancers' freedom. Then, slowly and secretly, the treasure could be enjoyed by the others, to give them new, and better, lives.

Eventually, perhaps Noble Paris could start a new Northlands Kingdom, one that was fair and generous with the people. Or, maybe, led by Oldsmith, the Matenne Palace in Calisay could once again become a place of beauty and justice. But, it would be a long and dangerous task. Prince Martellan would not like it.

Both Rings and Circles said that they didn't really need any of the King's Treasure, that the real treasure for them was traveling with the others, and finding it.

Window agreed that someday, as soon as he could, he would return to the Northlands and claim part of the treasure for himself. Panni said that she would keep it for him until he came to get it.

Then Panni thought out loud, "There are so many jewels, and so much gold, that maybe I could just build my own castle in Traepelle. It would be a place of beauty and grace for all to enjoy. I already know where I can find some excellent Palace dancers." Her idea brightened all of their spirits.

"I knew that you would be a princess someday, Panni," Window told her.

"You said that I already was a princess, Window." Panni
replied with a big smile. Have you changed your mind?"

"I will never change my mind about that, Princess Panni."

"And I will never change my mind about you."

+++++++++

The plans were complete. Rings said his leg was okay to walk
on, so he and Panni would leave in the morning. Tonight would be
the traveler's last night together. Window and Circles got a big
fire going, and they all sat around it, late into the night, one final
time. For a short while Circles sang and everyone sang along.
Then, they mostly just sat and quietly watched the fire dance
before them as their thoughts and memories danced in their
heads.

No one wanted to lie down to sleep because no one wanted the
evening to end. But, eventually, everyone was so tired that they
almost fell asleep just sitting there. Finally, Rings really did fall
asleep and so Panni told the others it was time for bed. Window
and Panni lay on their blankets and Circles curled against Rings
for the last time. Window looked across to Panni but she had
already closed her eyes. He did the same and drifted to sleep with
the cool, night breeze on his face.

In the morning, after a quiet breakfast, Panni gave everyone,
one of Mellie's picture-cookies. "To celebrate our great treasure
hunt, to remember our friends waiting for us in the Northlands,
and to honor Window's grandmother, the lady who helped us from
so far away."

They all slowly enjoyed the cookies, as they were reminded
again of how many things they had been through together.

Then it was time for the travelers to go.

Circles stood with Rings and spoke to him privately. The
others couldn't hear what was said between them, but it ended
with Circles punching Rings on one of his good legs. Rings
laughed and Circles hugged his huge friend.

Then Circles surprised Panni with the gift of the Amerand coin he had found at the cannon. He followed that gift with a kiss. "I will miss you, Panni. You are a fine treasure hunter. Please take care of yourself."

"The next time I go treasure hunting, I will invite you to come along," she replied.

"I would like that, Panni. You can count on me."

"I am sure I can, Circles. I have no doubt about that."

Panni turned to Window, "Window, may I please see the rose-diamond pin I gave you, from the treasure?"

Window, wondering about her request, got the silver hair-pin from one of the outer pockets on his pack and handed it to her. Panni took the pin and slipped it into his hair on the side of his head. "Please wear it today, Window. I would like that."

"Of course, Panni, I will wear it – for you."

Then Panni ran her left hand under her own hair and pushed a long strand of it behind her ear. She looked directly into Window's eyes and spoke from deep within herself.

"I don't need a trusting-ring to know how wonderful you are, Window. You have been everything to me. Our adventure together has been the start of my life. I will keep my bracelet close, and thoughts of you closer. My love is with you always – wherever you go."

Window returned her look of deep connection and spoke to her quietly. "When I left my home to find treasure and adventure, I never imagined that I could find both of them in one place – in one person. That is what you are to me, Panni – a treasure and an adventure, to hold onto forever. My love remains with you, too. I know that you will care for it always."

With tears in their eyes, the Windlands traveler and the Traepelle dancer held their gaze on each other for a long moment.

Then Window turned to his huge, brown, traveling companion. "Rings, you are as loyal a friend as any man could ever have. But you had better practice playing Northdraw, because the next time I see you, I will try to win your part of the treasure from you."

The Brarrie pushed his giant head against Window's shoulder. "You don't scare me, Window. I can beat you with two paws tied behind my back – as long as Circles is there to hold the cards!"

"I will be there, Rings. I will be there," the little Woot promised.

"I will be there, too, Window." Panni added hopefully, looking to the future. "I will see you then."

Panni reached out for Circles' hand. "Goodbye, Circles. You are a joy to me always. *Sae tou tresae tre-enne.*" She hugged him tightly. Circles returned her hug with a sweeping bow.

"Goodbye, Dearest Window." Panni took his hand and kissed him softly, just below his eye. He squeezed her hand, and returned the kiss.

"Goodbye, Princess."

Then, Panni grabbed onto a strap of Rings' harness as she had done so many times before. Rings nodded to his two good friends and started out over a slight hill, towards the west. He walked slowly, but only limped a bit, and seemed to be alright.

Panni walked along with him, as beautiful as she had ever looked. At the top of the rise they turned briefly, and Panni waved. With his heart aching, Window raised his hand in reply. Then his two loving friends turned again to the west and started their long journey home.

Window watched as they disappeared over the crest of the hill. He wondered when he might ever see them again. "Goodbye, my dear friends," he said quietly to himself. "I will miss you."

He looked over at Circles, next to him. Circles was wiping tears from his eyes.

"Well, let's go, Window. It could take us all day to find that ocean."

"You may be right, Circles," Window replied with a smile as they pulled their packs over their shoulders. "I hope that we get there by suppertime."

"What's for supper tonight, Window?" asked Circles as he picked up his bow.

"Oh, I don't know. How about some fruit or something?"

"I want another one of Mellie's picture-cookies for desert."

"Sure, Circles. We had better get eating those cookies before they get stale."

"I like your way of thinking, Window."

"I like your way of being my friend, Circles."

The two travelers turned to the southeast, and leaving the flower-forest behind them, started off together over the wooded grasslands alongside the river. Circles sang part of a new marching song he had been working on. Window hummed along as best he could. The early autumn sun was high in the sky. It was another beautiful day for an adventure.

Window and Circles didn't find an ocean that afternoon, as they hiked along the riverbank, but they did find some tasty leaves for Circles to eat, and some pleasant conversation. As they walked, they talked of Angels, and oceans, and the Silkie.

"The next time I come out here I want to be riding on Little Red," Circles told Window. "I bet that in the past few months I have walked more than any Woot in history."

You have done many things that no other Woot has ever done, Circles. Maybe that is what Raine was talking about when he said that you were special."

"Hey," Window continued. "How about using that bird talk you know and ask one of them if there is an ocean around here."

"That is a brilliant idea, Partner," Circles replied. "Do you see any birds?"

"Well, not right now – but we are sure to see one sometime."

"Let me know, and I will call him over. Hey, this is going to be really fun – and handy."

As they walked along, Window got out his notebook. Some of the pages were a bit crinkled from getting wet, but none of them were severely damaged. The pages were continuing to fill up as he drew more maps and pictures and made more notes about his adventures. Grandma Windowen would have a lot to look at when he got home.

He turned again to the list of names that he had stared at so often – his grandfather's expedition members. He couldn't help wondering once again if one of those men had a treasure-hunting grandson who stopped at the Summer Breeze and talked to Bill. Maybe it was Private Kensing. And, maybe that grandson was out searching for more treasure right now.

+++++++++

[NEAR THE CARATOUSAN RUINS]

Half a continent away, to the southwest, Cyenne Kensing dove into the undergrowth behind a fallen log. Three brightly feathered arrows whizzed over his head. Those three arrows were followed by a fourth, and a fifth. They were the long, poison arrows of the Golden Men of Caratousay.

The Golden Men had caught up with him, and they were not pleased. All he had tried to do was to sneak into their Sun Temple, and maybe take a couple of fancy carvings from a wall.

"I don't know why that should upset them so much," he muttered to himself.

Kensing had been in the jungle for weeks, trying to find the Car villages. Ever since he was a boy, all he ever wanted to do was explore the Caratousan jungle. At last, he got his chance. It was the first time he had ever been away from South Cape, and if things didn't improve for him in the next few minutes, it would be his last.

Kensing had hired on to the merchant ship, the Kathryn B., in Lissara, and worked his way north to Cillport, in the Horselands. Then he jumped ship and headed past the rolling grasshills to the edge of the jungle. After two weeks

*of a terribly, hot trek through the Deepgreen, he was there –
scouting out the best way to enter the ruins at Saydusay.*

*The jungle here was denser than it was back in South
Cape, so his exploration of Caratousay had been extremely
difficult. Also, the Golden Men were not interested in
sharing any conversation – or any temple relics.*
*The Car people were very tall, with smooth skin that
shone a bright, golden color. And, they had never liked
visitors, especially those who tried to steal from them.
Unfortunately for him, the Car were also excellent hunters,
using their game bows that stood even taller than their men.*

*Kensing had lost his jungle-blade crossing the Taracal.
He figured that, in only a couple of minutes, the Car would
realize that he was unarmed. And, of course, the Car
hunters were skilled in chasing game through the
undergrowth. He knew that escape from them was unlikely.*
*He had just one chance. In Caratousay, it rained almost
every afternoon. And, it was now afternoon. Through the
green canopy above him, Kensing could see the darkening
sky. If he was very lucky, today's rain would be an especially
heavy one.*
*Another arrow slapped against his protecting log. At
almost the same time, the sky crashed open. Instantly, his
world was filled with a drenching downpour of water.
Across the valley, a bolt of lightning burned the top from a
Fantou tree.*
*Kensing readied himself. At the next strike of lightning,
he would go. He couldn't see more than a few dozen feet
behind him. He hoped the Car would not see him as he ran.*
*His wait, of not more than a minute, seemed to last
forever. He thought of his home back in South Cape. He
thought of his grandfather in Reeltown. Then, with an eye-
stinging flash, a searing bolt of lightning crashed to the
ground somewhere near, off to his side.*

Cyenne Kensing jumped up from behind the log, and raced to the southwest. Giant jungle leaves slapped against his face as he ran blindly through the overgrowth. The pouring rain clouded his eyes as his feet slipped in the mud and tripped on half-buried roots. Through it all, Kensing never slowed down. He ran as if his life depended on it. It did.

+++++++++

It was a quiet, simple camp that the two ocean hunters set up that night. Window gathered wood as Circles got out some fruit and crackers.

"I think that it is time for me to learn to use the matches to light the fire, Window. I have never done that yet."

"Okay, Circles, I will show you. And, after we eat, I want to teach you a new game we can play. It is a game from the Windlands that only takes two players. I have been saving it, and now that there are only the two of us, I would like for us to play."

Window thought back to his childhood in Windtown. When he and his sister didn't feel like playing cards together, they would play Rainbow Chips. It was quick, easy, and fun.

"One afternoon, when we were at Dawson's," Window explained to Circles, "I spent a couple of hours in his workshop in the barn, making these."

Window opened the drawstring on a little cloth bag, and dumped a pile of several dozen, colorful, wooden coins on the eating cloth, in front of Circles. Well, they weren't really coins, but they were shaped like coins. They were round, and flat and could be stacked up on top of each other as coins could. They were painted different colors. Some were blue, some were red, some were orange, and some were light green.

"These are the Rainbow Chips," Window explained. "We each start with two of each color, and then we play them on the table, until one of us wins them all."

Window went on to explain about drawing more chips and matching with others of the same color, stacking them next to chips of the same color, and all of the other things necessary to win the game. It seemed kind of complicated.

"Did you just make this up?" kidded Circles.

"No, come on. Let's give it a try. I'll start with fewer chips than you, to make it fair."

"Okay, but take it easy on me, will you? Remember, I am a special Woot."

"We'll see about that, Circles. Okay, you play first."

Circles' first game of Rainbow Chips was not his last. They played long into the night. It really was fun, and he learned to play quickly. Soon, he and Window had forgotten, for a while, how much they missed their friends.

The next morning was a quiet and simple one for the ocean hunters, but in the afternoon and evening things changed quite a bit.

After lunch, when they had stopped for a break, Circles heard a bird calling from a high branch of the tree they were sitting under.

"Okay, Window. Here goes. I'll call him over, and ask this bird where the ocean is."

"Wee-it, wee-it," Circles whistled as loud as he could.

"Wee-it, wee-it," came the response.

In a moment, a big, black, crow-like bird, jumped down to a branch near Circles.

"We-ae wit-wit-wit," the crow-bird yelled at Circles, *"We-ae wit-a-wit-wit."* Then it immediately flew away.

"What did he say, Circles? What did he say?"

Circles had a very disappointed look on his face, as he answered Window, "He told me to get out from under his tree, and don't come back."

Window had trouble not smiling at his friend. "Oh, well. You can try again with some other kind of bird. That one didn't look much like a sea gull anyway. He probably wouldn't know an ocean if he sat in it."

Circles felt better after he heard Window say that. "Yeah, I wouldn't want to talk to that stupid bird, anyway. Where do they keep the smart birds around here?"

"We'll find one soon, I'll bet."

"Yeah," Circles replied, "Let's find a smart bird."

That evening the travelers stopped again and set up a camp along the river. They had their usual fire, and usual time to relax.

Window sat and, once again, took out the medallion that had started his whole adventure. He rubbed it, as he usually did, and wondered, as he usually did, where it came from. Wherever that was, it must be a long way from where he was now – far to the north and the east of the Windlands – far beyond the Newlands Wilds – past the Ancient Lands and the Moonlands. The medallion certainly could not have come from so far away. Still, he would like to discover where it came from.

"Oh, well, maybe tomorrow," he thought to himself, knowing that was not very likely.

Window stuck the medallion back in his right, front pocket, and reached into his other front pocket. From there, he pulled out his latest treasure – the glowing stone from the Underland. He wondered just what it was that gave it its light.

He looked down at the crystal stone lying in the palm of his hand, and that's when it happened. The clouds overhead drifted on past him, and the full moon shined down on him – and on his hand.

When the moonlight hit the stone in his hand, the blue glow inside of it seemed to come alive. Suddenly, the dull blue grew to brilliant blue. The light was so bright that Window had to turn his face away. The light in the stone was much brighter than their campfire. And, the light seemed to be jumping around inside of the stone.

"Circles, look at this! The light has come alive! The moonlight seems to have brought it to life!"

"Let me see, Window." Circles answered him, as he reached for the stone.

The light inside of the crystal lessened a bit, and Circles held it up in front of his face to examine it. He noticed something.

"Hey, Window. There's a crack in this stone. And the light looks like it is trying to get out!"

Circles shook the stone a few times, and the light bounced around inside of it. Then the light blazed bright blue again.

"Maybe I can help it get out," Circles suggested to Window, and he tapped the crystal stone on a rock near his feet that they had used as a barrier around their fire pit. As Circles hit it against the rock, the crystal cracked and split apart. The little ball of light was tossed out of the moon-stone, and lay on the ground at Circles feet. Circles laughed with amazement.

Window bent down and picked up the blue light. It vibrated in his hand, and it felt like he was holding a slowly buzzing honeybee. He set the light in his open hand, and let the moonlight strike it as before. Again, the light sparked brilliant blue. Then it jumped out of his hand and into the air!

The sparkling blue light flew up in front of Window's face, and then shot high above them, as high as the top of the big tree they were near. The blue spark looked like a blazing star, next to the moon, in the night sky.

Then the spark dove back near the fire, and began flying all around the campsite. It was a fantastic sight for Window and Circles as the blue light twisted and turned and spun in front of them like a wildly flying firefly.

Again and again it flew by them, as if it was celebrating its freedom from the stone. The moving light was traveling so quickly that sometimes it looked as if it was writing words, in script letters, against the dark, night-time sky.

Then the moon disappeared behind some clouds. Suddenly the flying light dimmed a bit, and flew more slowly. It came near Window and Circles.

Window held out his hand and called to it. "Come here, Spark. Come to my hand." The light stopped and stood still in the air, as if it had heard him.

"Look at that, Circles. What a fantastic spark of light!"

"I'll bet that Panni would say that it is charming," Circles shared.

"Window held out his hand again. "Okay Charming Light, bring your charm over here. Please come here, Charm. Come back to my hand."

And it did! The charming, sparkling, blue light flew back and landed on Window's open hand!

Just then, the moon came out again, and again the Charm blazed in brilliant blue color. But this time it remained in Window's hand. Window gave the charm to Circles, and Circles held it for a while.

"Do you know where the ocean is?" Circles asked the light. The charm flashed at him a few times, but didn't move.

"I'll bet that this light is smarter than that bird I talked to this afternoon," Circles offered with a wry sound to his voice.

As the moon stayed behind the clouds for the rest of the night, Window and Circles stayed up late, talking to the crystal charm. It seemed to understand them, and sometimes reacted to what they said to it. Once, Circles set it on a log next to him, and the charm remained there, as if it was just sitting around the fire with them.

Eventually, the charmed light faded more and more. Finally, Window decided to put the glowing light back into his pocket. It had faded to a very faint blue glow, as it seemed to go to sleep.

"Well, Window, I think that we may have found another bit of magic here."

"Yes, Circles, I believe that you are right. I wonder what Raine would say about this.

"I'll bet that he would say that our new friend is science – not magic. But this time he would be wrong!"

Window chuckled at his friend's response. Circles reached for a blanket and threw it open on the ground by the fire.

Circles curled next to Window as they lay down to sleep. "I wonder if Charm can help us find the Angels."

"That would really be nice, Circles. That would really be nice."

For the next few days, Window and Circles, with the sparkling light, Charm, in Window's pocket, followed the river as it wound its way to the southeast. The leaves on the trees were just beginning to change to their autumn colors, and the nights became a bit cooler.

Circles <u>was</u> able to talk to four or five birds along the way. Most of them didn't have much to say, but one forest-lark told him that the river flowed into the sea, just one day's flight to the east.
"I wonder if that bird is right, Window. Do you think that the ocean is really that close?"
"We'll know pretty soon, Circles."
"I wish I could fly."
"I would like that, too."
"And, I wish that the birds were smarter, around here."

Four days later, the two travelers stood on a high ridge. Their eyes followed the river as it flowed out below them to the east. In the distance, spread far to the horizon, was the sparkling water of a great sea.

EPILOGUE

+++++++++

[WHERE WISHES MIGHT COME TRUE]

"In the distance, spread far to the horizon, was the sparkling water of a great sea."

Their mother stood up from the edge of the bed and shifted her white-lace night-dress. The bright light of the table lamp reflected from the jeweled pin in her hair and flashed on the ceiling like stars in the warm night sky.

"I wish I could fly, too, Mama." Veri spoke with sleepy eyes, from beneath her covers.

"Where would you like to fly?" her mother wanted to know.

"I would fly out over the sea with Circles. It would be a grand adventure."

"How about you, Tressi? Would you like to fly?"

"Oh, yes, Mama. I would fly to the Very East and search for Angels."

The two girls each thought quietly for a moment. Then Tressi asked, "Mama, what happens to wishes when they don't come true?"

"I think that they just fly away," Veri answered for her mother.

But then their mother explained, "Sometimes wishes have to wait to come true. They have to be patient and not be in a hurry. Just like you girls have to wait for things sometimes."

A few more moments passed as the girls considered their mother's reply. Then Veri spoke up again.

"I wish that I wasn't so sleepy, so you could read to us some more."

"What do you wish for, Mama?" Tressi wanted to know.

"I wish that my Darling Daughters would be more patient and not always want to hurry things."

"Alright, Mama, we will be patient," Veri replied. "But I wish we didn't have to be."

"Veri, do you think that Window and Circles were always in a hurry?" Mama asked.

"Well, they seemed to enjoy each other's company as they went along – and they sort of knew where they wanted to go, but they didn't seem to be in a hurry."

"That's how it could be with you girls. Always try to know where you are going, and enjoy the adventure as you go along."

"Okay, Mama, we will," the twins answered with one voice.

"Yes, we will, Mama," Veri repeated. "But I wish we could hurry up and know where we want to go."

"You will, Darlings. You will. Just keep your wishes in your heart and someday many of them will come true."

"Will they really, Mama?" Tressi asked for both of the girls.

"Yes, Dears. Just like with Window and Circles. Remember that they searched a long, long time on their adventure before some of their wishes came true."

The girls sleepily half-nodded their agreement.

"And wishes can be very powerful," their mother went on. "That's why you have to be careful, and only wish for good things."

The sleepy nods came again.

"Now it's time for sleep. Close your eyes and think of some more wishes."

"I wish that we didn't have to go to sleep," Veri softly
spoke as her eyes opened for the last time that night.

*"Don't you want to save some of your wishes until later?
You wouldn't want to use them all up in one night."*

"Okay, Mama, we will save some for later," Tressi
promised.

"Good night, Mama," Veri spoke for both girls.

*Their mother expected to hear still another wish from the
girls, but she only heard the soft sounds of their breathing as
it slowed and quieted. They would both be beyond wishes
very soon.*

*The girls' mother reached over to the table-lamp and put
it out. The moon had drifted past the open window so just a
thin sliver of light fell on the smooth faces of her darling
Tresette and Vermillion.*

*With one hand, their mother pushed her hair behind her
ear. Then she leaned over and gently kissed each girl.*

*"Sweet wishes always, my Dear Ones. And may all your
wishes come true."*

+++++++++

REFERENCES

CHARACTERS, PLACES, AND THINGS
IN PARTS ONE AND TWO
AND THE PAGE WHERE INTRODUCED

+++++++++

A Mallen went to Calisay… – The first line of a Windlands
    children's rhyme. I : p. 20

A rumbling stumbling tumbling Zumbler… – The first line of a
    Windlands children's rhyme about a Deep Woods creature. I
    : p. 63

A star for the Old Countries and three stripes for the new… – The
    first line of a Windlands children's rhyme. I : p. 45

Ajer Hollen – Grandson of R. Holland of Grandfather Windowen's
    Northlands Expedition, from Ameran. II : p. 43

Alana – An angel friend of Caroline and Valentine. II : p. 27

Alezan – The last king of the Northlands, who gave his kingdom's
    treasures to his three sons to hide. I : p. 168

All Roads Lead To The King – A Windlands children's rhyme
    about the Northern Wars. I : p. 124

Alysse – A dancer at the Traepelle Castle. II : p. 133

Amarie – A dancer at the Traepelle Castle. II : p. 133

Ameran – One of the Old Countries, a less-developed, mostly rural
    land. I : p. 10

i

Linnaia – A world in the Fantessian Resenne star system for
      whom Raine delivered a message to the Prince of the Lettes
      before his ship was damaged by a storm and carried far from
      his charted stars. II : p. 6
Linner – An Ice Lands Brarrie, and snow-racer. II : p. 66
Lisette – A dancer at the Traepelle Castle. II : p. 133
Lissara – A port city in South Cape. II : p. 231
Little Red – One of the Silkie encountered by Window and his
      fellow travelers on the Northern Plains. II : p. 89
Locker – A kite-flying Deep Woods Owt, and friend of Frazzle,
      greeted by Circles on the Calisay kite field. I : p. 140
Longsea [Eastlands Sea] – The long, narrow sea extending from
      south of the Grasslands Kingdoms to the Far Ocean. II : p.
      200
Loren Briggs – The wife of Will Briggs in Woodmine. I : p. 103
Lowpoint – The Inlands town where the Windlands Road crosses
      the Windlands River. I : p. 6
Madam Trelesse – The woman in charge of dresses and costumes
      for dancers and actors at the Traepelle Castle. II : p. 136
Mallen – The language spoken by Mallen in the Deep Woods. I :
      p. 187
Mallen [pl. mallen] – A Deep Woods creature in a Windlands
      children's rhyme, believed to be a Talker. I : p. 20
Mama (mother of twin girls Vermillion and Tresette) –
      Unidentified, but most likely Panni Tresette – possibly Melli
      Oldsmith, Anna Bliss, Wendy Kesselle, or Mary Looking. I :
      p. 1
Maree Liysenne – A former resident of Windtown, buried in the
      Field Road Cemetery. I : p. 30
Market – The Atlandic Ocean town just to the north of Coastown.
      I : p. 32
Marrents – Ugly, rat-faced Talkers who sometimes joined with
      Deep Woods monsters to prey on other creatures. I : p. 141
Marsene – A jungle region in South Continent. I : p. 57
Mary [Mary Collette Looking] – Window's girlfriend, who
      promised to return to Windtown, and to him, in the spring of
      the next year. I : p. 9

Zumbler – A Deep Woods creature from several favorite
Windlands children's rhymes. I : p. 63

+++++++++

John Ernest Briggs

Creating the story of his lifetime, John spent thirty-five years in planning and design, and five years in writing the eight-hundred plus page three-part The Adventures Of Window Breesian, each part including approximately 20 pages of color drawings.

Master's Degree in Mathematics
Mathematics Teacher - College and High School
Vietnam War Era Veteran
Singer, Songwriter, Guitarist
Music Producer, and Recording Engineer
Author and Illustrator of Fantasy/Adventure

johnernestbriggs@gmail.com

Window's adventures continue in:

The Adventures of Window Breesian

Part Three:
The Search For The Angels Of The Very East